Sword of Rhoswen
Silver Dragon Series

By Brenda Williamson

A Samhain Publishing, Ltd. publication

Samhain Publishing, Ltd.
PO Box 2206
Stow OH 44224

Sword of Rhoswen: Silver Dragon Series
Copyright © 2006 by Brenda Williamson
Cover by Scott Carpenter
Print ISBN: 1-59998-119-X
Digital ISBN: 1-59998-014-2
www.samhainpublishing.com

This book is a work of fiction. The names, characters, places, and incidents are products of the writer's imagination or have been used fictitiously and are not to be construed as real. Any resemblance to persons, living or dead, actual events, locale or organizations is entirely coincidental.

All Rights Are Reserved. No part of this book may be used or reproduced in any manner whatsoever without written permission, except in the case of brief quotations embodied in critical articles and reviews.

First Samhain Publishing, Ltd. electronic publication: March 2006
First Samhain Publishing, Ltd. print publication: June 2006

Praise for Brenda Williamson's Sword of Rhoswen

"When Brogan and Brienna first meet the sparks fly both in combat and in lust. Brienna's fiery personality has Brogan craving her. Brogan seems to have a girl in every village and Brienna does not like it. As a result, their relationship throughout the first half of the book is full of jealousy and arguments as well as searing hot passion. Brogan is very handsome, as well as a good man. Brienna is delightful, beautiful and strong. I particularly enjoyed the final chapters of the book where the mysteries are revealed and the action and drama kick into high gear. Throughout the story, Brogan and Brienna's feelings for each other grow, but the end is where they really blossom. ...Brenda Williamson has written an exciting and erotic story with Sword of Rhoswen and I look forward to reading more from this author."

~ Nannette, Joyfully Reviewed.com

5 Ribbon! "Brenda Williamson creates the perfect blend of history and fantasy with her novel, SWORD OF RHOSWEN. This story is action packed from beginning to end. The main characters both have strong personalities that make it truly a joy to watch the passion ignite between them....The SWORD OF RHOSWEN is so easy to become engrossed in that I read through the entire book in one sitting. I can hardly wait to see what happens with the rest of this series. Ms. Williamson is an awesome storyteller in range of genres and I've truly enjoyed every one of her stories that I've had the pleasure of reading. This is definitely a keeper!"

~ Chrissy Dionne, Romance Junkies

Regarding Brenda Williamson

Brenda Williamson lives to write and create stories containing timeless love, with sensual, sexy, and spicy themes. Forgoing household chores most of the time, she has a great husband and one son who put up with her many long hours hidden behind a computer. For contemplation she sits on the porch swing and watches nature inspire from her country home. With nine cats, three dogs, and a quiet day, things can't be more perfect.

If you would like to learn more about Brenda and her work, visit her website at www.brendawilliamson.com or send an email to Brenda@brendawilliamson.com.

Sword of Rhoswen
Silver Dragon Series

By Brenda Williamson

~ ~ ~

In a time of castles, crusades, and lands divided, wars of religion and greed abound. What one might have, another would covet. The stronger preyed on the weak. Moreover, those that had the will to endure would triumph. Good did not always win over evil, but kept it in check while the circle of time tested the true convictions of its opponents.

Upon the rocky beaches or deep in the dark forests, the vastness of a country's differences often times are strengths. Amongst the clans of one such land lies the presence of a conflict yet unresolved for the people of a place called Avalbane and their potential ally of Kylemore.

It's been a long struggle with a seemingly endless train of problems. For one woman, it is her greatest challenge.

~ ~ ~

Chapter 1

Queen Brienna Rhoswen sat pensive. Many things weighed heavily on her mind. Her trip held promise, hope, and if all went well, the halt to an impending greater dilemma.

She tried to relax on the hard seat inside a covered cart, containing her and only one servant. She held her hands clasped together in her lap. Besides having the benefits of teachings in the ways of polite manners, she displayed all the signs of good breeding that provided an air of aristocracy instilled in her from birth. Her father would be pleased that while she had been a headstrong whirlwind in her very tender younger years, since she had come into power, she had retained all the pomp for her stately reign. She knew how to present every learned pose, each mannered nod, and eat with a refinement lacking in most. Her adventures, however, were not exactly conventional. She smiled to herself, knowing she had the very comforting assurance of her skilled abilities in using the Sword of Rhoswen.

"We should have an escort, Your Highness." Her handmaid looked nervously out the window of the enclosed cart.

"Could have, should have, but did not." Brienna smiled reassuringly. "We'll be fine."

Medora was more than a servant. She was a trusted friend. Only a few years older than Brienna, she was really the only constant companion Brienna had. Yet, Medora was so effeminate with her whining over trivialities that they were far mismatched as friends.

She let loose a labored sigh of sadness. Since her father's death, she didn't have room for more than a companion. The ruling of a country proved to be a lot of work.

"If we had waited for word, maybe Lord Torrick would have sent his son," Medora finally suggested, as if that hadn't been the dilemma Brienna faced for a very long time.

"I sent someone," she answered coolly. "I never received a reply; therefore, I can only assume my cousin, Thane, stopped him."

"All the more reason for you to stay in the castle, Your Highness. Your cousin will not stop until he has control of your lands." She parted the curtain of heavy canvas and peeked out of the cart. "We were probably being followed and will never get out of Avalbane alive." Her voice quavered with her fears.

"Medora, you didn't have to come." Brienna heaved an agitated breath. "I am capable of traveling alone."

"You are the Queen and you should never be left alone!" she exclaimed as if it were an unheard of act.

"Yes, a great downfall to my thrust into power," she groaned.

Up until her father died, she had flitted about the countryside on her own. Dressed like a commoner, she had mingled with people in the villages and saw the sights of her land, unhindered by her noble station.

"Nevertheless, we are on our way and you have not let me go alone. I will see to things personally this time."

Traveling for a day by horse, under the dark moonless sky, they had secretly made their way out of the massive catacombs beneath her castle. Not only did she sneak away from her home, she did so under the disguise of a peasant.

Brienna shifted to relieve the numbness in her rump and tugged the wrinkles in her heavy gray wool dress. She tried to imagine herself perched on the pillowed chair in her room. It didn't stop the bounce of the cart from jarring her back to the present, but it filled the space of time to let her mind wander.

Pastures came into view, and then faded once they entered the heavy thicketed forest. Brienna wiped a hand over her perspiring brow. A month had passed, and another time that her body heated with an expectancy to be filled. Each full moon since the marriage contract was signed, she'd felt the weight of a whole world on her. Her kingdom needed an heir to carry on in her place. Her power of healing needed to be preserved in the direct descendant of Rhoswen women. It was a gift. It was an honor. However, it also remained a secret because of an intolerable society.

Few knew of her power to heal wounds. Her mother had told her once she was the last healer, it would be up to her to have an heir. Of course, she had never understood the importance until adulthood. She never fully appreciated the path of her future, until now. Before her mother's early death, she should have been told more about the dying sect called Silver Dragon Healers. Maybe then, she wouldn't feel so confused about life in general.

"Do you really think this is a wise decision, Your Highness? Maybe the messenger was detained and we missed him in his coming and our going."

"I sent the most trusted man I know. His arrival should have been long before now." Brienna pushed the dirty canvas flap aside and looked out at the passing countryside. "I have waited long enough for Lord Torrick's rakish son to come for me. It's been over a year since my father signed the treaty and gave my hand in trust to that barbaric oaf. I can wait no longer, and I refuse to be harnessed by patience."

She looked at her fingertips, her palm, and the thin white scar. Memories of the blood smearing her skin reminded her of the vow. One year ago, almost to the day, she sacrificed her life for that of her people. She gave a blood oath to be bound to a man she had never met, a man she'd didn't know anything about. With her very own dagger, she had sliced her hand open. She had pressed the stinging flesh to her father's scrolled directive and shackled her soul to the eldest Torrick heir from the Kingdom of Kylemore. The laceration she'd made that day was the only scar she bore on her person, even though she had it in her power to heal the cut. This one she left with purpose. She wanted the testament of her vow to show her devotion to reign over her lands with strength and gentleness. Both of which, had been sorely lacking.

"You did not have to leave that unsightly mark, Your Highness. The young Lord Torrick will not appreciate the gesture." Medora frowned.

"Maybe, but I did this for myself. It is my reminder." She rubbed the white line on her pale skin. "Do you think he might be young?"

"We will pray he is a handsome and caring man."

"Oh poppy seeds, a man with caring would have come to me."

She stared at the scar. She had the gift and power to heal. The ancient and mystical religion paralleled with the one she had with God. The secret sect had virtually died out over the centuries, save one – herself.

To Brienna, her mother's sword became the symbol of the strength her lands needed. As a healer, she had the position of protectorate of that strength. As Queen, she had the ultimate power of Avalbane. She could bear the rule alone, but she could not conceive a child for the future without a husband. Nor could she stop the attacks of her enemy. She truly needed the alliance with Kylemore.

Brienna closed her hand and looked at Medora.

"I think it best if he never comes. Then you will be free to live your life as you wish," Medora said. "Marry a man that respects you as well as loves you."

Brienna longed to be loved. She also hoped to love. The Torrick she should marry was her chance at both and still, after a long wait for a groom whom did not present himself, she doubted she'd have either.

"Love is for the poets, Medora, not for me." Brienna tightened her fingers together in agitation.

Medora's hands twisted in the folds of her cloak. Her nervous shifting put more anxiety on them than necessary and Brienna didn't know how to dispel the air of foreboding other than to keep talking.

"Have you met a man that brings the promise of love?" Brienna inquired, thinking she knew the answer.

"Your Highness knows I have no time for such flirtations." Her eyes widened with a mysterious twinkle.

For the first time, Brienna realized that maybe she and Medora weren't as close as she thought. If the woman fancied someone, she thought she would be the first to know. Now it seemed, she was the last.

"There is someone that has turned your head, is there not?" She leaned forward. "Come, tell me who he is and I will see to your marriage at our most earliest of arrivals back at the castle."

"He doesn't even know I exist," she moaned and dropped her thick lashes to cover her eyes.

"I am sure he must." Brienna smiled. "You are pretty and charming to have in one's company."

The coach bumped over the ground and they both laughed, letting tension ease on their journey. The amusement, however, was short lived. Brienna couldn't control her thoughts and Medora couldn't contain her worries.

"Maybe Your Highness should consider sending another messenger." Medora offered. "We could return to the castle before nightfall and dispatch a man or even a half dozen right away."

"No, my mind is set; my road lay out before me. My father is dead. I have to come to some settling of this matter. My cousin, Thane, wishes to rule our providence and that can only happen by my death or our marriage. I refuse to ever marry Thane. First, because he is an evil, brutal man, and second, because I am betrothed to another." Brienna exhaled in exasperation. Betrothed! The word alone was a vulgarity now. What was she thinking? What possessed her to commit to the contract with her very soul?

"Promised to a man who appears not to care if he makes you his wife!" Medora laid a hand on Brienna's knee and patted it in sympathy. "He is a foolish man, as they all are. Once he sees you, his head will surely turn to do your bidding."

"Well, one way or the other, I am going to find out if he wishes to dissolve this agreement. As my husband, he will be able to thwart any actions Thane tries to make on my life and liberty. If he turns me away a free woman, then I will make an alliance where I will, to keep my people safe."

The cart bumped over another rutty patch in the road and then the shouts of men alerted her they were moving faster than normal. Brienna leaned out the window and looked behind them at the charging throng of a dozen men. Cloaked warriors thundering a few hundred yards at the rear was not an encounter she wished for. It seemed too soon for Thane to know she was on the quest of fulfill her marriage contract. Yet, there they were, large, powerfully well-built men carrying weapons. They rode fast and hard to overcome her trappings rolling down the dark forest road.

Sword of Rhoswen

Her disbelief that the men could be barbarian killers sent by her cousin rousted another threat she had not anticipated on having to deal with. If not warriors for Lord Thane Rhoswen, then she had to assume they might be criminals.

"Highwaymen!" she gasped, dragging her body back into the cart and sitting down. "Medora, whatever happens, do not divulge who I am. Since we have no escort, it will be believable that we are couriers for the Queen, on our way to deliver a message to her betrothed, to inquire as to his intentions. This will be the story we tell anyone that asks, until we've reached our destination."

She wished for all the world that a day could pass in pleasure. She'd battled the masses of ruffians Thane sent to the villages she was to protect and now, when she should stay to protect her home of Avalbane, she had to seek help. It wasn't much to ask for one day of peace and a leisurely stroll through the rose gardens. Someday, she hoped to have that little bit of heaven on earth.

Kylemore was her objective and no beasts laying siege to her journey would stop her. Beneath her to beg, she hated she might have to once she met up with William Torrick's wayward son.

"Yes, Your Highness." Medora's anxiety grew with the men outside.

"Now, let me see what can be done to avert these boorish men." She took off her black wool cloak and put a slippered foot upon the opening of the doorframe. The makeshift box over the cart was not of high quality and the whole contraption swayed as she scaled the side with a perilous expediency. She had always been agile so she did not find the feat impossible.

"Your Highness, what are you doing?" Medora asked with alarm.

"My weapons are tied on top. If I am going to defend you and myself from these libertine thieves, then I need to get to my bow."

The cart had little to grip when it came to climbing, so she found her heavy gray gown restrictive in her movements. A dark rider swiftly rode alongside and she kicked him in the jaw. Her movements paused as she listened to the stream of swearing. Vulgar words were not unknown to her ears, but she had never heard the elegance in which the man's rich baritone voice put them. It actually made her heart skip and a shiver race up her spine.

Brienna hoisted herself to the top of the cart. She flipped up a canvas covering her weapons and lifted her bow. The sleek and smooth leather grip fit her hand from years of use. The rigid ash wood flexed to just the right tension that made her aim, accurately lethal.

"Keep steady, man, I will attempt to slow some of them down," she shouted to the driver.

She had hired the man to make the trip and even he didn't know who she was. His momentary look at her displayed his surprise.

The first arrow she shot quivered a piercing trail through the heavily misted air. It went into the band of men and hit one in the arm, giving her some pleasure in hearing his yelp. It did not produce the satisfaction she wanted because it only slowed him.

The second arrow followed a similar course and she chastised herself for not practicing from a moving horse more. The hit landed in another man's leg. He too gave a howl of not pain, but determination, pushing him faster into the pursuit.

Brienna didn't want to kill anyone. Given the choice, she was left limited. The third arrow may have hit its target and made a kill if the cart hadn't bounced up and tipped her over.

She fell sideways and tumbled over the edge. She quickly sought to hold onto anything to keep her attached, but alas, the futile effort left her air-bound. Her slender fingers latched onto one item, her sword.

The blade, a finely crafted weapon of steel, had been custom-made in weight and size, solely for a lady's use and fit only for a healer. Said to be blended and forged with the scales of a mythically enchanted silver dragon. Her father gave her the sword, broken and beyond the repair of normal craftsman. Nonetheless, quite by accident while examining the lethal weapon, she found the power of her hands could heal the steel. Magically mended, she cherished the sword more once it had returned to its former beauty.

Her father had been impressed with her devotion to its use. However, he would have preferred a son who could wield one in battle. Her teacher, Jinn, thought her an excellent student. Although he, too, had the opinion women should leave fighting up to men.

Brienna landed on her back, knocking the wind out of her lungs. In the interim of regaining her breath, the thunder of horse hooves passed her. The voice she heard before shouted orders to continue after the cart and she tightened her hold on the hilt of her sword.

"Well, what have we here?" the masculine voice asked with a measure of humor. "A wee lass that looks more like a woodland fairy. Pray tell, what do you think you were doing to me and my men?" His condescending laugh came laced with warmth and kindness.

She blinked, looking up at his handsome face.

Chapter 2

Brogan gazed at the nymph with a newfound wonder of the world. Most things didn't surprise him. What he had not imagined was the Lass scaling the cart like a lizard and firing upon him and his men with the valiance of a warrior. Her lack of voice after slamming to the earth like the discards of the heavens was understandable.

"Well, Lass, be ye real or a vision to my weary eyes?"

He noted her fingers tightening on the handle of the sword at her side. The blade, short and fat, had no less lethal qualities than his. She scrambled to her feet swiftly and swung the heavy-gauged weapon in attack.

Brogan took a defensive stance and let her blow glance off his ready steel.

She stepped back, staring in surprise.

"Do ye think for a minute I have lost all me senses, Lass?"

He had a keen anticipation for her moves and had no wish to fight the woman. The unfortunate part was, female or not, she could be every bit as dangerous as she appeared. She knew how to stand, to swing, and to lunge at him with her sword. Her looks alone were enough to make him drop his guard. The beauty of her delicate face captivated him into noting details. Small nose, brilliant violet eyes set just right, and rose-tinted cheeks. He licked his lips and wondered what her kiss would taste like. His gaze wandered over her, lingering on the fine details to the way she was put together.

"You will leave me on my way, sir." She held her ground and her sword ready.

His nature never allowed him to think he could be defeated in a battle. Nor did the wee lass, a woodland pixie of extreme beauty, look to be a threat, other than to his throbbing cock. This dance of power only made him hard and aching to touch her in ways he knew would make her submissive.

"Ye, Lass, should put down that steel before ye get hurt." He watched warily as he had already seen her agility in climbing the cart as well. The added skill at kicking him in the jaw during that course of movement amazed him. He rubbed a hand over his rough unshaven face, still feeling the smart of her small foot. He looked down at her shoe. A soft covering that did not inflict pain, but she had put a lot of power into the punch it gave him. His consideration as to what her toes looked like made him laugh again. Now was not the time to be thinking of the girl's feet, nor if they might be pleasing to the eye.

The Lass sliced the air as she brought the sword around at him a second time, a third, a fourth and she kept at him. He knew his laugh fueled her determination. Not weak by any means, she still tired from the fight.

"Now, Lass, I really must ask that we stop. I do not wish to play this game any longer. One of us could get seriously hurt."

He stood his sword on end with the point of the blade resting on the tip of his brown goat-hide boot. He studied the golden-haired beauty in front of him. Her fighting like a warrior was out of place. In spite of that, she oozed excitement. The fire in her violet eyes and the glow that flushed her cheeks ignited flames of desire. If her passionate swordplay could be so hot, he wondered if she could as bring much fervor to his bed?

"Fine, we'll end it," she announced and took a final swing.

He narrowed his eyes as a violent storm washed over his calmness. The Lass hit his sword with such a severe blow in the hilt, it jerked unmercifully from his unready hand. A few more inches and she would have had his hand too. Instead, she managed a clean, razor laceration through his brown leather glove. He cringed slightly in pain.

"Damnation, woman!" Brogan yanked his glove off and pressed the clean slice to his mouth to quell the sting.

The Lass backed off and he thought he saw a glimmer of concern in her eyes. Yet, as he regained composure and continued his assessment of her, she really gave away no personal feelings.

When she raised a brow, a thin golden arch, he saw the twinkle in her eye acknowledge her readiness to proceed.

Strip off the dress and tan her hide. That was what he should do. Or... his grin returned. Slice the clothes from her young limber body and make love to her right there on the leaf-strewn forest floor.

He waited to give rise to any fear she had churning inside her, letting her marinate with the mystery of his next move. She remained a pillar of stone, with an expression that appeared contemptuous in nature.

Brogan could not hurt the Lass. He could, however, prevent her from hurting him anymore. The golden-haired angel had a wickedly dangerous side and to rush her could prove tricky.

He laughed. When had his life not been complicated with precarious confrontations? He charged, catching her off guard. Swift and sure, he offered no time for her to raise a defense. He tackled her to the ground. A man he would have fought to death's door. The Lass he could do no more than pin her struggling frame to the earth's floor. He crushed her under the entire length of his frame. He held her arms to the ground alongside her head and stared. Every ounce of strength she mastered in wielding the sword began to show with the depletion in some of her fortitude. He had the advantage of strength, size, and weight.

"This is how I prefer my women, Lass... on their back." He breathed heavily, regaining his composure.

He took in the delicate lines of her face. The soft feminine features were flushed. Her cheeks, painted by God's paintbrush, tinged them a burnished pink. Perspiration shimmered like diamond dewdrops over the bridge of her nose. Her lips parted, expelling sweet pants of exhaustion. Nobility, honor, chivalry—where were these qualities when needed most?

Brogan's head dropped so his mouth covered hers instantly. He plied her moist lips with a long hard kiss she did not resist. He gained no participation either. No fight, no win. He lifted his head to look at the lovely almond shaped violet eyes.

He felt the heave of her firm breasts as she gasped for the air he did not allow when he sucked at her sweet fiery breath. He kissed her again. Soft, gentle, and so deeply that he waited for her resistance to waver. However, something highly virtuous took root and he did not want her submissive. Not right at the moment when she was most vulnerable. No, he wanted her naked under him when she was eager for his caress and begging for his kiss. Both dreams were highly unlikely as he pulled free and studied her complacent gaze.

"What happened to the fight in ye, Lass? Are ye ready to yield?"

He watched the honeyed lips turn with a small smile as she nodded her head. It was a grand triumph; he could get such a surrender. She hardly seemed the type to give in and then when he should have questioned his instincts, he let her arms go.

"Very good then." He raised his weight up to get off her and in that second realized his mistake. The girl's knee caught him between the legs and he tossed himself off the seething Lass. A wolf in sheep's clothing, she tried to crawl away. He grabbed the back of her hair and dragged her up on her feet.

"This is the end, Lass." He strapped her against him with an arm around her narrow middle and one around her surging chest. Her heavy breath rose and fell under the constraints. He could not help glancing over her small shoulder at the pearly swells of her breasts, expanding with every deep gasp she took. How tasty she looked. How deliciously beautiful she was. How hungry she made him. She did not look built for brandishing such a weapon, let alone doing it very well.

"Let me go!" she demanded and bit firmly into his arm.

"Ye will have to do better than that," he informed her when she could not draw blood by sinking her teeth into his leather covered forearm. "Yield to me and I will let ye stand on your own." His thumb accidentally brushed over the tip of her breast. Through the heavy cloth, he felt the hard bead of her nipple. The protuberance seized his concentration. He could not stop his thumb from making another pass, firmer, more defined in cause.

When the Lass stomped hard on his foot, he released her with an annoyed grunt of pain. Then he grabbed hold before she could get away and her struggle caused them to fall.

"Ye are a real spitfire, Lass." He considered the beauty in her vehement stare. The violet eyes fired and ready to fight, yet calm and undaunted by her predicament. She had an amazing gift that most men could not possess. The Lass had an overabundance of true courage.

He wouldn't have touched her again if it hadn't been for the whimper he extracted from her. His fingers moved back up the hillock of her breast. Her chest heaved, pressing the mound tighter to his audacious teasing touch. The laces of her gown were loose and he took his gaze from her face to look at the ivory skin hiding beneath the fabric. The length of her slender neck and the appearance of flesh so soft drew his lips.

"Please," she whimpered when his mouth ran a rampage over the buttery smoothness.

He crossed her collarbone while his fingers made a steady project of loosening the points of her gown to give him access to her breasts. He kissed the top swell and followed the curve as the cloth gave way to his pursuit. He lifted his head and looked at the dusky peak, her nipple puckered in the aftermath of his stare.

"Please, don't...oh God," she whined.

The sound of her pleas weren't for his quitting. She squirmed and arched, presenting him with the fullness of her succulent tit. He took the advantage and swirled his tongue around the raspberry hued nipple before sucking the sweet nub into his mouth.

Her hands clenched in the throes of her rising excitement. Brogan slid his hands over hers and laced his gloved fingers to hers. She continued to flex her fingers, driving him insane with the thought of how she could be squeezing his cock in the same manner. The rhythmic pumping and kneading made him groan. If he didn't stop the torturing of himself, he knew the serious problem from his rise would make the insides of his britches extremely uncomfortable.

In all assessment, God had not put her together like other women. The ones he knew...and knew them well, were rounder, softer, meatier. This girl, whom he quickly corrected in his mind to deem a lady, was small, slender, and her contours were firm. Yet, she had a splendid, feminine softness in all the right places that made him want to melt into her embrace, if ever she should offer one.

He lifted his head and looked at her. The tint of a blush covered her nicely—from the pale rosy breast to her enflamed cheeks. He liked the way the Lass appeared so complacent.

"No more fight?" he asked.

She shook her head quickly. Tendrils of golden hair bounced with the action.

"Very good, my wee Lass, do not break a valued trust again unless ye wish to anger me more than ye have done thus far," he warned sternly, even though he felt not a drop of anger while his hand still throbbed from the sting of her sword.

† † †

Brienna sat up, gathering her dress together, tightening the laces to close the gap.

She wanted to rub a hand over her breast. It ached painfully from the graze of his fingers, the force of his teeth, and the tenderness of his kiss. The tingling tip begged for another gentle caress. Disturbingly, her mind jumped to the idea with an adventurous excitement.

"Who are you?" she asked, trying to distance her thoughts from the sensations coursing through her.

She felt ashamed for the betrayal of her body and her sentimental emotions. His voice echoed deep in her head when he spoke. The wild spearmint-infused breath mingling with hers provided a sweet waft of motivation for her compliance.

"Brogan. Now what has ye on this road without escort, m'lady?" He stood back and looked her over as if he inspected livestock.

"I'm on my way to Kylemore to deliver a message to Lord Torrick," she replied, hoping the name would offer her some protection from the ruffian.

She almost didn't want to consider protection from him as she turned her eyes from the devilish roving she did over his leather trousers. The worn animal hides showed a part of him too intimate for her to be considering. The movement of muscle in his powerful thighs intoxicated her with a yearning to feel them beneath her fingers. Worst was the flutter to her stomach so that she wanted to run...not from him, but into his thick and wonderfully possessive arms. It was written in his gaze that he was capable of holding a woman so she felt special. His kiss had proved wholeheartedly how much skill he acquired in that area of passion and she fully approved of the expertise.

He was too handsome to be anything but a vision in her dreams, where her imaginary world let her love a man and he love her. Her limited knowledge prevented her from knowing intimacy. A touch, a caress, an embrace—those were things she longed for and had indeed anxiously anticipated. She thought with a husband, but it seemed worth exploring with the man staring at her. He already proved himself capable.

"What is the message?" He leaned back on his heel against a tree.

"That is none of your business." She made the statement sound reprimanding of his insolence and then realized she didn't want him to know of her rank of royalty.

She watched him and couldn't even chastise herself for the thoughts hovering along his attractiveness. His green eyes danced flames around her and for a second she stayed mesmerized by a grin stretching wide and showing the flash of straight white teeth. A barbaric well-groomed thief was not something she was prepared to see. Nevertheless, Brienna couldn't let the fact that he was the epitome of a ruggedly virile man excuse that he was about to rob, rape, and maybe kill her.

"Where are ye from? If it is important, I will see that ye get to Kylemore."

"I'm from Avalbane," she answered, seeing no harm in the question.

"Ah, then I might hazard a guess to some of your reason for coming. Tell me, is Princess Rhoswen growing weary of her wait for a husband? No doubt, her father is behind this again. He has sent messengers every third turn of the moon requesting the union commence."

"I don't think it is a husband she wants, but finality to a contract." She felt compelled to explain. "She would accept dissolution as readily."

"Lord Torrick has given Avalbane a treaty. She should be happy with that alone because she will get no more. Torrick's son has no interest in wedding the shrew."

"Excuse me?" Brienna looked at him with open shock. "Princess Rhoswen is not a termagant for which you have any right to speak of like that. She may have some faults but no one would dare say she is a shrew!"

At least she didn't think anyone would. No, she knew there was no reason for anyone to have any but the highest regards for her. Friendly, even to the lowest peasant, she helped where needed and healed regardless of rank.

Referring to herself as if she were truly someone else came easy. Leaving him with the continued belief the king was still alive seemed even better. This was not the first time she had masqueraded as someone other than the ruler of lands vast and rich. She found people less willing to speak their minds if they knew she was of noble blood. It made many leery to voice honest opinions if they thought ultimately it would derive a decree that would quash them for speaking out.

"Lass, kings do not bargain off their pretty daughters haphazardly. I have seen nary a man wed through an arrangement get anything but a plain, dowdy woman. Each has wished he were dead rather than look at her. King Rhoswen had to think the Torricks were fools to give an offering of marriage without even seeing the intended maid."

"Lord Torrick saw her. He'd have relayed what he knew to his son." She trembled with anger making her weak in concentration. The man rattled her by his accusations and she didn't like it.

"No doubt lies in order to deceive his son and trick him into journeying to Avalbane to a damned marriage," he said with disparaging disgust.

"You are very outspoken for the Torricks. I'd almost think you had some ill will of your own against the Rhoswens." She cocked her head and waited for him to disband the idea she had of his enraging temper.

"Nay, I have nary met a one of them, but rumors are not always lies," he informed her.

"And they are not always truths either." She felt a hypocrite as she debated sentiment based on hearsay. She'd been just as guilty, thinking the Torricks were evil monsters when, as Brogan pointed out, they had a treaty and thus far had not broken it. Still, something had to be said by the way they were handling the conclusion to the contract. Brogan gave her details without being aware to whom he was really giving the information.

"We have thus come to an impasse in our conversation, m'lady. Before we turn our tongues loose on an argument, I say we retire the topic. I do wish to leave ye with one idea and that is to return to the Princess. Tell her not to hold her breath for Torrick's son will not come."

"You have no right to speak for him or his father. My message is for them regardless. Therefore, I shall be allowed to go on my way!"

"Very well. I will take ye to Lord Torrick, so that ye can deliver your message."

"How do I know you will take me there?" She challenged his words with tenacious distrust. He appeared to be nothing but a bandit, a criminal, a rogue out to steal a person's possessions... and a thread tugged inside. He could also steal a woman's heart.

"I assure ye, Lass. I am close to Lord Torrick. As a matter of fact, I am his most loyal subject. I will see ye safely to Kylemore so ye may deliver your message." He stepped toward her. "However, if I find ye are not whom ye say, I will not be very pleased." His fingers wrapped the hilt of his sword as a warning.

Chapter 3

Brogan paced a small area waiting for the return of his men. If not for them, he would have shucked the gown right off the Lass and buried his cock into her creamy core. Any woman as fetching and fiery as this one would no doubt be delicious.

Her mouth formed a rigid straight line as she waited with reluctant patience. She, however, did not pace. She stood as straight and hard as a tree. He felt sorry for her lack of understanding that he was not her enemy. He told her he'd get her safely to Kylemore. At the same time, he had to wonder if she wasn't whom she claimed, would he be laying his neck on the line giving her his trust. It would be just like Thane to have women trained in warfare, as well as men. The petite lady displaying all the brimstone of hell with her hackles up could be one of his spies. A kingdom of men and women warriors would be hard to conquer, let alone stand up against. His fight with Thane Rhoswen threatened his home of Kylemore. With the understanding Thane wanted King Padric Rhoswen's lands, Brogan took to heart how hazardous it would be to send an insult to the Princess. It could make matters worse.

Reluctantly circumspect, he would drag the Lass along under his watchful guard. It would be dangerous for them both. He'd have to protect her from Thane Rhoswen because if she were who she claimed to be then Thane would not want to hear of such a message being sent. At the same time, he'd have to protect himself from her sword... and worse, he'd have to protect his heart. Even he could not help the interest she stirred in him like no other woman he knew. The clack of wheels on the cart turned their heads. They looked to his men bringing the conveyance back.

"Where is my driver?" the Lass quickly asked.

One of Brogan's men, Sedge, drove the cart. He looked down and directed his answer to him instead of the Lass. "He is dead." He gave the news with a frown. "Fell and broke his neck, he did."

Brogan simply nodded. He could hear the Lass fuming with spits and sputters—her outrage ready to erupt. Instead, she gave him one hardened look of anger and hurried over to the cart.

"We got a woman inside screaming about Princess Rhoswen and how she'll not appreciate my lack of manners. She's squalling as if I touched her and I swear I have nary laid me one finger on the wench."

"Aye, well, she does not have a sword, does she?" Brogan raked his hair back.

If both women were skilled in weaponry, it would only mean double the amount of work he'd have to put into guarding or protecting them. "This one can wield one better than some men." He rubbed at his jaw, still aching.

She was a fighter and he could never trust what she might do next. He hoped she could not outwit him. She battled with the heart of a warrior and he would not underestimate her strength of will.

"No. She's scared out of her wits, wailing like a wounded animal." Sedge cupped his hands over his ears. "God, I wish she'd stop before she takes me head off."

"Aye, that would be an accomplishment." Brogan waved Sedge away from the door and locked eyes with the Lass. "Get in. We leave now and if ye can't silence that wailing instantly, I will do it."

Brogan walked among his mounted men and gave them their orders. Then all set to get aboard his own stallion, he handed the reins off to a man and climbed on the cart.

"I will ride up here for a ways, Sedge." He looked over the side at the door. "She is not the submissive sort. She will try to escape us again, I would bet my life on it," he whispered with some pride in knowing this certitude.

†　†　†

The cart jolted to a start and Brienna hugged Medora.

"What are they going to do to us?" Medora sniffed back her sobs.

"I don't know for certain. The man that seems to be in charge is called Brogan. He is not from around here. His speech is different from ours. He says he'll take us to Lord Torrick, and he may, for his brogue is much as I remember Lord Torrick's. But we are still close to Thane's land and we can't believe for a minute we are safe."

She lifted her head and wondered where he rode in the lot. Behind—guarded and wary of the lands they crossed—or out front like a preening pheasant, swishing his tail feathers proudly with his prize captives.

"Brogan is a sly scoundrel that may be in this for the riches he thinks he can steal from us, or he is a mercenary hired to find Queen Rhoswen. He is too far from Kylemore for me to believe too quickly he is as loyal a subject to Lord Torrick as he claims."

"Then they may take us to your cousin?" Medora dried her face and looked aghast with the doomed prospects.

"Never! We will do our best to be rid of these foul men and take our chance at getting to Lord Torrick on our own."

Brienna looked out at the men riding behind them. There were none in front and the escort seemed unconventional which further led her to believe Brogan only a hired lance-knight.

"Oh, Your Hi...Oh, my lady, you'll not be climbing out there again?" Medora wailed, watching Brienna rise up and shift her gown free of its inconvenient twist around her legs.

"My bow and knives will still be up top. I don't know what he's done with my sword. I have wounded two of his men. Maybe I can manage to wound enough men so we can get away."

She hoisted the burdensome hem of her gown up to her knees. The idea she could actually succeed seemed so far from reality, she chose not to think about it. If it were she alone, she may have managed. With Medora, a millstone around her neck, she had fewer options. Even though her handmaid exasperated her most of them time, she still loved her and would protect her with her own life if need be.

Unable to think of a better time, Brienna put a foot up on the framed opening of the door and swung out too quickly to climb up. She hoisted herself over the edge and a hand clamped her wrist. She looked up at Brogan's green eyes. The rich lush color of her homeland pastures appeared more amused than angered. He had awaited her with the cunning of a fox.

"So ye would like to ride up here with me?"

The glint of bright green mockingly twinkled and it infuriated her the way they sidetracked her for a second. He smiled and the wild spearmint of his breath flailed her. She inhaled the sweetness and returned to her senses, wrenching her wrist in the grasp of his thick fingers. He hung on with an unyielding strength, so she stopped trying when the effort brought no return. His soft chuckle, the way his eyes wrinkled in the corners with merriment, attracted and distracted all her concentration.

"Stop the cart," he yelled over his shoulder, "the Lass wishes to ride with me."

He had said it loud enough so all the men could hear and enjoy the joke he made of her. She did not take to humiliation well. Actually, she took it very poorly. Her mind buzzed around her next plan with a rapid succession until she inhaled to get the strength to commit to it.

"I do not want anything to do with you," she charged with outrage that he would try to make a travesty of her persistence. "I'll go back inside."

"No. I think I shall keep ye close. I have other things to think about besides the schemes ye are plotting in your pretty head." Brogan pulled her up to him, holding her against his chest, her breasts compressed to the hardness. "Sedge, go ahead and get down. The Lass and I are about to have a very private conversation."

Brienna waited until they were alone and Brogan eased his hold, then she moved faster than a lightning bolt could rip through a stormy sky. In seconds, she had her twin daggers, one in each hand, and her arms around Brogan's shoulders. She held a sharp tip to his neck and one blade to his ribs.

"I'll kill you if you don't send your men on their way and leave us be," she warned, sternly scraping a blade over the stubble on his throat.

"I cannot allow that. These lands are dangerous and I do not wish to see harm come to ye, Lass." He moved slightly and the blade pressed his neck.

Brogan gently kissed the sleeve of her arm, catching the cuff and a sliver of her hand. He nudged the fabric so his lips, framed by the scruffy stubble of his face, grazed the side of her wrist.

"What are you doing?" she asked nervously, the tingle of nerves picking up every caress of his kiss to her skin. It left wild streaks of heat as if she'd been touched by a flame.

"I want something good to remember if I am to die by your sweet hand, Lass." He kept his voice low, murmuring like a lover would, and kissed her arm again. Her resolve weakened, her hand trembled from the consuming odd foreplay.

She didn't want to be fresh butter but hard ice. Yet either way, he melted her resolve. He hypnotized her by the calming action. By the time her brain started to think, he grabbed her arm and spun her around so the daggers she held were against her own neck and ribs.

† † †

Brogan hadn't meant for the blade to come so close to her skin. The blood trickling down the steel spiraled over his fingers. His heart raced with an outraged panic. He threw the razor edged knives so they stabbed the ground.

"I could have killed ye." He directed his angry frustration on her, but was furious with himself. He had never inflicted harm on any woman before.

He jumped down and waved for Sedge.

"Get the Lass down," he ordered.

To touch her would be to burn with the wounded look in her eyes. When he managed to take his emotions and lock them away, he looked to see her pull a handkerchief from inside her sleeve and hold it to her neck.

"I'll make you wish you had killed me," she informed him coldly. "I'll not be kept like a captive."

"No?"

He could not get over the sedate way in which she stood her ground against him. No tears or wailing about how he hurt her. A warrior through and through, he took a measure of pride in capturing her. Women and weapons didn't belong together. If he were asked the night before which might have a chance at ensnaring his heart, he'd say a docile maid to do his every bidding. The Lass and all her beautiful passion needed some direction. Still, he could see himself in danger of truly wanting no one other than her in his bed.

"Well, we will just see about that. Duane!" He shouted for a giant amongst them. "Tie her hands and put her on my horse. Instead of my guest, she prefers to be my prisoner."

"You can't do that!" she shrieked with a pronounced indignation.

"I can and I will. Ye are proving to be a nuisance and if ye give me any more trouble, I will strap ye to the back of the cart with your trunk."

He didn't tire of her persistent inflexibility when it came to accepting his help. It only pressed him more into believing the pretty Lass an enemy to him. He cringed as the proud beauty held her hands out for Duane to bind them. Her eyes fixated on him and he could not give her the satisfaction of seeing regret. He watched her for any indication she regretted her challenges—something to give him reason to change his mind. Nothing came beyond the blatant defiance she wished to uphold. The Lass was a courageous vixen sent to plague him with new considerations in making decisions. She stood firm in her obstinacy and he in his.

"Put her on my horse," Brogan ordered.

He picked the daggers up and dropped one inside each boot he wore. His servant's assistance in getting the Lass on the horse was stifled when she kicked her foot into his shin.

"Don't touch me. I can manage on my own," she sneered, jerking her dress up with her bound hands and lodging it betwixt her legs.

Her foot hit the stirrup, her hands gripped the mane, and she leapt up like a cat to perch on the back of the horse. The grace and agility she possessed blended a beautiful skill with feminine countenance.

Brogan swung up on the big horse. The hardness of his torso took pleasure in the fit of her against him. He encircled her with his arms, locking her in the prison of his company. Once satisfied at having her in secure position, he relented in his vexation.

"Ye smell good, Lass." He sniffed the golden hair on her head, plaited in one thick braid that lay over her shoulder.

"And you don't."

He chuckled at her never-ending vehemence.

"These ropes are hurting my wrists," she complained quietly. "Do you think you could loosen them?"

Brogan knew he asked for trouble by obliging her. He lifted his leg and pulled out one of her daggers. He cut the rope, tossed it to the ground, and put the dagger back in his boot. The coarse hemp had indeed abraded the lovely translucent skin and he held her wrist to rub his thumb soothingly over it.

"You have a gentle touch," she complimented.

"Ye have a sharpness in wit, so don't go getting any ideas of overpowering me by charm."

"Are you always so distrustful of even words?"

"Only when they come from an enchantress such as I believe ye can be, when ye have only your mouth left to fight with."

She made it her last comment and for two hours they rode in silence. He could sense the Lass succumbing to the drowsiness of boredom. He also appreciated how busy her mind worked. Cautiously, he gave her a niche in his arms for her to surrender to comfort. She slouched against his support.

He did not glance down at the Lass reposing into the curve of his arm. He feared she would see how much he liked how she relaxed against him. With her head rested on his shoulder, he placed his chin against her forehead to keep her steady.

"When do we stop?" Her dreamy voice had an edge of sleepy coyness.

"Not for another hour. Then we will set up camp for the night."

He slid his hand further around, covering hers in a gentle embrace of intimacy to guide her into sleep. If anything, he knew she could stir no trouble in slumber.

"I don't think I can stay awake that long,"

"Then do not try."

In complete repose, the Lass drifted off. He knew she hadn't really intended to do so. The ploy to make him believe she could be docile had a flaw. Under his fortunate star, her weariness gave him peace.

Brogan slowed to make the ride gentle. He avoided looking at his men. They snickered with talk about his softening nature. Maybe he did have a weakness for females. It didn't seem so bad to have a heart.

"Lass?" He called her from her dreams.

Her lashes fluttered up and she looked at him with the arresting warmth his heart yearned for. He shook the complicated emotion from his head and slid from the horse, bringing her down to stand in front of him.

"We are going to set up camp. There are some rocks over there that ye can have a few moments of privacy behind." He gestured to the large boulders embedded into the earthen hill.

"My friend?" She looked to the cart.

"She will be given the same accommodations," he explained and then warned, "Do not try anything foolish."

Brogan found himself pacing and waiting her return. The Lass took forever. He took a step in the direction of his wayward charge and stopped when she finally emerged. Immediately, before she could tell his discomposure, he set his sights to something else. Ignoring her presence would suit him well. He'd been giving her too much of his time and he set about to disregard her presence, all but for the need to know her moves. Unfortunately, he had to look to accomplish that task. He noted her hands first and saw no weapons. It would not mean she hadn't already sharpened a stick and was waiting to retrieve it when he slept.

Haloed by the setting sun, the angel walked toward him. She had undone her braid and strolled along combing her fingers through the waves of long golden locks. A silhouette in vibrant color, her beauty far surpassed any he'd ever known. Her temerity refreshed his soul. He stared, awestruck. Her small diminutive frame was willowy, graceful, and elegant in contrast to the harshness of the men he traveled with.

"She's a wee bit on the skinny side if ye ask me." Duane offered the comment in a low teasing voice.

"She is perfect," Brogan responded and then coughed to clear away the wistful murmur of his contemplative thoughts.

"Do you think I could get something out of my trunk?" the Lass asked, her voice exuded the lethal charm of sweetness.

"Pray tell, what kind of torture devises do ye keep there to plague me with, Lass?"

He motioned for Duane to go ahead and get the trunk so he could inspect its contents. Duane hardly struggled under the weight of the wood casket he lugged over to them. He set it down and awaited further instructions.

"Well, need I worry about another attack from ye?" Brogan glanced at the trunk.

When she did not answer, he pushed her aside to look for himself. He gave no thought to delving into her garments. Lifting fine woven fabrics that were of the intimate nature, he picked up a leather pouch. Inside he found it contained an assortment of valuable jewels.

"Those do not belong to you," she hissed when he tied the pouch to his belt.

"I will just hold them for safekeeping." He looked everything over thoroughly and then motioned for her to get what it was she wanted.

She retrieved an elegant silver comb and handed it to Medora. Brogan watched them, supposedly two servants. One, far supreme when it came to her deportment, her clothes, and her learned skills. The evidence mounted against the Lass and he doubled his guardedness toward her. He watched for the moment, the golden hair of a goddess with fine silk threads, too richly beautiful for a simple messenger. The scent of lavender gave him further notice when she sat on the horse. He had not meant to mention how wonderful she smelled. The private thought simply slipped out.

She tipped her head back. The hair hung free in a waterfall of waves.

"Thank you, Medora." She took the comb. "That will be all. Go get some sleep."

She had forgotten his observance and he saw the surprise when her eyes drifted over to him. The initial disclosure faded and a new expression softened her features. She sat in front of the tent with the hypnotizing flames between them.

Brogan had the women sleeping apart. He told himself they should be in tents far enough away so there could be no plots made in the night. Yet, it was a hard excuse to swallow wholeheartedly as he looked over the Lass. Ulterior intentions thickly lodged in his thoughts. He decided long ago, with quite precocious wisdom, he'd personally see to the Lass that night. By sleeping in his tent with the pretty vixen, he was better able to know her every move. In the dark, the privacy would provide her with a way in which to submit to his lust.

He watched her yawn behind her hand. Her heavy eyelids gave her face an air of sleepy sultriness. The allure became innocently seductive. Shaking off his prurient curiosity, he smiled.

"'Tis time to go to bed, Lass. We will be leaving early, first light." He got up and held the flap open to his tent. When she crawled in, he followed.

"What are you doing?"

"Is it not so obvious?"

"No, yes, please don't do this."

The pitch in her voice was the first real alarm Brogan had heard from the Lass and wickedly, he liked he could scare her. She had been a very gifted adversary and he began to think nothing surprised or frightened her. Then, as his men pointed out, he softened.

"I am not leaving ye to sleep alone so ye can get up and disappear in the middle of the night. I would also recommend ye try not to attempt to slit my throat. I'm a very light sleeper."

"You can't sleep in here with me. It isn't proper, the others will think..."

"They do not think anything other than what they are told to think." Brogan stretched out so she could not leave the tent without climbing over him. "I can provide ye warmth if ye will scoot on over here."

"I will not. I am not cold and you will do well to ply a woman with respect instead of lewdness." Her reprimand rattled with the stringent demand.

"Ah, me fair Lass, if I meant for ye to be under me, then I dare say t'would have been that way in a second. Alas, I prefer my wenches to dote on me willingly. Therefore, I will bide my patience for that time." He folded his arm under his head.

"Arrogance! You'll no more get into my heart than you will into my clothes!"

"I have no wish to have your heart, m'lady. Your body on the other hand, t'would not be a man alive that would deny himself the pleasure if offered." He chuckled at the little disturbed noises she made under her breath. "Goodnight, Lass."

"Uncouth lout," she muttered.

He didn't bother to listen to her other grumblings. She had the enjoyment of a nap, where he had been awake far longer than his body wished.

When he awoke, he couldn't tell if minutes or hours had passed by. The movement of someone drew his attention. He looked to the Lass asleep, his hand wrapped in her hair.

He rose up and leaned over her. Of all the nights to have one so beautiful, this night had not been the one for tasting her body. It didn't prevent him from quietly squirming over her and covering her mouth to prevent a scream.

Chapter 4

Brienna woke abruptly to find Brogan over her. His hand clamped her mouth shut to cut off all sounds of her protest before they dared to escape. She couldn't see him in the dark. His hot breath came close to her head and he buried his face into her hair. His weight was comfortable, pleasing, and desirable. Immediately she wished they'd gone to sleep on better terms. In that way, she'd not feel so foolish in yielding to his covetous touch.

She had felt from the start, Brogan would not rape her. His opportunities to do so came and went. She, on the other hand, recognized her wicked actions practically goading him into the act every chance she got. When they came together, as she knew they soon would, it would not be under force.

The hardness of his arms, his legs, and his stomach slid up her side. It brought awake the dreams she had been having of him in her sleep. The secure, protective sensation spiraled around her soul. It tied to the belief here was a man with whom she might enjoy a sexual exploit. The man definitely could warm her heart to the idea of love.

The quietness of his voice prompted her to raise her hand to his broad shoulder. Not to fight, but to embrace, to urge him to squeeze the ache from her. Who would know what they did in the obscurity of the tent? Who would care, beyond her? Her fingers continued to glide over the edge of his thick muscled shoulder and touched a lock of his hair. That black as coal mane fell in layered wisps to cover the back of his neck. Soft and clean, the silky locks tickled her palm. A man who took care in his appearance and hygiene was a good sign. Even the way he smelled of leather and forest did much to arouse her sense of smell. The fragrance mingled with his body's salubrious headiness and permeated her feral senses. He was handsome beyond reason—forged from the best elements God had to offer.

Brienna tired of the fight against all her desires and wrapped her arm around him in surrender.

"Hush, someone is outside our tent," he whispered in her ear.

Her eyes widened. Mortified by what she'd been thinking of; what she planned to let the man do to her made her cringe. Embarrassment heated her cheeks. No, she had to be a crimson shade of red from head to toe. Thankfully, the darkness concealed her humiliation. It hid the cherry shade of red coloring her skin. She had to contend he'd not know how submissive she prepared to be.

She looked up and saw the shadow of someone with a torch moving slowly around outside. Nodding her understanding, he let go. All she could hope now, was he didn't pick up on the fact she wanted him to strip away her heavy gray wool gown so she could yield to the touch of his chaffed, work-hewn hands, and feel how they could enflame her skin.

Brogan's movements were quiet. She made hers as stealthy. The darkness left her with little option for guidance, so she put a hand out blindly. It touched him. She kept it there to follow his activity. The hardness of brawn rolled under her palm and a lightening shock skittered up her arm as if something hit her elbow and caused the funny bone to quiver. It laced a tingling thread around her veins so her pulse quickened with the strangulation of an adventitious yearning.

Then his solid back left her hand and she listened to the struggle that ensued when he leapt out of the tent. Brienna crawled out to assist, to support, or maybe she should escape. Her ponderous thoughts were thwarted by the impact she crashed into when a boot caught her in the jaw. She'd been wrong to think the fight further away when Brogan had just gone out the flap. This she had been made instantly well aware of by the throbbing in her jaw.

She held a hand to her face and sat back in the tent. She shook off the speckles of white starry lights floating in her eyes. The flap had closed her in the darkness yet it wouldn't be enough to conceal the glow of her fingers. She lay down, pulled a blanket over her head, and unleashed the power. The heated amber light healed and warmed her affliction swiftly. Before she completely finished, she heard a groan distinctively made by Brogan's voice. Extinguishing her healing powers, she lifted the flap and crawled out.

† † †

Brogan seized the intruder and took him tumbling to the ground. The double-edged knife in the man's hand showed evidence enough that he had come with a mission in mind. Brogan felt his foot hit something, but did not question if it were a rock or a tree. The man he held was a stranger. The brand on his neck was all Brogan needed to know—he was an assassin. Thane couldn't beat him in battle, so he had resorted to sending lone killers in the night, with the burnt mark of a skull tattooed in the flesh permanently, so all knew the man walked with death.

They rolled over the dwindling flames in a pit and while neither caught fire, Brogan gritted his teeth when heat whispered over his breeches, causing his manhood to shrink in protest. The skirmish of his men around him only made his fight fiercer and he quickly ended the brawl. He stood up and found they were back in front of his tent, he alive and the intruder dead.

"She's gone!" Sedge gasped, running up to him.

Brogan wheeled around to where he had last seen his Lass. His pulse, still pounding from the fight, increased at the thought Sedge meant her, but it was the loud wailing woman he meant.

"How?" he asked, looking back to Sedge for explanation.

In the back of his head, his mind held onto the fact he hadn't been wrong about the Lass. He had felt her arms snake around him in the tent. She had wanted him in the way he needed most. Unfortunately, her submissiveness came at an inopportune time.

"It looks like someone took her. The tent shows signs of a struggle, but I swear I didn't hear a sound," Sedge said. "I was watching ye and..."

"Ye weren't supposed to hear anything," Brogan countered with his acceptance of the situation.

"But you did!" Brienna hissed at Brogan, throwing a hostile glare toward Sedge. "You heard this man outside our tent!"

"I sent Duane and Reese after her," Sedge piped up with guilt, making him look at the ground instead of the Lass.

He could see her fears racing like a wildfire in the glow of her violet eyes. That she could back down one of his men reinforced his thought of her danger.

"Lorne, get things packed up. We'll leave now, before more return."

"Leave!" the Lass cried. "We can't leave with Medora in the hands of killers."

Brogan looked back at the Lass. "My men are looking to get her back. We cannot wait here for them to get the rest of us.

Now get out what ye need from your trunk. We will leave the cart behind."

"I need nothing from the trunk, but I would like my weapons."

He grinned at her. "Ye know I will not let ye carry them, but rest assured they will accompany us." He wanted to rub his crotch, a reflex that questioned if he indeed had not burnt the front of his breeches off, as well as his valued privates, as the ache grew intense under the Lass's fiery gaze.

"Who was he?" She strolled around the dead man.

Brogan glanced down. The corpse laid crumbled, his eyes dark lifeless black pools, his throat slit deep. The brutal sight was not fit for the beautiful Lass to look upon. If he could, he'd take her away to a place she'd never have to see anything harsh. Mindlessly, her hand touched her jaw. She stared up at him when he lifted her hand.

"Does it hurt?" He looked over her jaw. He put the clunk of his boot together with the squeak she'd made. Then his hand moved down to the nick on her perfect creamy throat. His finger grazed over the slender column of velvet to touch the unintentional infliction.

"No," she breathed.

"I think ye lie even when there's no need." He stroked the pulse in her neck with the curl of his one finger. "I suppose if I were to suggest ye wanted me to bed ye, I would get a denial there as well."

Her lips parted slightly with invitation, her eyes glimmered with desire, another misjudgment on his part. She didn't refute anything. The stir of men, the snort of horse, and the dire need of them to depart prevented him from really kissing her.

"Lass, ye are full of surprises," he chuckled.

He didn't know if it was intuition or the fact he goaded it from her, but he caught the hand she swung at him. He lifted her fingers and pressed a kiss to her palm.

"If ye wait by my horse, we shall leave shortly." He gave a slight bow and watched her stalk away.

She mounted the horse and he stood entranced. With her leg at eye level, Brogan looked at the long limb with the palest down he'd ever seen. It had to be because she had the golden hair of sunlight. The wenches he bedded were dark haired sirens or ones with flaming red. It was something new to see a creamy well-shaped leg and not be able to run his hand down it. The split in the gown allowed her to ride astraddle the horse, but was that how she would ride one herself usually? Her agility on mounting one suggested she was no stranger to riding.

† † †

Brienna couldn't believe how often she let herself fall into his teasing trap. Silliness seemed to come at the most inconvenient times. If he hadn't joked about her wanting him, giggles had been on the verge of erupting. The fact he chose to torment her with the prospect of a kiss to the lips and then refuse had really steamed her.

She looked at the man holding the horse, but he did not look at her. She slid off the saddle and stepped in front of him.

"What is your name?" she asked, folding her arms across her chest.

"James, m'lady."

She moved to the side of him when she saw he looked toward Brogan.

"How long have you been serving the ogre?"

She stroked the black mane of the horse. The beautiful creature had the power and size making a fitting mount for Brogan.

"Are you stupid, man? I asked you a simple question."

He grinned much with the same amusement Brogan always did, a cocky twist of his lips as if she were put on earth for sport.

"He's ordered you not to speak to me, hasn't he?"

She spun and marched across the clearing. She swept around the other men and went straight for Brogan. He happened to be bending over to retrieve his tunic when she reached him. She had no reason to capitulate to all his directives. Whether they were directed at her or given to his men. Her foot came up and she planted it squarely on his ass. One swift shove and he toppled over.

"I insist you tell them they can speak to me. How dare you put limitations on their words!" she screamed.

No one could miss the preeminence in which she forced her wishes to be heard. The laugher spread and silenced with equal severity.

Brogan jumped up on his feet.

Impressed by his tall wide stature, Brienna became more amazed at how he could make it appear larger when he towered over her.

"I will not have ye dictating what I tell or don't tell my men to do. They have neither the wish nor the time to deal with your whining and conniving ways!" He shot back at her.

His finger held up in her face as if to draw her mind closer to grasp the meaning of his words.

"I am done playing these games. We are in serious danger out in the open like this and ye will behave yourself."

His finger waggled at her as if she were a small incorrigible child. She didn't answer to his brittle undefined threat. She feared what would happen if they should leave Medora to fend for herself. The woman would get herself killed within moments of her shrill crying because no one would tolerate it any longer than that.

"Maybe I wouldn't complain quite so much if I could have a normal conversation with someone. All I asked James was how long he'd been with such a beast as you!"

Brogan looked up. His eyes darkened at the snickers from his men. She pinched her lips ready to stand her ground.

"The Lass," he grumbled. "Has...my...permission to engage whom she would like in conversation so long as it is she that instigates the conversation. And, as long as it does not hinder a man's job," he said so all could hear.

She smiled quite satisfied even as he took her wrist and dragged her to his horse.

"Get on."

Brienna was glad he did not insist on helping. She thought she might have to hit him again for his insinuation she was spoiled. She didn't make any comment when he ran his fingers through his hair to remove the crumbled leaves that stuck, or the fact he still had a smudge on the tip of his nose. He appeared quite mad about her shoving him in the dirt. However, she felt he deserved something, after spending a night in the tent with her and letting everyone think he had his way with her. It was plain stupid for him to believe just because he told people how to think, they would. People would do their own thinking.

Holding the reins, his arms wrapped her waist once he swung up behind her. She then realized her anger had been more for the disappointment she felt in missing him doing what he shouldn't to her.

"I will talk to ye, Lass, if ye desire conversation."

"I have nothing to say to you. You keep me hostage and I...I don't like you," she lied. "By the way, you have dirt on the end of your nose."

"I wonder how that could have happened." He rubbed a sleeve over his nose. "Would ye like to inspect that I have scrubbed it away?"

"No. I don't care what you look like." His hand never left her stomach and while it didn't bother her, she didn't like him thinking she enjoyed it. "You don't have to hold onto me. I won't fall off."

"No, I do not suppose ye would. 'Tis your jumping off and running like a jackrabbit through these woods that concerns me. Now that ye haven't the wee-wailing lass to look after, I don't see ye trying to stay with me. I would surely miss ye if we were to part company after all this time."

Brienna did not reply. She wasn't sure how to answer. He had to be joking, didn't he? The barbarian teased her again and she didn't at all like the way it made her suffer with dejection. He was to be commended for knowing how to hurt her feelings. Whomever he pledged allegiance to should bestow a prize on the man for his insightful ways of wielding not only a broadsword but words as well.

Chapter 5

Several hours took them into a town. Brienna looked behind her and found Brogan's men had disappeared. If someone had said the earth opened up and swallowed them, she would have believed it. Not one of them remained after their disbandment took them in many directions.

"Why are we stopping here?"

She felt the strength in his arms when he lifted her down. The large hands wrapping her waist so his thumbs met in the front and his middle fingers touched together in the small of her back, made her feel feminine.

"News, libations, sleep, and whatever other sin a man can find to get into." He pointed to the tavern. "We will go there, stay there and well...do other things there as suits us."

"Food, water, and sleep; it is all I require."

She hoped he hadn't intended on her filling the position for other things. She didn't want to repeat mistakes of her heart again.

"Then that is what I shall see ye get." He opened the door and bowed for her to enter.

She looked over the boisterous crowd. Men guzzled ale and groped the serving wenches as they passed. Brogan walked her straight through the throng of merrymakers. She found herself crowding to him to keep from touching any of the filthy lot.

"Now this is a right fine gal." A man jumped up in front of her and grabbed her breast.

Brogan went to push the man back when she squealed in surprise, but as usual, her reflexes to protect her own body were quicker than his. She drew a knee to the man's groin that doubled him over. The foot to his chest aggravated the situation when he came back at her.

Brogan instantly took charge.

"I do apologize, my Lass is out of your league, sir." He gave a placating bow.

"She's what?" The man stared, befuddled by the comment.

"Where she exceeds in beauty, she lacks in compassion to a man's sensitive areas. So if ye have not the balls of God so she might test them in her wee steely fingers, then I suggest ye leave her be." His voice, seriously mocked, but the man had no intelligence to understand the ridicule.

"Ah, the pretty young ones are always a might slow to teach." His dark eyes looked the length of her with a salaciously drooling stop on her bust. "Well, you bring her back in when you've taught her to serve a man well!" The lout laughed, accepting Brogan's warning.

"I will most definitely do that, sir."

She couldn't contain her disgust as it seethed out from her pinched lips.

"Of course, she may have castrated me by then." Brogan chuckled.

All patrons within earshot roared with the jest, all except her. Not given a chance to object to his use of her as a joke, his fingers dug into her upper arm and he dragged her to a table in a far off corner. A very private table situated away from the crowd. It appeared a safe place in which to watch the room as well as the entrance.

He immediately pushed her to slide over on a bench so she sat trapped between him and a wall.

"Can't you sit on the other side of the table? Must you station yourself next to me like a guard?" She squirmed away to put a hairline of space between them. It would have been more if the wall didn't look sticky from the filth. She couldn't identify what had been slopped on the stone. The putrid smell did a fair job on her gag reflexes. Each cough she made choked down the rising bile churning in her stomach.

"Unless ye intend on jumping over the table, ye will remain seated. And unless ye can control kneeing every man ye meet, I will be forced to let the next have your wicked body."

They both turned their attention to the comely wench standing in front of him. Her dull brown hair tangled of wiry curls had no semblance to an arrangement. Her high cheeks were rosy and her eyes sparkled with the indulgence of too much drink.

"Hello, Brogan" She dripped with sweetness and leaned toward him. "What is it ye want today?" She purred with exaggeration.

"The usual for two, Kate." He reached up and pulled the girl's face toward him. "Have ye missed me?"

"Always." She teased him with her breasts bursting at the seams and served under his nose, so that he need only stick his tongue out to lick over the ivory swells along the rim of her blouse. When she wrapped her arms around his neck to plant a firm kiss on him, the buxom tart insinuated herself further into his embrace.

Brienna stared at the stone wall, then the crud on it. It now looked more interesting than the whore fawning over Brogan. She wondered what the woman thought of him bringing her in the place.

The girl's obnoxious behavior turned her stomach. Brogan's groan when Kate pulled away made Brienna sick...and...and...jealous. It mortified her to even think it and yet there the thought stuck in her head like sap clung to a tree.

What would he do if she hung on him like the tart and lavished a big sloppy kiss on his lips, like a dog greeting her master? Would he enjoy her attention as well? He hadn't kissed her again since they met. Maybe he only gave one kiss per woman or maybe he hadn't liked kissing her. The sheer contemplation he would not find favor in her kiss drove an angry grunt from her.

"I think my guest is getting impatient with her hunger. Ye best fetch the food and make it quick." He smacked Kate on the bottom to send her away.

"I'm not hungry." Brienna told him. "Is she your wife?"

"Nay, she's another man's chain. Kate and I are solely friends." He tapped his fingers on the wood table, keeping time with the song of others surrounding them.

The people in the room seemed happy, but then inebriated men usually were quite jolly. They were also unable to make use of their judgment or their limbs. Brienna turned her eyes to Brogan swallowing his swill in gulps. If he drank enough, lost thought of her existence, she could probably just walk out of the tavern. She could take his horse and ride off into the night.

When Kate returned with their food, Brienna engaged Brogan in what appeared an intimate moment. She discreetly touched the goop on the wall, not much but just a smidgen to show him.

"Yuck, look at this filth." She held her palm up in front of him and moved it with a graceful sweep of the air.

"This spot." His thumb wiped away the drop in one sweep. "There, all gone m'lady."

"Thank you."

She leaned closer and smiled briefly before sitting back while Kate set Brogan's plate down with care. Hers got deposited in such a way that when the pewter platter clattered to the wood table, the liquid the food swam in spit in her face. It splattered the wall and she wrinkled her nose understanding how food got on the wall.

Brienna lifted what appeared may be a napkin. She couldn't be sure from its filth and then put it back down, not wanting it to touch her face.

"Here, let me." Brogan pulled his tunic up and dabbed the greasy drops from her cheek.

"Thank you." She smiled at him with a genuine sincerity this time.

Though, she did take a gander of the girl from the corner of her eye. Satisfied she had Brogan's attention to her face, miffing the tart. She didn't expect the tankard of ale to be knocked over by the busty witch. Ale sluiced across the table. A little went on her, much of it poured off the edge of the table into Brogan's lap.

Again, she heard the elegant slew of crude words spill from his lips. The rich resonance devilishly tickled her with laughter, which she honestly tried to suppress.

"I am plagued with wenches that hate me," he grumbled, rising up to let the liquid splash to the floor.

Brienna couldn't help the laughing. He had brought it on himself and she found a delight in his confusion.

"Ye would not find it so funny if ye were to feel as if ye wet yourself."

"No, you are right about that." She snickered.

Brienna ate the mutton with a hearty appetite. Laughter had made the tension erode. She took a swig of her ale and slid it to Brogan. "I seldom partake of ale since it weakens the mind. Besides I don't think she'll be back too soon." A fact that satisfied her immensely.

"Oh she will be back," he said, bursting her bubble. "Kate will not stay mad for long. Though I do not understand where her madness comes from at the moment." He picked up the mutton leg and began gnawing on it.

The singing escalated in pitch about halfway through her meal. Brienna listened to the uproarious way in which everyone joined in. She hadn't much opportunity to see so much uninhibited shenanigans at home. Too often people knew who she was and they kept to a demure tone set with whispering or silence.

"Come dance, Brogan." Kate bounced to their table very lively.

He did not refuse and Brienna watched him hop around with the girl and many others. Men and women rollicked merrily to the singing. The ebullient room grew loud. She had trouble repressing a smile until she watched Brogan's embrace of Kate. He pushed her up the stairs.

Brogan glanced her way, whistled, and gestured to someone in the room. He pointed at her, then snatched Kate up, and carried her laughingly up the stairs.

Brienna wanted to run. Not for escape sake alone, but the hurt. She should not care about who he spent time with, except she did. She stood with the idea of leaving fixed in her head. Then Lorne appeared and she sat back down.

"You're to guard me?" She looked up at him solemnly.

"Nay, Lass. I'm to entertain ye and protect ye from the rascally devils in this place. Alas, if nothing else, maybe ye will keep me hide safe," he chuckled.

She looked up questioningly.

"I have never seen anyone back down Big Tim."

She found his smile bashfully sweet.

"Big Tim?"

He gave a jerk of his head toward the crowd.

"Oh, the toad that grabbed me."

"Would ye like more ale or..."

"Dance, I would like to dance."

She gave a glance up the stairs and hoped she had the strength to dance for the length of time it took Brogan to return. She had a great urge to make him jealous of her merriment without him.

Lorne swung her around the room, and with each pass of a tankard, Brienna took a sip. Before she knew what happened, she took long gulps between bursts of singing and leaned toward forgetting about Brogan. It required too much energy.

"Brogan says ye have a coldness to your heart, but I don't see it," Lorne told her.

"Cold, aye, I'm as frigid as the deep winter snows, but only because he's so mean." She sat on the edge of a table and tilted back her head to take a long draught of the swill.

"He does walk with a hardened soul, Lass, but ye have the power to soften his tone." He took the tankard from her. "Of course not if ye can't stand before him and speak with words he understands."

"I talk good 'nuf for the beast if he listens...cares...to me." She giggled and put a hand to her lips. "Cares...to...listen..." she corrected.

"Ye have had too much, Lass." Lorne stopped her from taking another drink.

"You could be right." She put her finger up to his nose, distracted by the back of her hand. "I should have mended the infliction."

She thought of the cut on Brogan's hand. She had it in her ability to heal it and she hadn't. She spoke to herself visualizing Brogan's hand sliced diagonally through the black hairs of his skin. She was a healer, not a warrior. Although she had more skill with a sword, the abilities she possessed were for compassion. On battlefields, she worked the miracles of her restorative powers.

"Lass, is something wrong?" Lorne plucked her hand from the air in front of their faces.

She smiled and shook off the wanderings of her muddled mind. "No." She hopped off the table and danced around him. She let herself be sucked into the fray of other dancers.

Chapter 6

"Oh come now, me darlin' Brogan." Kate pushed herself against him with her wicked needs. "We always talk after we have our wee bit of fun. Come sit on the bed with me."

"Not this time. I cannot stay up here long enough to satisfy your hungers, dear girl. Now tell me of Thane's men. Have they been this way recently?" He pushed her back by holding her shoulders. He rubbed circles over her bare skin above the ruffle of her blouse and teased her.

"Two weeks ago. They killed the miller's wife because she wouldn't offer herself up to that rabble for their amusement." She shrugged his hands off.

"What plans have ye heard...precisely?"

He sat down on the edge of the bed. It creaked and sank under him. The ropes needed to be restretched, the stuffing in the sacking needed to be refilled, and the bedding could have stood an airing out.

Brogan shucked off his gray tunic. The wet wool put an added burden of weight on his shoulders and it felt good to shed something from all he carried. Whether in his heart or on his body, strength did not last under so many responsibilities.

"Just the same boast about takin' Kylemore soon." She swirled around the room filled with energy he wished he could steal. "They also mentioned somethin' about stoppin' a messenger from gettin' to Lord Torrick. T'would seem the Princess Rhoswen is antsy when it comes to her providence's welfare. They perceive she is very afraid of Thane invading Avalbane 'cause of her lacking of true support."

Kate tried to touch him and he brushed her aside.

"Kylemore stands ready to assist Avalbane even without the marriage."

"Maybe Princess Rhoswen just wants to have the man and nothing about the marriage matters. She's probably some fat, frustrated old maid. Ye do understand some women have honor when it comes to only letting their husband bed them. Might be she figured only a contract would trap her a man." She pulled her blouse further down her arm with an attempt at seducing him.

"Aye, but that has not been a problem for ye, has it?" He touched her cheek.

He wrapped his hand around the back of her neck and jerked her to his kiss. She tasted of stale ale, while the lass had the sweetness of honey on her tongue. The guilt of betraying the Lass made him stand back.

"How is that husband of yours?"

"Saw him last week, I did. That trollop he's gone and shacked up with in Herne is s'pecting a wee brat of her own. I have a mind to go over there and tell her he'll pretty much be done with her after that. Me husband doesn't come 'round here because he don't want to have nothin' to do with the youngin's."

Her cackle made him cringe. What had he found so attractive about the woman? Was there anything beyond her willingness to warm his bed? Even now, he had no desire to be with her. His standards seemed to elevate to that of the bewitching Lass downstairs.

"Go down and tell Lorne to bring me the Lass I brought," he ordered, immediately needing to see her.

He wanted to caress the sun-touched skin of her smooth face and convince her to let him feel more of her trim, but rounded figure. His lips burned to kiss her cool-tipped breasts and his imagination would only allow him to conjure what it would be like to slip his cock into the wet sheath of her tight cunt.

Kate glared at him. "Who is she?"

"No one of importance," he answered with a nonchalant flick of his hand at her. "Just a fair maiden I happened upon. I keep her for sport. Now go on with ye. I have some thinking to do."

He looked out the window into the darkness setting over the countryside. Many thoughts ran through his mind. Thane's men would be looking for them. The small band they had recently fought were scouts. They may not have such luck at their next encounter.

He waited for what seemed a long time. A hankering to have the Lass close by took over his wandering mind. When too much time passed since Kate's departure, he turned and looked at the door.

"What is taking Lorne so long?"

The words breathed out in a panic and he hurried down the stairs. His eyes went straight to the empty table. His heart stopped. He had to find her and to search the night would not prove to be an easy task.

Then he picked up his head to the lilting laughter in the crowded room. Not any laughter, but the tinkling of the Lass's voice drifting up from the dancers. His eyes followed the light aria and saw her floating around the room. The binds constricting his lungs slackened. He stared at her with a deeper concern than her disappearance. The affects of caring too much about her pained him.

She would give nary a consideration for him other than for her passage to Kylemore. That would be the reason for her to stay and he could not believe any other.

Lorne came to the foot of the stairs with an ill at ease expression.

"She won't come and Kate refused to go back and tell ye," he said. "She was a grumbling over sending ye her replacement."

"I will deal with the lass' disobedience. Enjoy the night for the morrow may be our day to fight and die."

Brogan made his way out to the Lass pirouetting around the room. When she spun around and bumped into him, she stopped. Her face had the heated flush of intoxicated energy. Her eyes shimmered with serenity.

† † †

Brienna wanted to stop smiling. Somewhere in disrupting his plans, she found herself having fun. Brogan's dour expression took away from it and for a minute of her time, whether friend or foe, she wanted to be in his company.

She lifted her hand to him.

"A dance?"

His hesitation made her feel a reprimand coming. She considered retracting her nerveless fingers when he took them. His arm coiled around her waist and they pranced amongst the melee. The muscles under her fingertips rippled with movement. The fact he no longer wore the tunic inflicted another stab of pain in her heart.

The white shirt, somewhat dingy, gapped open. She saw the curls of ebony hair like tiny fingers holding the edge of cloth. The temptation to touch grew but she just stared. The scar on his collarbone looked rough and grizzled. It had been a bad cut. Then her eyes drifted to the back of his hand holding hers. The crusty scab went diagonally, cutting across the tanned skin, dividing the black hairs. There would be a scar. Maybe a fine line, but she had injured him. Regret sunk deep.

All it would take was her hand to cover his and a little concentration. She glanced around. Too many people existed on a faith that did not allow for magic.

"How long will it take to get to Kylemore?" she asked.

He spun her around and the ale she drank began to take its toll on her coordination.

"Three, maybe even as long as five days." His boot hit a chair and made him stumble.

"Maybe talking and dancing is too complicated for you to do at the same time." Her quip was not an insulting attack on his intelligence, but a joke that rolled off the tip of her tongue like a fencing foreplay between lovers.

"Could be I'm just better at horizontal dancing, my bonnie wee Lass. Would ye care to make a personal judgment?"

"I don't understand?" She'd never heard the term and while she liked to dance, the expression on his face when he asked seemed truly wicked and wonderful.

She pouted with the cease to the music. The dulcimer twanged its last note and then started a new tune with lots of singing.

Brogan bowed his head and kissed over her knuckles. "Ye look tired, Lass."

The sensation of his brush against her skin left her speechless.

"This way and I'll show ye to our room." He made the first steps.

"I'll not have you…"

"Ye could have me if ye wanted." He waved his fingers so they caught the sweat-dampened tendrils over her eye. He pushed them back from her face. "Ye will sleep in a room with me." Her eyes met Kate's stare. It gave her the incentive to argue no more with him. It would be futile to think he'd change his mind anyway, so with a little selfish gratification Kate would not have Brogan, she took his hand and moved forward.

"'Tis early for you to be sleeping, isn't it?" she asked, mounting the stairs.

Her gaze went from him to everyone still swinging merrily about, a celebratory gaiety that made her smile. Her eyes caught back to Brogan's. Her lashes dropped and she thought of what might happen. The ale stunned her with thoughts which had no place in her mind.

What if she did let Brogan fully show her his sort of magic, the ancient ritual of coupling? It would serve her betrothed right if she came to their marriage bed no longer a virgin. She had waited a long time to experience the simple gifts of womanhood. What harm could there be in getting a little practice? It could be deemed training, the same as she had received in all her other areas of endeavor. Brogan looked well capable of teaching her the basics. He actually looked most competent if his carnal activities could match the blandish way in which he teased her with charisma.

"I could do with a good night's rest."

He opened a door and Brienna went in the room. He shut the door, turned a key in the lock, and removed it.

"Ye will allow me that and not have me up chasing ye." His brow lifted. "Correct?"

Brienna found his question did not deserve an answer, because she couldn't give the one he'd want. She saw his tunic lying on a chair. She looked at the bed. He had been in it with the tart from downstairs.

He lay down on the sagging bed.

"There's plenty of room for two, Lass."

He threw his long legs up to cross one over the other and closed his eyes.

She sat on a chair, pulled a shoe off, and rubbed her foot. It ached from using it for a battering ram on Big Tim earlier. All the dancing aggravated the dull throb. It made her lift her head and listen to the loudness of everyone still below.

For an hour, she sat and debated her options. The bed had looked good, but how could she just crawl on it and sleep so close to the brute?

Eventually, his light snore, giving every indication he slept, allowed her to creep quietly to the bed. She looked down at his face. Scruffy, slightly dirty, a few not so noticeable scars, and a well-defined shape to his nose all made the attraction worsen.

Handsome with an incorrigibly petulant personality, she believed much of his severity in tone was a result of her distrust of him. The black locks spread a dark halo around his head. The coal-fanned eyelashes were darker than any of his other hair.

Looking again at the empty place alongside him, fairly wide considering her narrow frame, she moved to the far side. She took a full minute to sit and another to lie down. She had thought it might be better to sleep with her back to him. An afterthought put her facing him. Petrified any more movements would wake him, she closed her eyes.

"It took ye forever to make a decision," he whispered.

"'Tis just to sleep."

"I think it more."

He rubbed his hand over her gown, over her belly, and up to her full breasts. She let him untie the laces. She'd not say anything and hope he'd not stop.

"Ye like this, don't ye?"

"I don't know what you're speaking of." She bit in her bottom lip and chewed on it, trying not to think of his fingers pinching and plucking the tip of her breast.

"Ye like that I want to fuck ye, but know I won't without your express permission."

"I don't believe you'd control yourself by waiting for me to say yea or nay to your lust."

His caress increased the speed of her pulse and forced her breathing to escalate.

"Oh and what knowledge have ye of a man's lust?" He cupped her breast and squeezed gently. "Maybe 'tis my thirst for a teat. Maybe I'm a naughty boy regressing to suckling a woman's ripeness."

"You'll get no milk from me!"

His laugh had nothing boyish about it. His lips claimed the aching nipple. She put her hands up to stop his advance and she could only hold his head. Her fingers knotted into his black hair to hold him to her breast.

"I may not get milk from ye and that's all right because I am not a boy. However, as a man, I know where to find the richness of cream."

He sat up and shoved her gown up her legs.

His hands held the garment while his kisses wet her thighs.

"I want to drink of your hot wet cunt, and I will not ask permission for that, Lass."

Chapter 7

Brogan went slowly up her soft legs. He kissed the quivering skin. She tasted exquisite, honey flavored, as if she bathed in the sweet stuff. He liked honey. He loved honey when it came coated on the supple thighs he licked.

"Oh Brogan, that tickles," she whined.

"Hmmm, I have not got to the real sweet spot yet." He slurped his way north to the dense forest of golden ringlets. "Ye are delicious."

He pushed the gown further. She struggled to help wiggle it out from under her bottom.

"Shall we just take it off?" He rubbed at her thighs, not letting her cool to the idea.

Her nod had a virtuous hesitancy. Instead of the gown going up, he lifted her to push the gown from her shoulders. The ivory of her skin stopped him. He kissed the curves to her neck, the muscle tensing at first, and then relaxing to his persistence.

"I shouldn't let you do this," she murmured with a delirious twist of her head so he could kiss behind her ear and nibble the small lobe.

"Until I am ready to shove my cock inside, ye have all rights to say no to that one final act. Until then, let me show ye the splendors of what my tongue can do." He licked behind her ear.

The Lass moaned a submissive agreement and he continued to lick every inch of her neck. He sucked on her throat, just under her chin. It made it hard for her swallow, but he loved the vibrations rumbling up from the depths. The purrs of her tranquil, sedated, and he knew, very inebriated state, were wonders he couldn't resist. She let her guard down by drams of ale. In the morning, she'd probably regret some of her compliance. Not all since he'd show her a full measure of carnal bliss.

He followed the line of her neck to the hollow wet with perspiration. His hand went to support her back as she dropped her head back. Her pert breasts, the color of moonlight, jutted up to his lips. He didn't tease or play at tormenting her. He gave her what she needed and suckled the blushing buds. Brogan drank in her nipples and nipped at them with his teeth. Her grip on his head forced him closer, sending him up and away from her succulent tits to her jaw and finally her mouth. He landed hard and she gasped with her frenzied demand to the union.

The Lass changed the location of her hands and he lowered her back to the pillow. He drew his lingering kiss from her puckered lips. Rising up, he drew his shirt over his head and tossed it away. Her short, smooth fingernails skated up his chest, sending shivers down his back and a distinctive throbbing pain of abstinence in his tortured cock. Returning to her mouth, he kissed her deeply, accepting her sensual hums as admission to her pleasure.

Her breasts, bare and hot, flattened to his chest when he lowered more to feel them brush his skin. She scratched his back in soothing strokes from his shoulders to the rim of his britches. She grasped his ass and kneaded leather and meat, making him thrust his tongue into her throat the same way he wanted to thrust into her cunt. She sucked on him and he could picture the luscious lips wrapping his hardness and whetting his full attention.

Sword of Rhoswen

Brogan tried to get his hand under the edge of the heavy gown except there was too much of it.

"Take it off," he insisted, shifting off her. "Take it off now."

"You're very pushy," she grumbled.

"Take it off before I rip it off," he growled with frustration.

Golden curls flew in his face as she shook her head.

He smiled and laughed. His arm reached out and grabbed her around the middle as if he were hooking a sheep with a pole. Her breasts jiggled until he had them securely against his chest.

"I am seriously in need of ye, Lass, and I think ye need relief yourself."

Her head shook again and he caught the side of her face, putting a halt to the flying coils of gold.

"I want to suck your hot cunt and make ye feel so good ye will beg me to do it again."

Her eyes fired a warning and waned into steamy violet. He kissed her gently.

"Please." He brushed his quiet plea over her cheek.

He'd never believe it of himself with any other woman, though he hardly ran into such a problem before. However, he nuzzled his face to hers and swept kisses along to reinforce his request. Him begging would be something new to the world if it got out.

Her eyes closed and she kissed him back. Not the wild ride over his lips. This came from deeper inside and he accepted he had won. Or maybe she had. It didn't matter.

Brogan worked the gown to her hips and out from under her without giving up his residence against her hot panting body. When he had her gloriously naked, he shifted off her, sat up, and pulled her up on his lap. He held her and tenderly stroked her back.

She spread her hands on his chest and he held her away. Awed by the beauty and curve of her mouth, he plunged into a kiss to take her breath away. They fell back onto the bed and he sought out her golden-covered mound with a probing hand. Parting the soft, damp curls, he swirled a finger in the dewy folds of flesh.

"Oh no!" She gasped and he didn't give her room to say more.

She dug her fingers into his shoulders and held tight. His finger dipped into the center of her cunt where he met with a surprise. He wiggled his finger in deeper, making her squirm irritably, yet it seemed a lesson he needed to learn.

"Ye are a virgin!"

† † †

Brienna's fingers held onto Brogan even firmer. She felt a sting to her insides and tried not to let him feel her tension, but he now knew the status of her womanhood. His announcement came like an accusation. He said it like it could be the worse possible thing for her and he wished no encounter with such a creature.

"Damn, Lass, when did ye think ye might warn me?"

"I don't...didn't know it was necessary. Does it change how things are done?"

His surprised features softened. The worry lines in his forehead smoothed. The crinkles feathering the corners of his eyes returned. Now all she needed to know was an answer and she'd feel better for her indecency.

"Aye, a wee bit, Lass."

"How?"

"I would be gentler."

"You wouldn't have before knowing?"

He gave her things to wonder about him and what they were going to do. She wanted him without understanding the reason. He wanted her and she believed it a male necessity. Her knowledge of sex seemed far more inadequate than she originally thought.

"I would have passion, for sure. 'Tis, well Lass, the first time for a woman is painful, and I wish to warn ye beforehand, that's all."

"Very well, I'm warned."

"And ye will let me into your body? Ye will let me fuck ye until the break of dawn?"

She nodded, hoping it the right decision.

He didn't say more. His kisses came sweetly and she rocked to the pumping of his finger inside her. When the sparks of heat came like striking flint for a fire, she kissed him fervently. The wide pad of his thumb rotated over her clit. She clung to him in need of relief of his torture and in want of the rapture entrapping her.

"Brogan, oh Brogan, please, I can take anymore," she cried.

He kissed over her breasts, suckling the aching nipple until it blossomed with a rosy glow. She looked down and watched him further his travels. His finger swirled inside, leading the way for his tongue.

"Brogan!" His name wheezed from her shocked lungs.

He pressed his face into her vulnerable clenching vagina and she shuddered. Between the fork of his positioned fingers, he drove his tongue into her hot swollen cunt. The tender spots could not accept the teasing and she tried to shrink from his attack. He'd not let her. He'd not give up his hold on her thighs. Every fraction she scooted back, his mouth suctioned to her throbbing core with more force.

Tremors rattled her violently. She thrashed on the bed as if she were a fish out of water. She had no control and he didn't ease up to give her any. He lapped at her clit and jammed his tongue into the depths repeatedly.

"Brogan, no more, please, no more."

He paid no heed. His arm slid up and his hand cupped over one breast. The calming never came, even though she liked the way he squeezed the mound of flesh. If anything, it agitated her body more.

When she couldn't handle the riveting sensations maddening her soul, she gripped fistfuls of Brogan's hair with the intension of pulling his face away. Only his hum into the cavern, his suckling sweetly sending her over the edge of all sanity, she forced him to her cunt. She bucked against his mouth. She fucked his tongue as it fucked her.

He slid up her stomach, the roughness of his leather britches touching her clit so she continued to flinch. His erection, still concealed by the covering, ground against her soreness. Her fingers remained locked in a death hold of his hair.

"Now what?" She panted, wanting to go on and at the same time not knowing if she had the energy for more.

He stared at her with an expression she didn't understand. In his eyes, were sentiments she didn't dare interpret.

"'Tis been a long day, Lass."

She could only nod in agreement.

"We could use some sleep and then maybe—" He paused. "Maybe in the morning we might resume this."

She wanted to shout *no*, no, now is the time to finish a deed worth doing. Except again she nodded and her whole body relaxed. The worry she did something wrong did not leave and she tried to figure out how to ask why he wouldn't, couldn't, or didn't want to continue.

He flopped off her to his stomach. A small moan of pain slipped out of him and he coughed, trying to cover up the sound.

"Go to sleep, Lass."

Brienna tried. She managed to flip the cover over her nakedness and then she lay there with a whole lot of unanswered questions in her head. She still had a jittery set of nerves enlivening her pores while Brogan, content as a baby, fell asleep.

She didn't know what possessed her but she put a hand over his large one that lay on the pillow near his face. He had truly fascinated her by the heights of an orgasm she thought she'd die from. She could not form words for the curiosity she had of him not sticking his cock inside her. She knew he wanted to and when he didn't, both disappointment and worry beleaguered her thoughts.

While he slept, she started to heal the riff within and then stopped. Everything told her to keep the barrier down, let this be the only man to tear the virginal veil. Something told her it had everything to do with his reasons for not fully making love to her. In a way, she couldn't fault him when she knew she should be pure for her future husband. If not chaste of heart and soul, she could be unchanged of the body, except she didn't want the soreness to be gone. Not yet, while she felt wonderfully at peace. The glow extinguished from her fingers rubbing her cunt. Each brush over her clitoris brought memories of Brogan's tongue, his fingers, and her imagination of what it would feel like to have his cock fretting her sensitivities.

She caressed the black hairs over his knuckles. Stroking with one finger as she might do mindlessly to a pet, she carefully avoided touching the gash she caused. Tracing an oblong circle, she went down each finger. His knuckles were rough and dry, callused from use and she liked them regardless. They had the strength and the toil of living in the real world, not the seclusion of a pampered castle life that left other hands unexploited of genuine work.

"Ye are a puzzlement, Lass." Brogan twisted his hand so he had a grip of her fingers.

"It's called curiosity," she explained.

"To stroke a man with affection t'would give rise for one to believe he was trusted." He opened his green eyes.

"Or lull him into false presumptions." She pulled her hand except his hold grew tighter.

"Or maybe ye look for me to satisfy something else. I will only when ye ask."

"Is that why you didn't?"

"Are ye asking me to do so now?"

"No," she snapped, afraid it wouldn't sound like it.

"I will not rush ye, Lass. I will not rush a virgin into something she may regret, no matter how much I lust for the chaste body of one."

Anger bubbled in her. He suggested any woman would do and having him lump her into a category with his other sexual affairs sat sourly in her throat.

"Go back to sleep," she demanded. "I'll not ask you to ever come into me, now let go of my hand."

"If we're to finish out this night with hope, allow me to feel ye have the desires I do." His hand relaxed and he closed his eyes. "Trust me, Lass."

"Brogan?"

"Aye, Lass."

"I want to trust you."

He pulled her hand close and kissed her knuckles.

She didn't know why she felt it important to tell him. She still had a lot of doubt and just because he happened to be an exquisitely beguiling man, she couldn't let good sex shut down common sense. She sighed and closed her eyes. If holding her hand gave him hope she'd not run, it only gave her rise to believe it would be to her advantage to let him have his imitation of optimism. Brienna turned her hand so it lay palm up under his and she went to sleep. What harm could there be in deluding him to think she liked holding hands?

How long they had been asleep, Brienna wasn't sure. The pounding at the door startled her. She groaned from the disturbance rather than wake. She had been comfortable, peaceful, and the succession of times she woke during the night from Brogan's turning had drained her of energy. She hadn't even opened her eyes to know the warm weight that had disconnected from her hip had been Brogan's arm over her.

She rubbed her eyes to see him, a blur crossing the room. He unlocked the door to a woman's chirp. Still dark outside, with a funny hazy blue in the sky, she recognized the coming of dawn.

"Brogan!" the hushed voice pleaded. "Brogan, it's urgent!"

He opened the door and Kate pulled him out of the room. She gave Brienna one nasty look of contempt before yanking the door shut. She cut her out of the conversation, but not for long.

Brienna climbed off the bed and hurriedly dressed to eavesdrop at the door. No tavern harlot would get the better of her. The she paused. A smile formed with a wicked happiness. It hadn't been the common wench in Brogan's arms last night.

Before she could finish dressing to cross the room and find out what the mumbling words meant from outside the door, Brogan came back in.

"Time to go, Lass." He grabbed his shirt, his tunic, and her hand.

"Wait. My shoes," she wailed at the door.

He stopped and let her slip them on while he held her arm. Then she trailed him with a stumbling gait.

The once rowdy group had passed out in chairs, benches, tables, and corners. Only Brogan's men were waiting, alert and ready to go.

"Lorne has gone to keep a look out," James informed him. "They came in about ten minutes ago. Kate shuffled them off to a room in the back with a couple of tired but fetching lasses."

"Then we go and hope they are kept happy for a long while."

"Brogan?" Kate looked sadly at him and he held an arm out.

Brienna yanked her fingers from his. The nerve he had, the conceited bastard had no idea of the humiliation she felt with him holding her hand while looking to lavish affection on another woman. He only gave a mild look of disappointment before turning back to Kate.

"Ye take care." He kissed her forehead. "Thank ye for the service ye do."

He came at Brienna and with a hand to her back, propelled her out of the tavern followed by the other men.

"James, get her to my horse." Brogan took two other men, walked them in another direction, and then stopped.

She watched him talking to them about the men that arrived. Who were they and why were they leaving so quickly? Were they Thane's men or Torrick's? Could they be that close to Kylemore? No, it couldn't be possible. How much had Brogan told her as truth and how much a lie? She still planned to escape him and yet, there in the pit of reasoning, she didn't know if she could leave. He proved to be a mystery she liked. She had the hangover of ale weighing on her ability to think.

Chapter 8

Brogan looked at the Lass mounting his horse. The flash of her white limb swinging over the horse gave him pause in his thoughts.

"Brogan?" Lorne questioned his silence. "Brogan, ye will have to stop looking at the Lass like she's a bit of sugar candy all the time."

"She is a comely Lass."

And a danger if he couldn't keep his mind on the matters at hand. She had a contrite look about her that always stole his thoughts. It left him feeling the inadequate bumbling warrior she frequently misjudged him for.

"She's cut, kicked, and bit ye. I think ye'd do better to stick to those wenches like Kate that want a poke," Lorne chuckled.

"Oh she wanted me. Last night..." He divulged too much.

The Lass muddled his mind and he shouldn't spout off about the quirky way he felt about her or what they did in private. What he and the Lass did together went beyond intimacy. It had to do with mutual respect and somehow it would be wrong to tell anyone the sweet noises she could make during an orgasm.

"Enough about your courtship of the Lass, ye are beginning to worry me with your lovestruck gawking of her all the time." He chuckled.

"I will have ye know I watch her closely because I do not trust who she is." He kicked the toe of his boot in the dirt to avoid looking at her.

"Aye, and I suppose 'tis the reason by which we have not heard her name." Lorne ducked his shoulder to allow Brogan a clear sight of the Lass.

Brogan looked at Lorne strangely and then laughed himself. He didn't want to admit, he had never asked her name. It would surely be a thing he'd correct shortly.

"Forget about the Lass. If we should have to split, go straight to the castle and wait for me because I do believe we will see Thane's pack of wolves today, even though their number is growing smaller. Ye would think he smart enough to replenish the assemblage before pressing on. His stupidity gives us the advantage and I must thank him someday for not being the cleverest dog in the rabble."

Brogan left Lorne and the others with their orders. He walked to his horse, a bit swifter step than usual with an anticipation of holding the Lass. She sat astraddle, a heavenly vision composed with a regal posture on his mount. He would like nothing better than to make love to her. She had undone her plaited hair and was raking her fingers through it.

"Where is your comb?"

"I don't know. I put it in my pocket, but it seems to have vanished. Maybe it fell out when I was dancing." She continued to use her fingers like combs, smoothing her hairs tangles. "It's unimportant."

One minute she sat tranquil and the next she jumped from the horse in a full-out run. Brogan turned to see her headed straight for Kate poised against the open doorframe. The Lass' shiny silver comb waved in her hand with a taunting only a woman could do.

"Lass!" Brogan ran for her.

She reached to grab the comb from Kate's teasing hold over her head.

"Looky what I found," Kate sang. "It must be me lucky day."

"That is mine and you very well know it!" The Lass held her hand out and then made a lunge for the comb.

Kate backed into the tavern while the Lass followed.

"Kate, give her back the comb," Brogan ordered.

"I found it, so now 'tis mine," she replied with a glare of anger directed at them both.

"Oh no, it's not." The Lass charged Kate and knocked her over a chair.

They fell to the floor and wrestled with the purpose of holding onto the comb.

Lorne looked at Brogan and then at the two girls tussling on the floor. "Ye want I should stop them?" He ran a nervous hand over his head.

"Hell no! Ye will get hurt." Brogan slid a tankard over and took a position on the corner of the table. He propped a foot to the bench and watched.

"But Kate—" Lorne cringed when she smacked the Lass on the cheek. "She might hurt your Lass."

"The Lass is playing. Believe me when I say she is going easy on Kate."

He chuckled over their staggering swings.

"That's my wee Lass," he cheered.

He knew it was wrong to encourage the brawl between the ladies except he could hardly see a reason why he shouldn't let them vent as men often did at times. Kate could hardly be considered a wilting flower and the Lass, a scrapper to be sure.

"Brogan?" Lorne looked at him shocked.

"Ah, 'tis only a bit of fun. The ladies need to exhaust some of their frustration that there ain't two of me." He chuckled. "Give 'em a few more minutes and they will tire of the game."

The Lass sat up and turned an angry glare at Brogan's shout of approval and his comments.

"A game indeed!" she fumed.

He thought that maybe he should have stayed quiet before her wrath turned on him.

She grabbed the comb and swung at the harlot. "This is mine, you fat cow!"

Brogan's eyes widened. There weren't an ounce of fat on the statuesque Kate, yet it seemed an insult to her nonetheless. The Lass jumped up and backed away as Kate, not willing to give up, came at her.

"Hold this, please." The Lass leaned close to him.

At the same instant he took the comb with a smile, he saw the formulation of real danger. She had reached in his boot and retrieved one of her knives.

"Oh, no, ye do not want to do this, Lass." Brogan grabbed her hand as she stood with the steel dagger.

It might not have caught his attention except the open door let a ray of morning sunlight in so the blade glinted under its beam.

"I'll kill your whore, if you don't get her to back off." She huffed with her arm clenched in his hand.

"That will be enough." His voice, intolerably loud and commanding, brought Kate to a halt. "Tis the Lass' comb because I have seen it in her hand before."

Kate wheezed a disgruntled noise and folded her arms together.

"I found it fair and I say 'tis mine."

"Next trip, I'll bring one bought special for ye." He held her chin in the V of his hand. "Would ye like that?"

The Lass fumed behind him. He could hear her annoyance hiss with each panting breath she took. Then a door opened which made them all look.

"What is going on out here?" a gruff, sleepy-faced man demanded, rubbing his eyes.

Lorne wandered over to the opposite side of the room.

"Take care of him, now!" Brogan hissed low to Kate. "Be very convincing or ye may wind up by way of the Miller's wife." He pushed her away and reached back to take Brienna's arm.

"What are you doing?" she gasped.

"Saving our hides, Lass, now t'would not be the time to argue or fight me."

He took the dagger from her hand and dropped it in his boot as he nuzzled his face into the silkiness of her hair. She smelled of honey, lavender, and sex. His cock jolted with the renewal of her scent.

"He is one of Thane's men," he whispered.

"Thane's men?" she questioned nervously.

She tried to look, but he blocked her view. His mouth moved closer to hers. "Try to pretend ye are having a good time."

"Did we wake ye, sir?" Kate purred, sauntering over to the man. "It was only a bit of fun we were 'aving out 'ere. How 'bout I show ye me special sort of fun?" Her arm slithered around the man's. "My ye are a strong one, aren't ye?"

Brogan looked over the Lass' shoulder at Kate's magical way with the man. She went in the room with the man and the door closed quietly. While he kept a close watch on the door, he kissed the sweet lips under his. It gave him a few minutes of pleasure he could thoroughly enjoy.

He felt Brienna's responses. They were reserved, unlike the night before when she kissed him hungering for his saliva. Her palms lighted on his shoulders, soft like a butterfly. He moved his hands along the dip between her shoulder blades and grasped the back of her neck. Not in a threatening way, but so his fingers could burrow to gently caress the back of her head.

When her fingers crept across his shoulders until one brushed his jugular, he involuntarily stiffened. Her whole body livened with a sensuous writhing so he forgot they had to go.

The immediate threat of Thane waylaid, he found a tempting danger to take precedence. The lass and the way she became a hazard to his thoughts.

"Brogan," Lorne whispered. "We should go."

Withdrawing his kiss from the Lass, his eyes flitted over the creamy complexion. He touched her soft and satiny cheek and stayed riveted by the contours of her features. Her mouth hung in that last puckered pose. A magical lure, tugging, pulling, and insisting he go back to kissing her and be damned with what else happened. Only he couldn't endanger her life.

"Here, put this somewhere safe." He wrapped her fingers around the silver comb and took her outside.

With a wave of his hand, Brogan had her get on the horse. His patient stallion, Goliath, had not taken a step from where the Lass flew off him.

"Brogan!" Duane called out, riding toward them.

With a light touch to her knee, Brogan left the Lass and went to him, not wanting her to hear bad news.

† † †

Brienna placed the comb carefully in her pocket. The deep fold in her dress would have made it hard to fall out and she immediately assumed Kate had stolen it from her. She'd put nothing past the wench including the skills of a pickpocket. She couldn't imagine what Brogan saw in the girl other than her endowments that were mostly bared for display to all.

She watched the men talking and strained to hear what they said, but their voices stayed low. When Brogan looked at her with a sorrowful stare, she thought the worse and it shook her insides.

Not thinking through a plan, Brienna dug her heels into the horse's flanks. The man had been sent for Medora and he returned alone. The overwhelming rush of fear pushed her to ride blindly. She couldn't help it if Brogan had trusted her to stay his docile puppet. He would ruin everything she set out to do. She rode fast and found the horse swifter than any steed she ever owned. Only, did she really think she could escape by riding off on his horse?

The thunder of a horse gaining ground behind her challenged everything she knew to go faster. It was of no use. Brogan let out a long loud whistle. The stallion stopped with such abruptness, she thought she'd fly over his neck. Regaining her equilibrium, she dismounted and ran. A useless attempt against a man on horse, but a desperate fortitude she could not forsake for quiet defeat.

Brogan jumped down, capturing her around the waist. Both their momentum and collision put them tumbling to the ground. The landing, less than graceful, ended with her in his lap, with a vivid memory of her that way before, all hot and naked. She wiggled in his grip, yet with her hands held behind her back it gave her nothing with which to swing.

"Where's Medora?" she yelled, inches from his face.

"Duane said they saw her try to escape by using a knife. Her skill is nowhere equal to yours and she was stabbed." He relayed the dismal information and hung onto her firmer.

"No!" Brienna felt the tears boiling up.

"There were too many men for them to get to her, but she was being taken care of. Now tell me, who took her and why?"

"It's my fault." Brienna started to sob, the upset too great to control her emotions. "It's my fault."

"Aye, it is. Ye will find no sympathy with me," he told her harshly. "Ye should not have been out on your own to begin with."

She cried harder and when Brogan let her hands go, she fought him trying to tenderly hold her. All her strength fizzled in his deep soothing tone telling her things would be all right.

"We will fix everything, Lass," he whispered against her head.

She needed his consoling. She didn't want to be brave anymore. Her struggle ended and she pressed her face into his chest. Her crying shook her and his embrace only reassured her more that everything could get better.

"What's your name, Lass?" His hand came up and stroked the soft wisps of gold hair back from her temple when she lifted her face from his shirt.

She angled her head back to see him. "Brie," she replied, giving him the nickname only her father had ever called her. It wasn't a father figure she required, however, that deep masculine resonance had brought the comfort she needed.

"Don't cry, Brie." He grazed her forehead with his thumb and rubbed the wrinkles from between her brows.

She closed her eyes when his thumb traveled down her nose and rolled over the tip as if to inspect the shape. His touch swiped away another impulsively quick tear. Her heart missed a few beats and then the rhythm escalated at the perusal of his inspection tracing her mouth.

The palm of his hand cupped her face. His thumb rubbed her lips, ventured into the cavern, and explored her teeth. The inside of her lip he drew down and squeezed her mouth gently until he puckered it partly open. Her soft sigh invited him to taste the liquids in which he bathed his thumb.

She put her arms around his neck and kissed him. She wanted to relive the moment where he filled her with happiness. She plied him with a vision, the one she knew he wanted to recall as well. She reached down between them and wiggled her fingers beneath the band of his britches. She knew not all she did, but she had the willingness of an adventurer. Stories did not pass her ears lightly where men and women were concerned. The fascination of this man enthralled her exploratory nature.

"Here, let me." He slid her off his lap.

She watched him unfasten the britches and produce his long thick cock. Her fingers wrapped his fist, holding it and she bent down, kissing the tip.

"Oh God, Lass." He stiffened with a deep groan. "Are ye changing your mind?"

"No, I'm returning a service."

She held the thick shaft and fit his cock in her mouth. The silky skin surprised her. She sucked on it with a lack of skill, yet an instinctive action he seemed all too satisfied with if his moans were any indication. His fingers wove into her hair and he gave wordless instruction, pulling her head and pushing it back. The deeper his maleness plunged the more her nose was tickled by his pubic hairs. They were not as soft as her own were, nor as short and curly. He had crinkly coarse hair in a wild wiry bush surrounding the base of his cock and balls.

She kneaded the sac with twin stones and it frustrated him. Something she fully appreciated since her ordeal.

"Ye suck it wonderfully, Lass," he praised. "Ye take it as deep as ye can stand for it to go."

She swallowed, relaxing her throat muscles and shoved her face into the dense bush. His cock jammed against the back of her throat. His fingers squeezed her head and she drew back quickly.

"Faster, Brie, make it fear your devouring hunger. Faster," he repeated.

She thought it went deeper the second time, though she didn't know how when his body stopped at her face. The third plunge made her think it grew. She gagged slightly and he withdrew almost all the way.

"Are ye all right?"

Brienna held his cock and took it from her mouth. She looked up at his strained features, his passionate mouth hanging open as he panted heavily.

"Fill my mouth with your essence." She breathed over the swollen head. "Fill my throat."

She took his cock between her lips. Swirling her tongue around the pulsing vein, she raked her teeth back and forth until he roared. The sounds of culmination shook the leaves from the trees and she gulped the hot spurting liquid into her raw throat. It soothed and slid freely into her belly.

The spring went dry and in a flurry of movements, he jerked her up to his mouth. His kiss went hard and his tongue bathed the traces of his come from her breath. She had accomplished what she sought, he'd not go lightly again with her feelings where another woman was involved.

She hated the jealousy, the envy she had for the time others had pleasured him and been pleasured by him. She had no right to those feelings or to lay claim to a man she could not call her own. It brought a horrible shame on her for wanting him so desperately and not able to offer herself to him as a lifelong partner. She hugged him fiercely, hiding her tears in the moist heat of his neck. His hands roamed her back and made things truly seem they could be all right.

Deep in her mind, she had so much conflict she couldn't see anything ever being right again.

Chapter 9

Brogan held her head to his shoulder. His cock softened in her hand. He could sense it beginning to get new ideas as she mindlessly fingered the tip. Nothing could please him more than to have her sweet lips suckling it repeatedly until he died from the rapture. However, there were other things to consider.

He cupped her cheek and wiped the wetness of her saliva blended with his come over her mouth. It glossed her scarlet lips so they were as delicious looking as the ripest apple. He had savored the tantalizing samplings over the course of knowing her. Wishing for more time now did neither of them any good. They had frittered enough time away on carnal play.

"'Tis time we got back to the others," he said, taking his hands away from her before his mind's progression went further.

The hardest part of getting up was her fingers coming undone from his cock.

She stood up and he rose with her, readjusting himself, tucking his cock back into the tight britches. They seemed tighter with the chubby devil's desire growing for the Lass. Unfortunately, he fought the erection and won. Whistling loud, both horses came instantly to the high-pitched sound as if it tethered them. He allowed that the Lass was quite capable of mounting the horse herself, but his need to touch her made him put his hands on her waist to assist her anyway.

"Thank you."

Her voice had a happy lilt, drawing his smile wider. "Ye are welcome, m'lady."

She looked down oddly for a second and then went to adjusting her seating on the saddle. They rode back to the village in silence. He didn't know her thoughts and he didn't want to talk of his.

"Duane, come take ye horse," he called when they rejoined the group waiting on them.

He noted the Lass didn't raise her eyes to a single one. Her cheeks tinted with a blush of adorable pink and he understood her discomfiture. He slid from the horse and walked to her.

"They will not ever know." He mounted behind her and whispered.

"They already know."

"They think they know and I'll give them no helpful clues."

"Men brag, it's natural." She sighed.

"I suppose, except..."

"What do you think will happen to Medora?" she interrupted.

The topic of his swaggering vanity fell by the wayside. She did not wish to discuss their intimacy and he wished no further embarrassment to her feminine delicacy.

He swung his horse around and they all headed out.

"I would guess she would be tended to and treated as a slave." He turned the conversation to the other woman. "Reece has followed them and he will come to Kylemore and let me know what has become of her. More importantly, he will tell me where and by whom."

His belief as to who and where had already fixed on Thane Rhoswen at Thorndale. Reese was the right one to send as he could best serve the girl.

"You have a suspicion though, don't you?"

He let his men go on ahead of him while he enjoyed Brie's fingers lightly caressing his forearm around her middle.

"We have been in battles for several months with Thane Rhoswen. I suspect it was his men. Thane wishes to rule the world and some of his men have been trailing us. We have waited for their attack for days," he explained. "It may come to that before we get to Kylemore."

"Yet, you came after us, why?" She eased back into a comfortable position.

"Trust is hard on the road. Ye could have been or might be a spy for Thane. Ye are a powerful adversary with a weapon, Lass, and therefore a threat."

"I'm not in league with that devil!" Her vehemence sat her up and startled his horse.

"Whoa, Goliath, the Lass is not our enemy."

She took her reposed posture with a shiver. "Thane Rhoswen is an evil man that will do everything he can to rule Avalbane. It is why my message is so important for Lord Torrick. If his son does not wish to wed the Queen, he should let her out of the contract so she can wed an ally that would be of real benefit."

"The Queen? I thought this message came from Padric Rhoswen." Brogan heard the urgency in her voice.

"King Rhoswen is dead and his daughter is ruler now."

A great sigh of sadness shuddered through Brie and he hugged her, feeling the loss as if the King were his own father. Never had there been a better King than Padric Rhoswen and Brie's loyalty gave him an ache in his chest. It tightened the air in his lungs and made the first breath hard and he choked. In all his life, he didn't think he'd ever know or hold a woman who had more compassion or spirit than the Lass did.

"Thane will be no threat to Avalbane when I get hold of him."

"He already is. He's the greatest evil to ravage our lands and he plans on having my...our kingdoms by marriage or force."

"If Thane takes control, he will increase his armies and come even stronger to Kylemore. Ye are right to question what our futures hold."

It left him questions he wished might have complete answers. Things were preparing to evolve and he wasn't ready for change.

"Do you think there is a chance Lord Torrick's son will honor the contract?" she asked and her hopeful tone disturbed him. He wanted to say nay, the son would remain a stranger to his betrothed, except he couldn't and she already knew that before he did.

"With this information, he will have no choice."

"Do you think he has enough mettle to be a King?" To find an ally to marry her and stand against Thane would not be easy. With Torrick already at odds with Thane, their alliance would serve them equally.

"He will rise up to the occasion. Tell me, what is she like?" Curiosity got the best of him since Brie talked of the Queen in such high regard. He had never given thought to what his father did in making a contract without his sanction.

"Oh, she's pleasant enough. Her father would describe her as headstrong."

"Is she plain, fat, short, tall..."

"You do want to know a lot."

"I have never heard about her. I do not even know her name," he said with a small amount of wistfulness and then cleared his throat. "Lord Torrick's son will want to know," he imparted brusquely.

"Let's just say I could change places with her and the opinions would be a mirrored image."

"Ah, then she is beautiful because ye are nothing less than exquisitely ravishing." He lightheartedly laughed, looking at her face redden.

"I guess some think so," she replied with a brash glare.

Brogan reached his hand up and held her face turned to his. "Ye are far prettier than any woman should have a right to be. It turns a man's head and creates a puddle of mush in the place of his brain. Ye could get me in a great deal of trouble, Brie, and this is knowledge I do not impart lightly. I often welcome trouble and ye would be no less desired."

He captured her mouth in a long kiss. His horse continued on his own accord behind the trail of others. Offering a bit more privacy, the animal even slowed and Brogan saw a great gap between him and his men when he looked up.

"Is that why he has not come? He doesn't wish to have a fat ugly wife at his side?"

He laughed at her insulted tone. He needed her understanding and relished her not giving up her persistence. She had a mission and while she hadn't divulged it all, he quite suspected she was sent to bring her Queen's Torrick to task. He also thought it very clever of the Queen to present him with a problem. With a woman messenger as beautiful as Brie, she had the power of persuasion. With her fighting abilities, she had the potential of force. If it weren't for the reason in his arms, he could consider he might very well like the Queen.

"I think 'tis safe to say no man wants that, but then what one man thinks is ugly, another may think perfection. 'Tis more likely Lord Torrick's son does not wish to have the obligation of a wife at all, especially of Rhoswen descent. His father had not consulted him on the matter and if he were to have a say himself, he would find it disagreeable."

"Well then, they should be perfect for each other because she doesn't want to be married either, other than to save

Avalbane from the hands of Thane. However, it's a shame he would be so narrow-minded to discard her because of a wayward cousin tainting their name."

"'Tis not all the name, Lass. We of Kylemore have heard many rumors of the Queen's mother and the sect of healers she belonged too. Ye are from Avalbane. Is it true they still practice sorcery, or are the myths really a storyteller's vivid imagination?"

† † †

The question made Brienna uneasy. She didn't like the cadence of his skepticism. How did she answer something so volatile where beliefs were challenged? Brogan sounded distrustful of such people and she feared his opinion of her would change for even knowing of such truths.

"Legends are not created by unfounded threads of fact, they are events given to distortion, yes, but it makes them nonetheless real."

"So it is true. The Queen is a practitioner of deviltries not common amongst mortal man. What of her people, what of ye, Lass? Do ye hold such a woman in high regard when she commands with magic?"

"I don't think the question is appropriate for me to answer," she said quietly.

"Your loyalty to your Queen is commendable and I will not ask ye to go against your tenets as a subject of Avalbane." He rubbed her arm affectionately. "Ye are a smart woman and I trust ye have your reasons for any beliefs ye guard close to your heart."

"Brogan?" It seemed as good a time as any to tell him all truths.

"Hmmm?" He nuzzled her chin with kisses.

"Nothing."

She saw the men stop ahead. She wondered their opinion of mystic healers. She wondered their opinion right now about their leader toting what appeared to be his doxy along for their adventure.

"Please stop." She pulled her face away.

Brogan's mention of myths made her think of the silver dragon. The power of healing she inherited from her mother made her recall the higher command. She didn't ever hear the details beyond how the taking of one drop of silver blood from a legendary silver dragon could give the ultimate capabilities of a healer. Her mother died leaving her to find out all she could do on her own. As for the dragon, Brienna liked to believe it true, but she had no idea where it could be found or if it even existed anymore. Over the years the fact became more of myth to her.

The group waited for them to catch up and Brogan took lead. They rode for a better part of the day until they reached a village of peasants that welcomed them. Brienna watched as some of the men dismounted and were greeted by name, by woman of varying ages. She considered it might be their home since the last village had not been.

Then Brogan was rushed upon by a pretty woman slightly older than herself. Her eyes were bright with affection for him, but when they took notice of her, they darkened into a jealous quagmire. Brienna couldn't help the small groan at having to put up with another of Brogan's tarts.

"Duane, watch her," he said, pulling Brienna off the horse and posting the man as a guard on her.

She resented his swift regression to distrust. She watched him go off with the woman. Jealousy began a slow torturous suffocation. The woman hung on his arm as if she owned him. It dawned on her that maybe this one might be his wife even though he claimed to have none.

At the far side of the village, Brogan and the she-devil disappeared into a hut and it broke her heart. It crushed her with a hopeless pain she could not even fight. The last lingering detail stopped her from challenging any woman. She had agreed to be another man's wife.

"Do ye want something to eat, Lass?" Duane swung his head toward the festivities accruing near a modest hovel.

"No," she answered crisply but went with him anyway so he could eat.

Someone brought out a horded barrel of mead and the cups filled with great enthusiasm. Musicians of the group gathered, one with an elongated fretted sound box held on the man's lap and played by plucking strings much like a harp. Another man had a reed flute that played the most beautiful melody.

The impromptu party put good spirits at their best and no one seemed to look as glum as she felt. Medora had been abducted and there was no one to feel the tides of despair for the loss, save herself.

An hour passed before Brogan joined the crowd. He gave a smile and wink to her as he passed by. His outright flaunting swagger at what he'd been up to disgusted her. She reached to the table to take a piece of pheasant and he came back to sit with her. In his hands, he held a mug of ale and a leg of lamb.

"Enjoying yourself, Lass?" He tore a piece of the meat from the bone and chewed it.

"This is not a trip I take for pleasure," she muttered, taking another delicate bite of pheasant.

"Ye have not a drink, Lass." He offered his cup to her and she shook her head.

"Aye, I forgot, ye prefer not to dull the senses." He rolled his eyes skyward. "Like last night, huh?"

The woman he had left with came into the circle, laughing and joking with her friends. Brogan waved her over. She no longer had a smile for anyone. Her bright orange hair twisted in fringes around her oval face came loose of the knot fixed on top her head. Brienna locked her jaw in place to keep from making a noise of utter disgust with Brogan.

"Elaine, bring a cup of water for Brie." His shout bespoke of a man giving an order instead of a request.

"She can bloody well get her own cup of water!" Elaine snapped. "There's the well, her legs work for I seen them me self, and if she needs waitin' on, then ye fetch her water."

Brogan stood seemingly ready to chastise poor Elaine, but before he could speak Brienna shot to her feet.

"Who are you to command anyone to do bidding for you or anyone else?" she charged with her unbridled vehemence. "I told you I wanted nothing to drink and if I do, I'm more than capable of getting it myself."

His chest puffed out, his face turned red, and he prepared to match his self-importance with her own. His men had cocky grins daring him to fight and she could see the anger dissipate from his eyes. The men would like nothing better than to be spectators in a heated brawl. She and Brogan in a shouting match or she and Elaine in a hair-pulling, eye-gouging contest would be their favorite sport. The air expelled from his lungs and he sat to take another drink of his ale.

Elaine sauntered off and sat with Sedge.

Brienna stormed away and eventually took a place outside the ring alone. Drinking and song went on for hours. The merrymaking only aggravated the situation more for her. She gave some consideration to running away. It would be so easy. Most everyone had fallen asleep or passed out drunk. She could slip away and reach Kylemore on her own. Brogan would no longer tempt her morals. She'd be free to finish all she started out for.

She kept a watchful eye on Brogan and not once did she ever see his gaze drift to Elaine. He had on occasion looked to her. The terse stare became a haunting seduction to make her nervous from the longing she had for him.

How tents ever managed to be erected, she didn't know. She couldn't believe what staggering men could accomplish when assembling structures anymore than they could open their britches to relieve themselves.

"Lass?" Duane pointed to a tent. "That t'would be yours and...well that t'would be yours for the night." He stopped short of mentioning the tent as also Brogan's.

She wondered how guarded she would be as she crawled inside and laid on her back staring at the hole that let her see a single star. Her stomach growled with remorse for not eating more and she closed her eyes to sleep.

What the men did after she left, she didn't want to know. She was sure it included heavy drinking. When she woke abruptly, the strong odor of mead, assailed her nose.

"There is me fair Lass," Brogan exclaimed in the dark with a slurred speech giving away his inebriation.

His hand glided over her hip, which made her jump more than the sudden sound of his loud voice had. She wanted him and refusing his advances never entered her head. Then his hand was gone and she heard him drop down next to her. Seconds later, he snored so loud she pushed with vexation to stop the infernal noise. He grunted from the persistence at which she kept pushing him until he shifted so his back went to her. The snore rumbled low enough she could sleep.

She hated the way he seeped under her skin the past couple days. She didn't like his gruffness for sure. The attractive way his eyes lit like the summer lawns outside her home. Green clover spreading over the pastures for as far as the eye could see gained any woman's fancy. She had left a lantern lit for him and it had nearly gone out. Reaching to put the flame to bed, she looked at his hair, a mass of wavy black locks. It gave her a wish to run her fingers through and remove any tangles.

She puffed a breath over the firelight, leaving the trances of smoke in the tent. Brogan rolled over and his wild spearmint scented breath had vanished. He smelled of soured ale and her nose wrinkled. Hers, she knew, could not be much better.

"Ye are too far away, Lass," he mumbled.

"Too far, ha! I should be further."

"And ye are too loud."

"You're drunk so everything will sound loud."

He rolled toward her and snaked his arm over her middle, clinching her waist and hauling her to his stale mouth. He kissed and she hung there waiting for him to finish his wet slobbering over her lips.

"Mmmm, ye taste good."

"Mindless drivel spews in your head from that swill." She groaned with a little disappointment for he would not even know who she was come morning. Tonight should not bring her aching desires relief, as long as Brogan remained muddled. He had been with yet another woman, and right under her nose, and it vexed her to no end. She hit him in the arm not expecting a fired reaction.

"What! What's wrong?" Brogan rose up on an elbow.

He couldn't see her in the dark. She could feel his heart beating quicker and she hadn't meant to scare him.

"Well?"

"Nothing," she answered, surprised at how he suddenly seemed so alert.

She stroked his chest in a calming manner. She'd do it for anyone with the hard pounding excitement coursing through them. She never imagined her hasty annoyance would sober him so well.

"Let go." Brienna pushed against the solid body when he pulled her tighter.

She didn't want him coming to her after Elaine. He had a woman in every village and it felt degrading the way he flaunted her in front of them and them in front of her. He had no morals, not a one, and she refused to give into his caress again.

"Oh, Lass, do not fight me," he cooed, laying his head back and dragging her up his chest.

She really didn't want to fight what had been twisting in her every thought for three days. With what they already shared, emotionally she already felt trapped. Her fingers extended and massaged the tight muscles in his shoulders. She rubbed the thick cords sweeping up his neck, knowing he would have the same stiff tension as her aching body.

"Ah, with that magic touch, I am but a servant to do your bidding, m'lady."

She slid up further and kissed him.

"I bid you go to sleep."

"Mmmm, a plan to be sure."

It only took minutes for him to drift off. She didn't seriously believe he could be sober enough to perform any sexual acts upon her. The idea did cross her mind to pull his cock out and suck on it. Elaine's fluids dried on his skin made her discard the notion.

Brienna's fingers stopped rubbing his shoulders. He slept peacefully, unaware at how much she would do right then. It had to be fate stepping in and watching out for her. Yes, her fingers were more magical than he may ever know. Invoking the intrinsic warm vacillation to remedy all that pained him, she put a lone finger to his jaw. A light amber glow emitted instantly and went out quickly when his snorting snore startled her. She withdrew her hand, afraid he would wake and find something he did not want to know.

Slowly, she slid off him and resumed her place a foot away even though she didn't want to go. Sleep came easily to her tired muscles. The nightmares that soon followed, jarred her upright. Medora, Brogan, and all others she knew were dying because of her. Waking up should have stopped the struggle her mind had, except she found herself against Brogan's rigid back and she immediately thought him dead. Her arm around him was caught under the weight of his arm over it. She tried to jerk free and couldn't pull herself from his grip. She panicked and pushed at his shoulder for leverage.

"Five more minutes, Lass," he muttered sleepily.

"No more minutes and how dare you indecorously hold me like I was one of your whores!"

"What are ye going on about, Lass?" Brogan groaned, rolling to his back. "Ye were the one hugging me like some pup ye found."

Brienna didn't know whom she could vent the anger on. She looked to her side of the tent, empty of her and then examined that he was right where he had started in the middle of the night. A small, infuriated sound funneled up her throat and she swallowed it down. His laughter did nothing to help her temper as she kicked a foot at him.

Brogan held her hand to his chest. The beat of his heart had been evident all along. She tried to tug again and his grip tightened.

"Lass?"

She didn't know what to say. Something terrible would happen all because of a choice she would soon make. She'd had premonitions before and hated they were not clear until too late.

Chapter 10

Brogan sat up and held Brie's face. "Lass, what has frightened ye?"

She leaned against him and his compassion went out wholly for her trembling.

"A nightmare, it was only a nightmare."

"Oh, they can be bad at times, I know." He smoothed a hand over her head and stroked her back. "Seems so real, as if ye were really there."

The splitting ache in his head pounded harder with talk. Drinking did not mix with women, Brogan decided. Their voices were too high pitched to deal with afterwards. She crawled out of the tent before him. When he followed a short time later, he looked to see where she went. There was nothing good about Brie and Elaine together talking. Women comparing notes over men only led to trouble. In his case with the Lass, she would learn more than he wanted her to know about him.

"Elaine!" he yelled to her. "Come here so I can see your pretty face this morning."

His words didn't come out how he wanted them to and she hurried toward him, smiling. Brie's expression cut him deep with one swift flash of her violet eyes. He wished he had reversed the person to whom he spoke. Now the woman he didn't want excitedly held his arm as the one he began to need took his comment as a rejection of her.

"I knew you'd come 'round. I don't care if ye marry the woman in Avalbane. That's so far away I'll gladly bring ye comfort each visit you make here," Elaine declared.

"What were ye and the Lass talking about?" he casually asked.

"She wanted to know how far Kylemore was from here." She fingered the strings tying his shirt closed. "We could go to me hut now."

"What else did ye talk about?"

"I don't know, just things."

Brogan gripped her hand tight. "I need ye to tell me everything ye said to her about me."

"Ouch, Brogan, you're hurting me hand," she wailed. "I don't know. I told her how long I've known ye, how often ye come here, and..." She hesitated and Brogan squeezed her hand harder.

"All right, so I lied, and told her ye loved me. I know ye don't, but I don't like her. She wants ye and I don't like sharing." She stomped her foot with a childish pout.

"Anything else?" He wanted to be amused, but the seriousness to what she might have said was uppermost of his concerns.

"No."

"She does not know I am a Torrick?" He looked at Brienna combing and braiding her hair.

"I don't know. I didn't tell her anything like that. Why? Is she not supposed to know?" Elaine stared at him confused, the way he wanted her to remain.

"Not yet." He rolled her fingers in his hand. "Can I trust ye will not tell her?"

"The less she knows about ye, the better I like it." She grinned and hugged him.

"Elaine, I told ye, we are finished." He let her hand drop. "I will be marrying Queen Rhoswen of Avalbane and I will be a faithful husband to her. I have not the stamina to tell lies or keep them between women."

"What about her?" Elaine gestured toward Brie. "You'll not give her up, will ye?"

"There is nothing between me and the Lass. She is a messenger for Queen Rhoswen and I am escorting her safely to Kylemore. Hell, Elaine, the Lass doesn't even like me so what makes ye think I have any say over her?"

"Ye could if ye wanted. There isn't a woman around that wouldn't love ye, if ye asked." She stroked her hand over his cheek.

"Elaine, no more talk of love. Find yourself a husband." He swept back some hair from her face, feeling sorry to have led the girl on as far as he did. "We will be leaving shortly so stay away from Brie."

"Will ye at least kiss me goodbye?" She tipped her face up to him.

Brogan didn't want to but he had to keep her on the single thread of loyalty to him. He looked around and didn't see Brie anywhere. He held Elaine's jaw and gave her a kiss. Her whimper broke his heart because he liked her. He never meant for her to fall in love with him. He knew a long while back he shouldn't have let things go on. That was one reason he hadn't been to see her in the last six months.

† † †

Brienna closed her eyes tight after watching from the shadows of a tree as Brogan kissed Elaine. She moved behind the tree and before she knew it, she ran. Five, ten, fifteen minutes she raced through the forest until her legs gave out and she dropped to the ground. Thorns of a briar vine pierced her gown and pricked her knees. They scratched over her palms and she lifted them up to see the speckles of blood on her pale skin.

She wiped her hands on her gown and hung her head to cry. It wasn't fair her father had her assigned to the best choice of marriage he could obtain. It was not right for her to lay the full blame on him. She had agreed when she didn't have to. Now she found love did exist but it was not to be for a husband, rather for some rogue mercenary leading a band of men on attacks to thwart the onslaught of her cousin Thane's men.

She got up and looked at her blood-streaked hands. Putting them together, she let the healing begin. It took less than a minute for amber rays to spark from her fingertips. She held palms together and then pulled them apart. The scratches were gone and the light extinguished as if it never existed.

Brienna wiped her face with the hem of her dress. "I'm Queen Rhoswen of Avalbane and feelings have no place in my life."

She tilted her head up to walk proudly back to the village. Brogan would torture poor souls as to which way her disappearance took her. She didn't hurry but when she arrived to the outskirts of the village, she wished she never left in the first place. For then she might have been able to assess what had transpired with knowledge.

The carnage of some battle had swiftly twisted the place into smoke and wreckage during her two-hour disappearance. All that could happen in the blink of an eye devastated the tranquility. She wandered through the village looking for Brogan. Too ornery to die, she resolved he'd be safe. Then she saw him kneeling. He held someone and she went to see if she could help.

Draped over his arm, limp and lifeless, lay the body of a battered and dead Elaine. Brienna put a hand to Brogan's shoulder. "I'm sorry." She sniffed back the cry.

"Aye, Lass, so am I."

He glanced up at her and then hoisted Elaine into the cradle of his arms. He didn't physically cry. He wouldn't because a warrior had to be toughened to all forms of death. Still, she saw how much it hurt him not to shed tears and she cried in his stead.

His look to her had been empty. He had nothing left to give in affection. Or he had discovered something about her he didn't like. Either way, he left her behind and carried Elaine to her home. She had no idea who would be there, if anybody. Maybe he simply wanted time alone with the dead woman. She slowly followed to comfort him, lingering, afraid he might not want her to be around. For all the lives lost that day, she wished she had the gift of life in her healing hands to bring Elaine back.

"Ye like giving him rise for alarm, don't ye, Lass?" Sedge situated himself between her and Elaine's hut. "If we weren't here, maybe none of this would have happened."

"I don't understand." She stared at the wide man. His face grim beneath the full dark beard and his brown eyes dulled by a disturbance he clearly blamed her for. They hadn't had contact since Medora had been kidnapped from his charge. She forgave her rash accusation. He appeared not as forgiving of circumstances.

"These are our countrymen, they fight for the Torricks and when Thane's men came, we had no choice but to defend ourselves. The villagers chose to fight with us. They are not skilled and while we did triumph, lives of these people were lost."

"But if it was their wish to fight...then they...it's because...I wasn't here! Oh no, I didn't mean to stay away so long." She looked at him, horrified.

Brogan's blank stare had the same indictment. If she hadn't run off, they would have all been long gone. Thane's men would have passed through and Elaine...Brienna bit her lip to keep from crying.

She looked at Sedge and then surveyed the others gathering together, readying to depart. Brogan came back and she didn't know what to say. It was her fault that a woman Brogan clearly had feelings for was dead. He couldn't forgive her and she understood, but what of his promise to protect her. Could he still do that?

"Do you think I could ride with someone else?" she asked him as they neared his horse.

He looked at her and while it looked like he was hurt by her request, she decided it was his chagrin she even spoke to him in light of the events.

"No."

Surprise stunned her. She was sure he wouldn't want to be anywhere near her after what she'd done. Empathy kept her quiet as he boosted her up on the horse and he swung up behind her. They had no conversation and the day went long on horseback when he remained silent. She'd heard a comment about them reaching Kylemore lands, but she wouldn't ask when. She had no wish to disrupt Brogan's steady contemplation.

Another night fell upon them.

Brogan selected a secluded area in the cliffs so any attack would have to be head-on. He had his tent offset from the others. Brienna did not question his motives. Something in her wanted to trust him. He made his reason clear when she announced she was going to sleep.

"I will be out here if ye need me," he pointed to a bedroll not yet unfurled.

"You won't be sleeping with me?" The query spilled out.

It crushed her with more regrets than she'd ever voice to him.

"No. I think I will trust ye not to run from me anymore. If ye do, well, I am done chasing."

Brie thought his tone sounded cross. All the while she thought he had put the tent away from everyone to be alone with her, he had done it as punishment or preventative. While her secret desires all required him to be close to her so she could comfort his grief, he protected his men from her as if she had been the one to have personally killed Elaine. She looked at her hands, wishing she still had the scratches. She had knowingly healed herself when she could have healed another.

Brienna's sleep became distressed even more. Medora's abduction and the guilt of a woman's death made her sick. Her impending meeting with a man she might wed also held a place in her troublesome slumber. She had not contemplated the gravity of it until she had met Brogan. His arrogant, officious manner made her stomach churn and knot with each touch or look he gave her. She wanted to think it didn't mean anything. Deep inside, she knew it was a start of something dangerously disruptive. Anything tied so strongly to her feelings proved hazardous to her spirit.

She awoke abruptly from the nightmare and wiped a hand over her sweat-dampened face. She thought a drink of water and some fresh air might help. She prescribed the false needs and crawled from the tent in search of Brogan.

"Leaving?" He was sitting against a tree.

"I wanted a drink," she replied, quietly assessing the area for others who might be awake.

He handed her the water bag. She took a long gulp and handed it back. His hand grasped hers and tugged. It compelled her to drop down next to him, not by his will but her own need to give and receive comfort.

"Are you all right?" She cupped her other hand over their locked together ones.

"I will be." He lifted her hands and kissed them both.

"Is there anything I can do?" She almost didn't think the words would come out.

"No. Go back and get some sleep. We will be traveling far tomorrow." He released her hands.

Brienna wanted to scream, *no!* He couldn't turn her away when she requested his attendance to her despair. He had no right to reject her offer of affection. She was a noble woman and with that position she was due respect to her wishes. During her hesitation, Brogan reached out and pulled her to his lap. Her smile formed out of an unreasonable belief he had read her thoughts. Her heart pounded with relief he didn't hate her for Elaine's death.

"Truly amazing," he murmured at the edge of her mouth, where he kissed her cheek lightly.

Brienna looked at him shyly, afraid he'd make fun of her desires surfacing so swiftly. He combed his fingers into the hair at the sides of her head and brought her back for a longer, much deeper kiss that bordered on desperation. She leaned on him, needing every ounce of his strong embrace holding her.

"Oh, Lass, sit up!" He groaned and put a hand to his side.

She looked down at the blood on his palm. "You're hurt!" She moved off him and pulled his shirt further open to look.

"Aye."

"It's not bad." She let out a slow breath to carry away her sudden fear.

"Hurts like hell though." His stomach shrank from the sting of her touch.

"It should be cleaned so it doesn't take on a blight that'll rot your flesh." She tore a piece of the hem from her dress and opened the water. Her mind debated fiercely with healing it. Only what would he say, what we he do? She couldn't risk rejection. Not since they had found a neutral ground on which to exist.

"Lovely image ye portray, Lass." He clenched his jaw as she dabbed, wiped, and washed the area surrounding the laceration. Her fingers shook against her will and she could feel the heat building in the tips.

The muscles moved under her strokes, his skin in that particular spot had a softness like a baby. It reminded her of his velvet cock. Skin like that didn't seem to belong to a man made of hard muscle. From that point, black fibers of hair circled his navel and thinned to a fine path up where they spread out like a black shower of rain. Brienna took her time to cause the least amount of pain as well as survey his torso. The blood stopped on its own, but easily started again when he shifted to give her better access to the wound and to her grateful gaze.

"The blade was sharp, not jagged such as a dull worn sword might make."

"Mine as well, Lass, and I made the attacker aware of that reality." He rubbed her arm as she worked. "Sit down here next to me."

Brienna took the place he tapped at on the ground. She positioned herself in the niche, and when he put an arm around her shoulders, it gave her the comfort she had sought. He encouraged her to lay her head against him and she did it freely, feeling safe in his arms. She was tired. Exhaustion, warmth and the snug fit she made to Brogan put her to sleep within minutes.

Chapter 11

"Brie, wake up." Brogan covered her head with his arm as the first drops of rain fell. "Come on, Lass, 'tis starting to rain."

She rubbed her eyes and without a word crawled to the tent. Brogan climbed in behind her and found a surprise when her lethargic squirming limbs clung to him. She wiggled herself up against his side and went right back to sleep. She was a wonder every moment he spent with her, and while she slept, he played with the damp golden tresses. His exam went to the perfect way the locks curled his fingers and how the humid air drew the ringlets tighter.

"Lass, ye should go home." He kissed her head and she hummed a pleasant unconscious response. "Except after today, I do not know if I can ever let ye go," he murmured and closed his eyes to steal a few minutes of sleep before the sun came up.

It came as an impossible notion. His thoughts somehow remained plagued with Brie's attitude and her actions. From the time they met, a wild vixen unwilling to give into his lust, she was able to seduce his common sense with her care and an unexplained fondness for his feelings.

The men stirred in the camp. He took a long breath, wishing the night had begun as it ended when the Lass lay wrapped in his arms, more lovingly than a wee babe.

The rain spattered the canvas in big plops. He thought over how he would treat her since doubt of her trustworthiness had rooted in his head. He had to remind himself her unassuming nature could be another ploy. Her assertions of going to Lord

Torrick could be only a ruse to gather information on them. It would be a highly unconventional subterfuge having a woman as a spy. The possibility, however ludicrous, could not just be dismissed.

"Brogan, is it time to get up?" She tilted her head back and looked at him with her weary violet eyes.

"Uh-huh, but ye can have a few extra minutes. I will get the horse ready."

He kissed her forehead and crawled from her embrace. It ate him up inside to think for a minute her affections weren't genuine. When it was time to leave, he had considered offering her a horse. She was a skilled rider and it would be a good enticement to keep her affections from vanishing. Yet, he had to keep reminding himself she could be a threat.

The fact remained Brie had been gone for over a half hour when the attack came. She'd been nowhere to be seen by anyone for two hours.

Brie approached with an expression he assessed as nervous, timid, and almost scared. It rattled him to begin thinking the worse again. He then did something he hated. He distanced himself from her.

"Duane, the Lass will ride with ye," he ordered.

He waited for her to question the change and couldn't have felt worse for her silence. It increased his suspicions more for her actions. He checked for himself—Duane had no small weapons the Lass could use against him. They were set to depart when Sedge came riding into their camp fast.

"Brogan!" He shouted as if the devil were on his tail. "Thane's men...twenty at least!" he announced, winded from his swift scouting return.

Brogan surveyed the area in one turn of his head.

"Up there!" he shouted. "We will make a stand in those trees. It will offer us an advantage which we will need since we are outnumbered." He looked at Brienna. He hated having her to deal with. "Duane, take her up behind those rocks and keep her out of sight." He pointed to the furthest buttress of stone.

"Give me my sword!" Brienna commanded. "I'll not sit passive and let them take me, nor will I let you dictate my safety to the hands of another!"

"I do not have time to argue this. Ye will stay out of the way and out of sight!" Brogan took her arm and walked several feet. "Do not fight me on this, Lass, or I will have ye tied and gagged so they will not know your presence here!"

"Fight you? I'm trying to help."

"Help is not needed." He motioned for Duane, then his finger slid down the graceful line of her jaw and he spoke softer. "Ye would only distract me, Lass."

"Well, maybe you should learn to keep your mind on what's at hand rather than what I look like naked!" She fumed as Duane's fingers firmly wrapped her upper arm with Brogan's nod. "You conceited bastard! You're afraid I might show you up in front of your men!"

"Take and keep her safe, Duane, but do not give her a weapon." He turned his back from her shrieks of resentment and rode to take his place in a fight against Thane's band of raiders. Everywhere they went, these men pillaged and killed people of his providence. Others of the surrounding area were not safe either from the slaughter if they resisted the taxes placed upon them.

† † †

Brienna turned her attention to the tall, wide young fellow. He didn't appear to be any older than her twenty years. His beard while long was not as full as she first thought. Light filtered through the hairs, showing it sparse on his baby face. She thought a good washing might take it as well as the dirt off.

It made her wonder Brogan's age, if he was ever married or if he had children. Maybe he had always been a warrior without ties to a family. He appeared older if only by the weathered lines around his mouth and eyes and his dark complexion. His inky hair, shorter in the front than what lay on the back of his neck, showed no signs of graying. The scars were her only clue he was older than many of his men. He had seen battles and healed from them.

She hated the way men thought and treated women as inferior. She hated that his words sounded distrustful of her altogether. She had wondered whom his allegiance was to and she finally trusted it to be the Torricks. That he did not believe the same of her was disheartening.

Brienna did not stop her quiet complaint as Duane steered his horse up the hill. The rocks didn't provide as much protection but they were the furthest removed from the melee about to befall them.

"Give me my sword, Duane. I can take care of myself."

She watched over the rock at Brogan directing the men to lay in wait in strategic positions. The magnificence in the move of his arm—pointing, ordering, and aligning everything for the fight—gave her goose bumps.

"Brogan's orders, Lass. He says no, but I have it guarded safe with me." He looked over the hilt and the craftsmanship. "'Tis a very fine blade, but small."

"That's because it was made special for the women in my clan." She huffed and took a seat on a small flat rock behind others. The position almost looked as if someone prepared it for observance of a battle. "Look!" She pointed down the hill at the riders charging up at them.

Her attention became ensnared by the men clashing into Brogan's group. She thought if she could see Thane, maybe she could find some compassion in him to stop this aggression. The

Sword of Rhoswen

count she took of twenty-seven to Brogan's nineteen teemed with an unfairness she wanted to right.

"Go down and help him," Brienna commanded, watching Brogan taking on three men by himself. "Please, just go down and I'll stay here."

"Alas, I cannot. Brogan said to keep ye safe and that I shall."

She saw the concern also in his face for the odds were growing against them. Three of Brogan's men fell and all of Thane's remained active in the fray. The clang of swords progressed upward and Brienna saw no choice but to abandon her forced docility. She backed away from Duane's peripheral vision, picked up her skirting, and made her way down the hill beyond the direction Duane watched. By the time he could see her, she would be halfway to the throng.

She first came upon Sedge holding his own against two men. She saw his eyes flicker with a puzzled expression as she picked one man in which to drop down behind his knees. Sedge forced him back a few inches and he toppled over Brienna.

"What are ye doing here, Lass? Brogan will not be pleased ye have not stayed hidden away." He continued to swing his sword until the man he came up against fell with a blow to his middle.

Brienna, in the meantime, had the man on the ground cowering under the knives she'd taken from him and held like a scissor at his throat. She contemplated her moves and everything seemed just right for the kill. Only she couldn't do it. He groveled for his life and she couldn't take it.

"Here, Lass. I will handle that." Sedge took her arm and pulled her back.

The man came up on his feet. His attempt at saving his life was lost to Sedge's quick reaction. His sword slid in and then out. The blood sluiced down the blade and Brienna turned her face with a grimace. She then looked about for another place she could help. The plan became thwarted by the clamp of Duane's hand on her shoulder.

"Are ye trying to get me in trouble? If Brogan finds that I have..."

"'Tis too late, he knows." They both turned around and Brogan glared at her with a vexation that shouted his anger without sound.

"Take her, Duane, and if ye have to tie her up to keep her..." His words were shut off when he turned to fend off another man coming for them.

Duane towed her up the slope of the hill. She stumbled over uneven ground. Duane continued to keep the pace, swiftly retreating. She was surprised when the knives were not also taken from her.

Two men came rushing at them and Duane pushed her. "Go, Lass, I will take care of these scoundrels."

His sword rose and she watched, in one flailing blow, a man drop. The second, a man much the extra large size like Duane, proved more formidable. He kept his blows coming with a sword slicing the air so fast the sound of the swish echoed.

Another man joined that one, but Brogan was there in an instant. When the third traveled toward them with no one in his path, Brienna noted his eyes take a recognizing assessment of her. He knew who she was. His course changed and he skirted the others to come for her.

"I will take these two. Ye get to the Lass," Brogan shouted to Duane.

Brienna managed to reach the top of the cliff and the horse that carried her sword. She pulled it free from the lash strapping it to the saddle and swung it at the man.

"Your Highness, we have come to take you home." The man grinned. His wild rust colored hair hanging in strings around his face flopped around like the frayed threads of a peasant's worst dress.

"You can go back and tell Thane he'll never have me or you can go to hell!" She swung the sword at the man, knowing there was little he could do to her. His mission was clearly to bring her to Thane. She would assume if Thane wanted her dead, he would want the pleasure himself.

Duane stepped in the path between her and the man intent on claiming her as some victory prize. She backed off ready to help as needed, and took her eyes to Brogan. He fiercely fought another man and she sent a silent prayer to help him.

The reflection of her thoughts on Brogan put her at a disadvantage. In the moment her attention diverted from her own safety, someone grabbed her from behind. A filthy hand covered her mouth so she couldn't give any call to Duane. He wrenched the sword from her hand, but left the unseen twin knives sheathed inside her sash.

Brienna struggled while the villain dragged her beyond the crest of the hill. The foul taste in her mouth was the filth that seeped in from the man's grimy palm. She had cast one glance to see if Brogan was aware of her predicament, but he was unable to help. A tall skinny man, stinking like the fecal waste putrefying his clothes, came up and tied her hands. He gagged her with a strip of his clothing. Brienna felt the rush of bile burn her throat. Swallowing down the revolting substance, it left a trail with threats of repeating. Then, with nothing more than a fling of his arm, the man threw her up on a horse with the rust haired man.

They immediately took off in a full-out gallop. Darting and hurtling the battlers, she saw his goal was to take her directly away from the skirmish. She reached her fingers toward the knives, each finger stretching to grasp the handles. With her hands bound and the horse galloping over the rough terrain, the task proved hard. When she finally had her fingers wrapped on the handle and the knife came free of the tie on her waist, she plunged it deeply into the man's leg. He shrieked in a thousand languages of pain and fell from the horse. His hands became more interested in the blade protruding from his thigh that he lost all thought to her.

Brienna spurred the horse on with the quick tapping of her soft-soled heels. She hoped this horse hadn't been trained to halt with a mere whistle. Those fears left her when the man went to shouting and the horse paid no heed to the orders for her to stop.

The steed obeyed her commands with a will to race and she locked her knees tight. Keeping balanced while jumping logs, ducking limbs, and turning corners required concentration. From the sidelines of her ride, she saw Brogan. He rode bent low for the least resistance against the air. No one followed her and no one appeared to follow him. She worried when he wouldn't accept her pleading look to untie her and remove the gag. Instead, he didn't slow. He grabbed the reins of her horse and galloped through the forest.

The unforeseen river's bank tripped up her horse and she went careening off his back into the water. The fall could have been harder if she hit the ground, but she saw no satisfaction when the icy wetness claimed her.

She held her breath as she went under the surface.

"Brie!"

She heard Brogan yell to her, but why was he not there? Did he not understand she couldn't last forever under the froth of rapids? The currents swept her over rocks, forcing her to gasp each time she came to the top. Water snuck into her mouth.

"Brie!" Brogan continued to shout.

The pressure became too great on her chest and she involuntarily inhaled. The water flooded her lungs. Panic overcame her senses to fight death. Blackness gathered her mind into finality and everything disappeared.

Chapter 12

Brogan snagged a fist full of her gown and did not let go even though they were splashing over the rumble of drops in the river. Rocks were unavoidable obstacles he hit. He did his best to shield Brie from them.

He put his feet against a boulder and, with a powerful thrust, forced them to the muddied bank. He hauled her from the river and carried her limp body. The slippery mud tried to reclaim them, but he forged up the slope until he knelt with Brie hanging over his forearm. He cut the knotted rope from her wrists and her arms dropped. They dangled like broken limbs of a tree and he just stared at her.

Tendrils of liquid gold clung to her skin and he pushed the hair from her face. The Lass appeared to be a lifeless angel and it was his fault. If she had been untied, she could have swam. He cut the gag off and covered her mouth with his. He breathed his life into her lungs.

"Come on, Lass. Breathe!" He let another breath out into her cold mouth. The still icy pale lips didn't move. "Breathe, damn ye! All the fight in ye cannot be gone!" He shook her.

The eruption of gurgles quickly followed with a drowned choking. Water spewed out of her mouth and sprayed up to his face. He pulled her close and held her gently while more water regurgitated down his chest.

"Brogan," she croaked, coughing up more water, "I'm not dead."

"Now how would ye know that?" He laughed at her observation. "Could it be ye would go to heaven and I would not be there?"

"Oh, you'll be there. I'm destined to have you follow me through eternity like a burr in my shoe." She coughed some more and grasped his shirt to stay close to him.

They joked out of a life threatening fear. It deeply stirred sentiments in his heart. When she stopped coughing and tipped her head back to look at him, Brogan captured her wet lips with his. This time instead of giving life, he wound her very soul into his heart. Her arms, draped in sopping wet sleeves, wrapped his neck. She fully accepted all his devouring kisses until she panted, out of breath. He released her mouth and stared into her glassy violet eyes. Regrets ran deeply. Honor paralleled carelessness. The illicit lusts crushing and grinding at his soul were forbidden.

Her fingers curled into his wet hair. She took more and more of what should be prohibited into her kiss. His tongue played over hers and she met it with aggression. Her moans were accentuated with a staccato of breathless gasps for air. He couldn't stop the pent-up frustration any longer. Regardless of his prearranged future, he had to love the angel until the very end.

"Brogan, no...please no." She kissed him more even while protesting.

"Lass, I want to make love to your very soul."

She stroked his wet hair back behind his ear. Her finger swirled over the rim and lingered with no sounds of protest.

"Lass?"

"Do you have a wife?"

The question tried to shame him from his present goal and the truth should never hurt his glory. "Nay, Lass, I have no wife."

He hated to think her reason for asking. With greater effort than he wanted to deliberate on the matter, he pushed the thoughts from his head. Lovingly, he lowered her to the ground. He pulled the tunic off over his head and then worked the wet knotted laces free on her gown. Brie no longer denied him access, and within minutes, he parted the fabric. His gaze impatiently beheld the turgid nipples, all puckered from the water's chill. She shivered and reached for him. His lips claimed hers and he didn't think he'd part from the joyous whimpers.

"Ye know I need the gown out of the way?"

"Yes."

He kissed hurriedly down her neck. He made no delay in getting to her quivering wet breasts. He didn't stop slurping over the chilly mounds until she was warmed.

"Oh, Brogan," she purred, raggedly choked up with emotion.

He drew the sodden gown from her shoulders, worked it free from her slight curved hips, and tossed it aside. The river left the flanks of her thighs gleaming with droplets. Kissing the corded muscle on the inside of her thigh, he traveled into the valley of her legs. The golden ringlets tangled over her entrance opened with her legs. The way cleared. From the glistening ivory mound covered in hair, the opening of her cunt appeared. Pink folds peeked out and his fingers pressed wide the entrance where he watched her sphincter winking.

He brushed his thumb over her clit, tempting the nub to swell. His cock stiffened against the inside of his leather britches. He ignored the insistence of the rod of flesh to come free. Brie would have the first pleasures and his body would have to accept his mind's choice.

He fingered the labia and caressed the delicate layers. She wiggled each time his stroke dipped into the tunnel of dark desires. The creamy nectar leaked to his fondling and he massaged the glistening moisture into her folds. Around, beneath, and alongside each rosy seam he lubricated Brie's sex. His touch went with an unhurried cause. Circling and swirling in and out of the mouth of her vagina, he teased her sensitive sweet nubbin.

"Ye are ripe for the sampling, Lass."

He swiped a tongue through the fissure.

She twitched and hummed.

"I will try to make the pain as small as possible," he told her wiggling his tongue into the hole.

Her receptive cunt tweaked and he allowed her gentle orgasm to warn her body. She squirmed to the slap of his tongue on her distended clit. Wrapping his arms under and around her supple legs, he lifted her ass from the earth. He could see paradise in the vivid cherry opening. Burying his face into her hot core, Brogan sucked at her sweet succulent juices. He hoisted her higher pressing his nose into the glorious scent of her womanhood, her sex a fragrance to make a man's cock harden.

She twisted her hips in his grasp and her panted whines escalated. He freed one hand to unfasten his britches. Then placing her back on the ground, he teased her clenching pussy. He rubbed the head of his cock against her clit before pushing into her just a little.

"Brogan, please, oh please..."

"Please what?" He leaned over her while his cock hung in limbo outside the gates of ecstasy. "Do ye want me, Lass? Do ye want me to fuck your tight cunt, Brie?"

"Yes, oh yes, please," she whimpered.

Her fingers squeezed and released in spasmodic clinches on his biceps. His muscles flexed to her fretting. He dipped his fingers into her wet cunt. Fisting his thickset shaft, he coated the swollen head of his cock. Pressing it to her golden gated vagina, he guided it slowly into her wetness. His body undulated from his knees up until he shoved himself into her. Then he held still, kissing over her adorable face contorted with the unexpected pain.

"It will hurt no more than this," he explained.

He kissed her trembling lips, his tongue exploring hers. The arms surrounding him offered affection. Brogan kissed her cheeks, her nose, and her eyes. He had himself immersed in pleasure with the precious Lass and he didn't know how to express every feeling he had without offering a commitment as well. She wouldn't know he couldn't. He longed to tell her who he was, but given their position, it wasn't the appropriate time.

"Can ye rise up your legs and put them around me, Lass?" He wiped the tears from her cheeks. "That is it, Brie. Just relax and all will get better."

† † †

Brienna lifted her weak limbs. Cramped into place, she found extending them lessened the tension in her hip joints. She folded her calves over Brogan's back and shivered when contacting the wet fabric of his shirt. With her ankles together, she dangled like a dew drop hangs on a blade of grass. His effortless rock against her no longer hurt where numbness set in and she panted in synch with tremors building to small explosions. His cock had not touched upon the deepest ache. She let her body hang loosely from him, deciding he knew best when and what to do. All she wanted from the moment was to hold him, to have this experience she'd forever carry in her heart.

"Are ye all right?" he asked while kissing along her jaw near her ear.

"Yes." Her breath stuttered.

She imagined men taking and never giving. She'd heard their braggart boasts, their vain talk of conquests, and she'd not think less of Brogan for those very masculine traits she expected. His light touch, the affectionate whispers, and the care in his voice were things she'd never suspect of a hearty warrior. Made from stone, forged of steel, he had the strength and brawn she so foolishly took for granted. Beneath the hardness lie a compassionate, loving man and her heart shattered with the thoughts of losing him to her life's path.

"Brogan." She said his name yet didn't know why.

"Aye, Lass?" He didn't seem to mind she had no reason.

The moment slipped by and the sensations she'd been having lifted her hips to his movements. She bit her lip, finding a discomfort she could handle. His cock, thick and long, went in further.

"That is nice," he moaned.

She didn't know what he talked about. She had only moved with him, or was it away? She couldn't be sure until he nearly came out. Upon the reentry, he stretched her wider. He thrust faster and she liked the friction against the very places that had been annoying her.

"Hold on, Lass, hold on tight."

She did. She hugged him so hard she could have broken a smaller man. His hand went under her bottom and cushioned her spine. He rocked into her harder and she squeaked her pleasure.

"Oh, Brie, if the day had no sun I could live with ye there to shine for me," he groaned.

Sappy but sincere, she kissed his whiskered face. The rough bristles scraping her smooth skin and prickling her lips made her feel so alive. Her insides ruptured with a gushy heat and she cried against the pulse in his throat. Ecstasy came with an orgasm so intense, she froze. Brogan's followed and for a moment, she thought his roar would tumble down the forest. If they were being hunted, he surely gave away their position.

"Lass, Lass, ye took me last breath," he rasped against her head.

"And you mine." She panted.

For several minutes he lay draped over her and she held him. She held dearly, wishing for all the world things could be different in her future. When he lifted up, she didn't want him to leave his place nestled warmly in her wet cunt. She didn't want to think of the repercussions of the carelessness of their coupling. She could only hope, by divinity's plan for her, she would not conceive his child this time or any time he should come to her. Because she could not foresee herself turning him away, not until she was duty bound to another.

Cherishingly, her hands glided slowly over Brogan. Filled with admiration and wonder, she still felt amazed such a handsome man as he had no wife. Her palms skimmed lightly across his chest. His nipples were hard beads beneath his shirt. She smiled and imagined taking them between her lips so she could suckle him.

"Ye have a delightful happiness spreading on your face, Lass. Did I give ye pleasure?"

"Yes," she answered shyly, aware his gaze continued a hot inspection of her.

"Me manhood has no complaints as well."

Her hands slid to the juncture of his cock and her cunt. She rubbed the soft skin and trailed a finger up to her clit. The sensitivity withdrew her exam, but his grip wouldn't allow her to go far. He pressed her palm to his groin and from there she skated up under the cloth of his shirt. The mat of hair covering his hard chest was short and soft. She loved the feel of it tickling her skin. Then she touched one of his nipples. His position didn't allow her to kiss the pebble so her fingers pinched it gently.

"Oh, Lass, things such as that will harden me again and I do not think ye would welcome me so soon."

"Why?" She liked taunting his sexual needs.

"Ye would be sore and uncomfortable."

She smiled again and closed her eyes. She could handle the soreness. For that matter, she could heal herself and experience the newest all over again.

"Brogan, have you seen many battles?"

Her fingers heated near his wound and she pressed on to feel the firm ripples in his stomach.

"Aye, Lass, I have been in too many to count."

"You're a careful man, I hope." Her fingers touched over the white scored lines in his tanned flesh.

"Now, Lass, would I be sitting here lodged between your glorious legs if I had not been careful?" He chuckled.

She felt his cock soften and his laugh caused it to slip free. She sighed at the loss of him. He leaned over and planted a kiss on her lips, drawing her mind away.

"Time to go, Lass."

He rocked back on his heels and stood up between her spread open legs. She watched his cock, limp and still impressive, get tucked into his britches. His expression hardened oddly. His jaw clenched and the muscle, what she could see beneath the shadow of whisker, ground with indecision. He bent down and held his hand out.

"Lass, ye are a beautiful sight to behold all day, but I can't handle much more of ye sprawled out there for me eyes to devour."

She took his hand and he pulled her up before him.

"Looking at ye all tinted pink makes my cock ache in reminder of your inner warm depths, so ye would be favoring me with some clothes now." He snatched her dress from the ground and handed it to her.

After a slow perusal of her length, he gave a low whistle and turned, supposedly to find the horses. She felt all tingling and for just a second wondered what he'd say if she asked for him to make love to her once more before they left.

Chapter 13

Brogan searched the immediate area for the horses. He couldn't find either. He went back to the clothed Brie and held her arms for a minute. His hand swept her long golden hair back and he studied her violet eyes for regret. They were watery pools beneath a fringe of translucent golden spiked lashes. Losing her to a watery grave was not acceptable and he was glad she was all right. They both had lost themselves in a moment of pure grateful passion and now there were other things that had to be tended to. Burdens, obligations, and duties they each had been on paths to fulfill.

Brogan guided her over to a log to sit on while he contemplated which way they would need to go. He dropped the tunic over his head and tried not to think of how much he wanted to strip the wet clothes from Brie once more. Warm her with ravished hot kisses in areas meant for her future husband. Nor should he think on how he wanted to make love to her for the rest of his life. He knew he shouldn't succumb to those desires knowing his future. As the son of Lord Torrick, he had to marry the Rhoswen woman, even though his heart had quickly stitched to Brie's.

"Can ye walk?" He held his hand out to help her up.

"Yes, but not very well. This gown outweighs me."

"I did not ask because of the dress, Lass."

He adjusted his britches and saw the spark in her eyes.

"I can walk," she said again with a pinched mouth as if he didn't know how much she liked their time together.

She gathered up the skirt and twisted the water out as best she could.

"Which way?"

"We go north." He began walking and then looked back at Brie when she didn't move.

"Thane is north...those men that took me are that way," she replied, challenging his choice of direction. "Kylemore is east."

"If we stay out of sight and head where they are not prepared to find us then we'll head east come tomorrow morning," he offered in way of explanation.

"We should just stick with heading east!" she argued in opposition to his tenuous plan. "It will just take us longer and we don't have that kind of time to spare!"

"I say, it will be quicker if we head north and circle around where they think they might find us. Since I am in command, we will do things my way!" Brogan stopped when he heard the small puff of disgruntlement further behind him than she should have been. "Come on, Brie." He looked at her standing like a drenched child. Her bottom lip pouting, her arms crossed over her chest, and a scowl wrinkling her face.

"Tomorrow is a day away," she groaned.

Brogan went toward her with a placating smile. "Ye think we should just go east?"

"Yes," she answered adamantly.

"Well I do not and I know better." He picked her up and slung her over his shoulder.

"Let me down you...you brute!" Brienna kicked and struggled on him.

"Not until ye agree to obey me." He began his trek again to the north.

"Obey you?" she screamed and wiggled more. "Never!"

"Then I will carry ye until ye see it my way." His arm tightened around her hip and his hand firmly gripped the curve of her delicious bottom. He had many ideas of what he could do with that part of her bared and facing him.

"Put me down, I say!" She hit his back, not fisted but open handed. "All right already, we go north, now put me down!"

"And what else?" He continued without hesitation. The only thing that had changed was she did not jiggle around and his hand rubbed over her rump with a mollifying stroke.

"What do you mean what else?" she grumbled.

"Ye will obey me?"

"Obey? I'm not your lap dog!"

"Say it, with meaning, or I will continue to carry ye like this." He brought his other hand up not to caress her backside, but to let her down. Only she thought differently and it brought an immediate response.

"All right, I'll obey your decision." She wiggled again. "Now let me down!"

Brogan put her on the ground and pushed her to walk. "I know a place that will offer shelter so we can dry out," he said, watching her shiver.

He wished he could build a fire for them now, but they had to get moving. His impetuous frolic with her could have very well put her in danger. The men that had taken her would come looking. Having his horse would be nice, only Goliath was nowhere to be found once they had rode the rapids down the river a ways.

"We can't walk all the way. Can't you whistle for that horse of yours?" she asked as they climbed a hill following the river.

"My voice does not raise to the shrill pitch yours does," countered Brogan. "If we get through the night alive, we will worry about a fresh mount then."

Hours dragged. Each time he looked back, Brie lifted her chin in defiance of his choice in direction. Weariness showed in her eyes. He knew more about the Lass now and she'd not show her weakness unless necessary.

The surf of the ocean resounding across the rolling hills brought Brie up along side him.

"Is it the sea?"

"Aye, Lass."

He watched the energy return to her slumped frame as she lifted the skirt of her dress. She ran toward the cliffs with all the excitement of a child.

"I've never seen the sea before," she called. "I've heard how magnificent and vast the rolling waters spread upon the horizon. This is beyond my dreams."

"Come, the way down to the beach is over this way." He held his hand to her.

She put her fingers into his palm and he led her down the natural formed path. The shelter he had in mind sat in the secluded cove along the northern shore of Kylemore.

"The sand is getting in my shoes," she squealed with delight and slipped them off her feet.

"What is this place?" She danced along, looking up at the high cliffs.

"'Tis called Dragon's Dare."

† † †

Brienna had never seen the ocean, she'd had never been very from far Avalbane. It didn't make the place she stood any less familiar.

"Don't you mean lair?" She shielded her eyes to the sun and looked at what he did with a concerned expression.

"'Tis been said centuries ago, dragons inhabited these caverns. When a man wanted to impress a maiden, he would come here to slay one." He continued to stare at the stony face of granite.

"Dragon's are to be revered, not slain. I think it a horrible story, if true."

"I do not know if true, Lass. The legend is it was their lair but it was also their dare to men." He let a soft chuckle out. "I suspect they lost the provocation because man still comes and the dragons are no more."

"How can you be sure there are no more? Dragons were as plentiful as birds one time. People still claim sight of one from time to time." She looked at the fissures in the stone and wondered how big a space was needed for a dragon to enter.

"I have seen their bones, but never anything remotely close to having been alive in my time." He reached for Brie's arm when she stumbled. "We will go in here."

Brogan pointed to a cave immense in size and extremely dark.

She felt a wave of apprehension. Her skin prickled as if danger lurked beyond and when her hands heated, she had a sense of what compelled her to go forward. Beads of perspiration moistened her palms. She wiped them on the damp gown.

Brogan gathered driftwood for a fire as they went.

"We will set a small fire far enough in so the smoke will not be noticeable and maybe the scent will not travel too far."

"You've been here before?" she asked, letting her eyes adjust to the dimness.

"Aye, a few times." He pulled off his tunic, then his shirt.

She stared into the blackness of the cave. "How far does it go?"

"I do not know. I never came to explore, just take shelter." He struck a piece of flint to spark the fire.

"Do you hear that noise?" She should have stepped back instead she went further, hypnotized by the hum.

"What noise?" Brogan came up behind her.

"It's like breathing," she whispered.

"Ah, the dragons come alive" He chuckled. "Come Lass, 'tis the echo of the surf. The tide is coming in and the waves resound through the caves."

Brienna turned around, unable to argue with his theory. Although she had to wonder when the sound continued to drum in synch with her heartbeat, a heartbeat that broke pace and quickened with Brogan's methodically slow removal of his clothes. Her eyes scanned his physique with great interest.

"Ye can take off your dress and put on my tunic, 'tis dry now."

She untied the laces binding her gown closed, wanting the very thing he did, to be free of the damp fabrics irritating her skin. She'd seen bits of him with his tunic and shirt off, and she'd not forget the details to his cock. He, on the other hand, had her not once, but twice, as naked as a newborn babe. Her pulse accelerated each time he bent over to stir the fire. The rocky surface of his muscles rolled under his taut dark skin. His stomach made of stone blocks with deeply grouted lines stacked three high melded with black hair funneling up into a canopy on his chest. She had touched it all in the confines of his shirt. She had no idea how beautiful he'd be to look at with no clothes.

She found her hands shook trying to work a knot free and Brogan came to help. He hadn't said anything, but she heard him by way of his eyes burning into her chest. She wondered if he relived every moment from their coupling. She had. She couldn't forget one second of how he gently brought her to full womanhood.

The laces came free. He peeled the dress down her shoulders, slowly staring at first to the contours of her breasts, and then his blue eyes lifted to her face. It mirrored her hunger, it harbored doubts, and she saw a sinister darkness snap inside him.

"Can ye manage on your own?" he asked brusquely and turned from her regardless.

"Yes." She took the wet wool off and set it on a rock. In exchange, she put on the tunic.

She could smell Brogan on the cloth. She resisted the urge to hold it to her nose and inhale his scent deep into her lungs and further into her heart. She picked the dress back up and held it in front of the fire.

"Do not get too close or the cloth will catch fire," he said from the darkness.

It made her jump back and she looked to him, wondering why he had left his more personable manner outside.

"I was trying to dry my dress. It's getting cold and all you have is your shirt and this tunic."

"I will be fine," he grumbled.

"Why are you barking at me?"

He didn't answer.

"Brogan, what's wrong?"

He looked the length of her and she glanced down. The tunic came to her knees. It modestly concealed her shape for as much as the sleeveless, thin woven muslin could do.

"Sit over here," he commanded. "I want a clear vision of the entrance if someone should come."

She considered he meant for her to be next to him to remove temptation. It wouldn't work. She didn't want him to deny his feelings, because she wasn't about to reject hers for the time being. A cool breeze drifted through the cave. Brienna perched herself on a rock and rubbed her arms to chase the shivers away. The space between her and a silent brooding Brogan shouldn't have been so uncomfortable.

Periodically, he got up and turned the clothes over on the rock near the heat. His shirt dried first and he held it to her. "Put this on too."

"You haven't anything, you should put it on."

He continued to hold it out to her.

"You're a very stubborn man and I'm cold so I'll not argue it another minute." She took his shirt and slipped it on. The prominent scent of him swept up her nostrils and she hugged the shirt to her body.

"We should get some sleep," he finally said.

"I'm hungry," she complained, hoping for a suggestion they'd search for something.

"In the morning, for now we stay hidden and get some rest." He scooted down on the sand, leaned upon a rock, and closed his eyes.

It did not look relaxing and Brienna contemplated making the most of her own comfort. She picked up the gown and spread it out on the sand. The dampness had been warmed by the fire. She watched Brogan for a long time. The shadows of the flames danced over his face and she noted his beard had grown more. Black hair practically buried the lower half of his face. Wild spiraling locks drooped over his forehead to his thick brows. The heavy crescents of lashes fanned his cheeks. If he had been playing in coal dust, no one would be able to tell. Then she noticed the brilliance of green staring at her.

"Are ye warm enough, Lass?"

"As warm as can be expected."

He crawled over behind her and lay down. His arm went over her without hesitation. She held her breath in anticipation of his hand upon her heaving breasts. Her heart surged with the heat of his palm pressing into her belly. He pulled her tight, fitting her every curve to his.

"This can't be warm for you, away from the fire with no shirt on," she whispered.

"Believe me, Lass, I am as warm as I need to be right now so go to sleep without worrying on me."

"Brogan, I'm sorry about Elaine." Each time he held or kissed her, he had stopped with an abruptness she thought might be because of his feelings about the woman. She couldn't shake away the faults that fell upon her childish running away.

"I know ye are, Lass, but it really is not your fault and I do not want ye thinking it was." He gave her a gentle hug.

"Sedge said it wouldn't have happened if you weren't looking for me."

It was the wrong time to bring it up, however she had to confess her guilt if nothing more than to free herself from the awful nightmares she'd had the night before.

"'Tis not your fault Lass. Do not be thinking it is. Sedge was spouting off from the pain. He loved Elaine and ye happen to be first to blame. He did not mean it and I know he has regrets in making ye feel bad for something that was not in anybody's control."

"But she...you...I didn't think Sedge..."

"I will not deny I am a selfish man. I had noticed his interest, but it was not until some months ago I gave her up. Unfortunately for the sweet girl, she held onto the notion of loving me and I did nothing until now to tell her we were to be no more."

"Didn't you love her?"

"I was fond of her for sure, but nay, I was not in love with Elaine. I am not offered that privilege in life."

Brienna wiggled for the warmth he provided. With a moan he moved his hands and she placed her fingers over his. Slowly, she pushed his hand down and pressed it to the center of her legs. She didn't have to do more. Brogan already knew her wants, her desires. She could only hope he didn't stop the caressing over the cloth covering her cunt, not until she felt the rapture.

Chapter 14

The tunic and shirt were easily lifted so Brogan could fondle the Lass. He knew lying next to her would be the start of trouble. Her squirming ass teased his cock, which needed no extra prompting. Hard and ready to insert himself into her channel, he played at the entrance.

Her wet pussy throbbed. If a chill stirred the air, it hadn't reached her hot enlarged clit. His finger pushed at it gently. She wiggled and thrust her hips forward for more. She cried out with elation when his fingers plunged into her cunt. They withdrew immediately and attacked with a steady priming of her juices.

"Get to your knees."

He went to his and helped her up into a position he wanted to explore.

"What are you going to do?"

"Fuck your cunt from behind."

"You can do that?" Her head came around to look at him.

She had an amazed sparkle in her eyes and he saw her quite the adventurous minx.

"Aye Lass, with your permission."

"Aye, Brogan, ye have me permission." She giggled, making fun of his brogue.

From the first time they spoke, he knew she came from inland by her speech. Only those people along the Emerald shores talked with less refinement to their words. He hadn't met many who spoke like her. But, he liked the way she spoke so clear, never a word slurred as if the annunciation were everything splendid about the language.

"Ye are a playful Lass when cold, are ye not?" He smacked her bottom.

"Ooo..." she squealed with excitement.

He lifted the tunic and shirt up. Her shapely rounded bottom faced him with the glow of a split moon. He smacked the cheek of her ass and her reaction intensified.

"Oh again, Brogan."

"Ye like a spanking now, do ye?" He slapped her other cheek and a guttural moan made his cock jut with no satisfaction in getting into her.

He pushed the tunic higher and bent to kiss the inflamed red print on her milky white bottom. He kissed every last heated spot and licked down between her cheeks. He tasted her sweet skin, like a preview to a delicacy. He licked up into her parted vulva, and enjoyed her pleased hum. With his fingers well placed, he spread her ass wider. The rose puckered ring of her anus closed.

"Press your delicious bottom out so that I may charge into your tightness here." His thumb poked the closed gap.

"I...I can't."

He smacked the fleshy cheeks of her ass several blows until the white stained with a red blush. She remained clenched tight until he stopped his spanking and she relaxed. It pushed her bottom out in relief and he thrust his finger into her anus.

"Oh, I don't think I could take anything wider."

He continued to pump his thumb in the hole while his other fingers stretched and buried into her wet cunt. The already swollen folds of skin hugged his knuckles. The labia caressed his touch as he fondled her. He delighted in watching the two hemispheres of her enflamed bottom lift with each thrust he made. From hip to shoulder, her skin quivered under his palm. He pulled his hand out with the creamy essence of her dripping to his cock. He greased the plump head and immediately pushed it into her anus before she could seal off the entrance.

"No, oh no please, it's…it's too big and hurts me," she cried.

"It will not very soon." He gripped her hips to prevent her from forcing him out.

"Brogan." She gasped in big gulps of surprise.

He moved slowly, yet vigorous. Her body heaved with small bursts of discomfort and pleasure. As he felt her give in to his thrusts, he drove further until he reached his personal limits. Inserted to the hilt, his scrotum slapped her wet cunt.

The sounds from her then were stuttered whines as she climaxed with small quakes he felt sure she'd collapse from. Her arms wobbled, her thighs quaked, and he moved more aggressively to spend himself. With an extended length of time coming to a head, he felt the time right to hold her more fashionably secure. He slid his hands up under the garment and lifted her up so she arched back upon his chest.

Her body heaved and he latched hold of her plump breasts while sandwiching her in that grip and his hardness.

"Oh, Lass," he groaned against her head.

His cock pulsed and pumped a copious amount of liquid into her quivering body. He rubbed his hands up and down from her sensitized nipples to her belly. Her head twisted in the private sensations she experienced. He fingered her cunt and tickled her clit so she jerked with spasms. Her face came around far enough so he could kiss her cheek, then her lips.

He took his hand from her cunt and held her face. Her delicate features contorted in her strained position. He kissed her harder, loving the cries of her orgasm echoing in his mouth. He backed quickly away from her ass clenching on his softening cock. She had wicked strength in areas that delighted with dangerous repercussions to his sensitive area.

Brogan gathered Brie to him and lay with her in front of the fire. She didn't say anything and he didn't attempt to delve into her what her thoughts were regarding his lust. He needed to fill her with the hot liquids built of his desire and when done, it left him empty. The act had been void of the real passion, the emotion of why a man and woman should come together. He fucked her in much the manner a dog humps a bitch in heat. He closed his eyes, hoping the morrow would bring insight into his actions.

†††

If it were not late summer, Brienna might have noticed the coolness spreading over her right away. However, She opened her eyes to find the fire out and Brogan missing. Rays of light cast a glow over the sand in the entrance. Dawn created a sparkling glint like jeweled dust. She stretched her arms above her head and then brought them down to touch her breast. Every time his name moved in her head, she felt an ache, a taut grab to her bosom.

She had no way to describe the moments before she went to sleep. She'd never thought a man would come into in such a fashion, and yet, he handled everything so well. She sighed upon the idea he left her satisfied in an intimate way.

The growl of Brienna's stomach practically doubled her over with pangs of hunger. Her father used to marvel over her slimness since she had always been a rapacious eater. She contended it to be the over-active lifestyle in which she kept a trim, healthy figure. Not eating was simply out of the question and she stood to find out why Brogan hadn't awakened her. Considering he might be off fetching food or on a private matter to relieve himself, she hurried to a shadowy corner of the cave to take care of her growing urgencies.

Removing Brogan's shirt when she came back to the camp of a dead fire, she collected her gown and shook out the sand. She put it to her nose to the dry garment and inhaled the comingling fragrance of her and Brogan. She reflected on the sound sleep she had gotten in his embrace. At least she thought she had slept next to him. Looking about, the idea it may have been a dream entered her mind. She shook off the thought. He snored and every time she might have awoken fully, the peace of it lulled her back to sleep.

Something else lulled her with tranquility. The hum from deep in the cave he said was the surf echoing. It didn't feel right, and unable to accept his conclusion, she retrieved a stick with fire. She went carefully deeper into the large cavern. The whirr, an animalistic moan, compelled her in much the same way a flame attracted a moth. She could only hope not to get burned by her curious investigation.

A rumble, like a distant thunder, suddenly rotated her to the fork in the cave. A foul heated air blew out of the bowels of darkness. Her hair fluttered. Guardedly, she stepped forward. Bravely or foolishly unafraid of what awaited her, she went to the source of unknown excitement. Her body tingled with the powers within and she dropped the stick of fire lighting her way. Unable to fight an urge, her hands rose up and glowed. That which lay before her called upon her in a way only destiny had preordained.

A smile caught her lips. The warmth from her magic made everything so alive in her she could not believe what she felt, what she knew, or what she experienced. She had wanted to know so much about her heritage for a long time and the moment seemed before her.

"I can sense you watching me," she said, advancing. "I feel your breath upon me. When Brogan told me what this place was, I knew legends never die and I understand how all should not be forgotten because reality is no longer seen."

The twin reflection of her glowing hands bounced back at her like a mirrored image. The hum she had followed deepened. Like a sigh of appreciation, she closed her eyes for a moment and opened her mind to the rush of knowledge sweeping into her soul. The Silver Dragon opened the portals of communication between them and she gathered an insight to her reason for living.

He shuddered with an anxious pause to his deliverance of information.

"I am a divine healer and you need not fear my presence," she said soothingly.

Her mother said in ancient times, dragons were one in thought with the healers. Communication would come easy because conversation between two like minds had no limitations. The train of contact stopped. The dragon, in the recesses of an eternal midnight abyss, went silent.

"Do you understand me?"

The glow from her hands brightened and extinguished. Instantaneously, her mind flooded with a wondrous flash of hindsight. Things her mother never had a chance to explain came as swift as a bolt of lightning. Then cut off just as swiftly when a warning severed her concentration.

Brienna ran for the exit. She gathered up Brogan's shirt, tunic, and a knife he'd left behind. Her heart pounded in great fear. Something in the transference of information left her with a need to find him. The Dragon gave her the ability to sense danger surrounding Brogan and she never ran so fast toward anything.

Sword of Rhoswen

She emerged from the cave and scanned the beach. All the while she had assumed he might be getting food, he was in the middle of danger. Without any sign of him on the shores of sand, she put on his shirt and tunic to have her hands free to climb the rocky cliff. Her foot slipped on the stone, wet from the heavy misty morning. Her teeth sunk into her tongue to prevent a scream from escaping. For the very reason she hadn't called out for Brogan, she didn't want to add to his danger.

Men shouting drew her deeper in the thickets and she crawled low to see who they were.

"Ouch!" her muttering curse was inaudible as she continued to creep near the loud and extremely angry voice overpowering everyone else's. Briars slid over the top of her foot making her skin burn.

"Where's the girl, Brogan? We know you've hidden her." The man talking backhanded him across the jaw.

Brienna saw Brogan hang with his arms tied around a fat tree. She cringed when the man hit him again and blood slung from his mouth. Her hands tried to fire to life but she couldn't let the healing out yet. Each hard hit the man inflicted to emphasize his words dropped another tear from her eye for Brogan's valiant heart. She could have jumped up and presented herself and put an end to the momentary abuse he took for her. Only she could not let his heroics die in vain. It would not solve their problems. She had to use the opportunity available to free Brogan.

"She is just a messenger, Mackey. And she has already delivered Queen Rhoswen's message, so what need have ye of her now?" Brogan spit a mouthful of blood out as he talked.

Brienna, with a sympathetic pain for the salty residue of his sweating pores stinging his split lip. Her fingers trembled with the intensity of which her healing power wanted to be released. She'd never known it to come so readily without her invoking it.

"If we have to do this the hard way…" Mackey hit Brogan in the stomach with an elbow. "Then I guess I'll not complain too much."

He stepped away, but the false reprieve came back as a punch to Brogan's jaw. She crawled quicker to circle the men and get close to Brogan. The merciless lot of Thane's butchers closed in as if they might get a turn having sport with their captive. She resisted all urges to stand up. She wanted so much to stop them from hurting him it made her physically ill. He protected her location so nobly it brought a tremor to her heart again.

How she longed to be free of all encumbering clothes as the gown snagged on a root. She had to stop and work it free. The threads knotted to thorn and twigs, the hem already a rag of fringe. The silence may not have been broken by the swearing she did, but God would hear every one of the cussed words she thought.

"She'll be found, Brogan!" Mackey thundered. "I've got a half dozen men looking and one of them is McCollum. He's got an axe to grind with the bitch for putting that knife in his leg. While Thane said to bring her to him alive, he made no limitations on what we do to her between here and there."

Brienna's lip hurt from biting down on it hard. She couldn't believe he really thought she'd be so submissive. She'd kill the first bastard that tried to bed her without her consent.

Brogan laughed and she stopped crawling to listen.

"She stabbed him in the leg, Mackey, next time I doubt he would be so lucky. I do believe the Lass would castrate a man for trying what ye suggest, if given the chance. Ye are better off killing me and going back to Thane with the news we are both dead."

"Don't worry. You're only alive until we find her. Then we'll be leaving your dead hide strapped to that tree for the wolves," Mackey informed him. "The rest of you start looking for her. She can't be that far away," he yelled irritably to the men standing around. "Brogan is too honorable to leave a lady alone."

Mackey would, of course, be right about Brogan. She saw for herself he bravely would not give away her whereabouts. Though, he still had much to learn about her. She had more strength than she wished, only because of Thane. Her cousin would not tolerate weakness. Thane hated anyone to weep and whine like a girl—even her as a child. When they were both young, he didn't like that she wouldn't accompany him hunting. He thought it was because she couldn't draw a bow and kill so he had showed her how easy it was by shooting an arrow straight into her favorite dog. She had cried so hard, her whole body shook and while trying to stop the bleeding, it was her first real knowledge of healing. She had been eight and when she told her mother, she learned more about herself, at which time she had been sworn to secrecy about her gift.

From that time on, Thane had only worsened in his actions. About that same time, her father and uncle had a falling out and she never had to see Thane again as a boy. When he became a man and his father dead, he came to her father seeking a kingdom not his. Her mother died and left her a twelve-year-old girl with little guidance. She hadn't even considered the special attention Thane had paid to her could be anything more than a cousin's affection. It seemed natural then, now she wondered with his threat to marry or kill her, how far back had his evil plot began?

"Ye will never find her," Brogan spit more blood on the dirt. "She could be sitting under your nose and she would outsmart ye and your degenerate cohorts."

Brienna wanted to groan with the irony of which he was not aware. Indeed, she lay in wait under all their noses. She ducked beneath a patch of bright green ferns and lay still until the rush of passing footsteps faded. Mackey paced with his irritation. Fully understandable since she didn't know how Brogan withstood the brutality. The first moment she could take a chance, she moved forward. The closer she came, the greater her fears became. Brogan made no sounds. His low groans of suffering were stifled.

She quietly inched forward on her knees. Her fingers slipped into his palm and still she got no response other than a weak pulse. She peered around the edge of the tree to see which direction Mackey faced. Her hand heated and in seconds, she had begun the healing. His outward appearance could be left and she concentrated on the internal injuries. She couldn't risk him or Mackey knowing what she could do.

† † †

Brogan gathered his thoughts to the hand in his and he squeezed it firmly. He didn't have to see her to know his Lass. She had a way about her that drew his mind. Her warm fingers chased the chills from his body and he felt a renewed energy radiate into his limbs. She cut the leather binds from his wrists. Her delicate fingers wrapped his and her kiss pressed firmly to his knuckles. That alone made him stronger. He took the knife she placed in his palm and flicked his wrist to motion her away. He looked to his enemy.

"So, Mackey, what is Thane going to say if ye return without the Lass?" Brogan goaded to draw the man back to him. "He will have your head on a stake, will he not?"

"I'll not be returning without her." Mackey stalked back toward him.

His intent clearly vivid, like a red sunset or a bright blue sky in the morning, Mackey wanted him dead. Yet, striking him another blow would equally satisfy. Brogan liked that the man had such confidence. It made the lunge he took from the tree much more enjoyable by the expression Mackey had on his face. Brogan ignored the fact the pain in his ribs had vanished. His full attention had to go to getting Brie safely away.

Mackey managed to dodge the knife and when he came up with one in his hand, they collided in a struggle of will. Cunning like a fox, dangerous as a snake, Mackey came at Brogan with pure hatred. The feisty brawler had to have some competency as well as fortitude to hold a place in Thane's army of cutthroats.

The fight took the men wrestling over the uneven ground. When they rolled so Mackey was atop him, Brogan caught a glimpse of Brie charging out from her hiding place. With a rock in hand, she brought it down hard on Mackey's head. He looked up dazed and no doubt surprised. The Lass never failed to surprise anyone. She swung again sideways and caught Mackey alongside his head. It sent him falling away with Brogan pushing.

"Lass, I do not know if I should strangle ye for your boldness or kiss ye for your valiance." He got to his feet and pulled her along. "But I will decide that later."

"Where will we go?" She stopped him and picked up Mackey's sword. "They'll find us."

"They will find only me, Lass. Ye are going to get on this horse and ride southeast to Kylemore." He hoisted her up onto a horse tethered to a line with a half dozen others.

"You're hurt and I'll not leave you."

"Please, Lass. I appreciate your bravery, but ye are in danger."

Half mindless of his hand rubbing over her thigh, he pulled her down and kissed her.

"You're in greater danger and I'll not go. You can't make me leave you here to fight Mackey's men alone. So unless we are going to argue until we're found out, I suggest you get on a horse and let's go together."

"Ye agreed to obey me!" he growled without much threat.

"I did no such thing." She smiled. "I agreed to obey your decision to go north, nothing more."

"Ye indulge no man with control, do ye?" He took another horse and put all efforts into swinging up on the steed's back.

"Why should I? Have you learned nothing about me? Am I not capable of making decisions for myself and often better ones?" She rode up along side him. "You did say southeast?"

Brogan nodded and watched her ride off ahead of him. He smiled at her chin held high and thought how sad he could not get to know her in every way possible. How much he wanted to learn every intricate detail about the feisty minx.

Chapter 15

Brienna rode fast through the forest. She only gave a fleeting glance back when she wanted to make sure Brogan followed. Surprisingly, no one followed them. They went many miles in a couple hours before she slowed to give rest to the horse.

"We can stop if ye think I am allowed to make the suggestion," he said, pulling up alongside her.

"I'll grant the request," she remarked regally, laughing with goodhearted humor. It filled her with thanks to the heavens for both of them to be alive and safe for the moment.

"Good, because I think I may have to take the break with or without your permission." Brogan slid off the horse and dropped to a knee, holding his side.

Brienna jumped down and knelt in front of him. "How can I help?" she asked, putting a hand near his ribs and touching lightly over the purple bruising. It was close to his other recent wound in his side. Her hand drifted up to feel the raised knot on his cheekbone that had his eye swollen half shut. Everything in her wanted to heal him. Her fingers burned but the fear he'd hate her with an old prejudice against healers backed her away.

"I do not think there is anything ye can do to reverse Mackey's damage. Though I do believe a kiss could make me forget it for a time."

Brienna's hand wavered to perform the miracle. Instead, she leaned forward to give only what he requested. She kissed lightly over his swollen cheek and then his brow above the puffy eye. She pulled away but not very far as his hand held her arm.

"Not quite what I was looking for, but it will do, Lass." He grinned. "Now if ye are not in need of my clothes..."

"No, I brought them for you." She quickly removed the tunic and the shirt. "We should tie the shirt around your ribs in case they're broken."

She didn't look up at him. His remark had flushed her cheeks and left her lacking any sort of response so she concentrated on his wounds.

"I will be all right. Just give me the shirt."

"Will you at least sit down? I'll take care of the horses." She reached for the reins and he let her have them.

"Tie them well, Lass." Brogan lowered to the ground.

She took them to a stream of water and let them drink. Glancing back to Brogan, she felt the heated tremors of his lust. The devil in him eyeing her so bold made her feel naked. He'd take her to his arms and do things of which she'd enjoy and worry over. Each day brought her closer to him. Each touch drew down her guard. He'd own her if not for the problem she faced with the Torrick she might wed.

She knelt and scooped some water in her hand to sip. Carefully, she carried some back to Brogan. He drank until his tongue licked her palms.

"I'll get you more." She breathed heavier.

"I need no more than what I can get from your lips." He brought her head close.

Brienna went with a willing need to feel his strength surround her. His kiss traveled slowly. He took tender care and she put her cool hand over his swollen eye. Her other hand held the back of his head. The kisses she gave back, he ate up with great relish. She could have sat all day with the energy she had from their day's ordeals, but she could feel his exhaustion.

"Lass, if I had but the strength to ravish ye, I would." He leaned his forehead to her shoulder and smothered his face into her neck.

She held him with love.

"You could put your head on my lap and rest," she offered.

"Aye, Lass, a pleasure I will accept."

Brogan said nothing more and lay down so his head fit in the cradle of her gown draping between her thighs. A twitching, a fiery flame-tipped sensation within her vagina flexed muscles right through to her bottom. Her body still recollected that point as it still harbored a glorious soreness from his hearty intrusion.

"I never tire of this country. I've talked to people that have gone far and visited places beyond where most men go. I wonder why they would want to venture outside their homeland. So much can be seen here. A day is never lacking in mystery or..." She gave a little laugh. "Or adventure."

She looked down at her fingers combing and twirling Brogan's hair around them. Handsome, well built, and polite, in some ways he had ventured far from her initial assessment of him. In other ways, he really had not behaved any different. Far from being immature, she pondered whether anyone ever considered him a lad even when a boy. She could picture him as a handful for his mother. He liked to be in control with no appreciation of anyone questioning his decisions.

Without her insistence to rest, Brogan fell asleep and Brienna brushed the hair from his forehead.

"We have to get you some help," she muttered to herself.

She swept her hands over him, wondering if he'd wake to the heat, to the amber glow of her healing magic.

"You are truly brave, but also an idiot to think you can go on as you are. Even I need food or I'll not be moving another step."

She moved carefully to leave him. Her path took her to explore the territory. The smell of smoke grabbed all her attention and she followed it until she found a village. The first man she came upon, she asked of for help.

"Excuse me, but my friend has had a mishap and he's not well. We've traveled many a mile to get this far and I don't think I should make another day on an empty stomach." She watched the man's face twitch and mull over the information. "We're on our way to Kylemore to help the Torricks against Thane Rhoswen."

"Say no more, m'lady. That is not even a man you speak of but the devil." He turned his cart and waved to another man. "The Lady needs help with her man."

Brienna smiled at them both. They'd get no argument from her of Brogan being her man. She liked the idea instantly and maybe too happily since he really never could be.

The kind people offered to her and Brogan a modest, but warm hut. It took the two men to get Brogan on the cart when she found he wasn't just asleep but unconscious and burning with a fever. Immediately she wanted to heal him, but now was not the time to reveal her mystical aura.

An old woman pointed out the bloodstain on Brogan's legging. They both were so filthy she hadn't taken notice to the thin worn leather molded to his solid legs. The cut in the garment had a dark dried stain spread around it. She sat quiet while two women pulled his boots off and then his britches. Before she could move, she stared at his exquisite manliness. His bronzed skin had the beauty of nature and it included the wrinkled skin of his penis. She didn't get much chance to study the drooping extension of him all nestled in the rich black wiry patch of hair. The eldest woman laid a piece of sackcloth over his privates and set about examining his wound. That too had the obscurity of black hair concealing it. They washed it thoroughly, applied ointment with a horrible odor, and bandaged it.

"He may get worse before better," the old woman told her. "Keep him cool and try to get as much water into him as possible. Your man is a strong one, so have faith." She pushed a heavy flap away and disappeared outside.

Brienna would never let him get worse. If it meant exposing herself to ridicule and distrust, she'd use her power right in front of the lot of them. Shortly after they left, a younger woman returned.

"M'lady, you would do to get some sleep this night and I've brought you a nice shift."

"Thank you." Brienna took the under-dress made of muslin.

The girl's eyes drifted past her to look at Brogan. Obviously there were two reasons for her visit. The dress seemed more a ruse to see the handsome warrior. Brienna felt obligated to move aside a bit to let her look.

"He's very handsome, your man is, and very brave. I hear tell he'll be stopping Lord Rhoswen's attacks on our farms."

The girl said the name Rhoswen as if it were evil. Thane had swallowed their whole family's legacy of good into his vat of evil destruction. No one would ever believe the whole of Rhoswens were not the spawn of the devil.

Once the girl left, Brienna took off her gown and put on the under-dress. The air chilly and unable to snuggle to Brogan's warmth, she pulled her brocade back over her head. The two pieces of clothing felt good.

The groan brought her back around to sit next to Brogan on the pallet of furs spread on the floor making a bed. She positioned herself next to him and wiped a wet cloth over his face. She carefully bathed his facial cuts as well as treating his fever. The black inky locks on his forehead were slicked back over and over while she trailed the wet rag around his face to cool him.

The prominent features prompted her to outline his eyes, nose, and lips with her forefinger. Never had she been able to so audaciously inspect a man's face or body before. Her hand left his face when he moved. Her intentions were good to adjust the sackcloth that had slid to the side and exposed his hipbone. Black curly hair peeked out from the edge of the cloth and she touched his flesh at the hip joint. Finding it as smooth and soft as the skin on her belly, she leaned to put her lips there.

"Brie," he moaned in his sleep.

She kissed his stomach. The muscles retracting and moving with her long, languishing journey up as high as she could push his clothes. The advantage she took seemed no different than that which he would take. She touched her fingers lightly over his cock and watched it spring up. Fascination made her probe it more. Her fingers wrapped its pulse and she brushed a caress over the tip. His moan stirred in her and she quickly pulled the fabric back in place leastwise he see her rudely toying with the notion of him coming into her again.

Wanting him well, she crawled to the door and peeked outside. It appeared they were alone. With a well-judged cause, she went back to Brogan and spread her hands over the worst of his wounds. The amber glow emitted warmly and she mended everything from inside to out. She left only the barest marks for his unquestioning inspection.

Time progressed and Brogan came conscious for a few minutes at a time where she forced him to drink the spring water. The villagers supplied them with bread and cheese. All of which Brie could have eaten herself.

"Lass?" he called and she touched his face.

Sword of Rhoswen

"Feeling better?" She smiled, happy to see he kept his eyes open.

"Aye, Lass." He tried to sit and she pushed him back.

"You have to eat as much as you can," she said and let him lift just his head.

She pushed one wooden spoonful of food in after another. She begged when he tried to refuse. Her vigilance through the night paid off when he finally spoke again.

"Ye need sleep, Lass," he commented with his deep resonance expressing authority.

He tugged at her arm to make her lie next to him and she set the food aside to give him any peace she could. Her head went to his shoulder and she let him bind her to his side as close as clothing could touch him. Hours later, she woke to the dampness of sweat through her clothes and her hand tucked under Brogan's tunic around his waist. He had rolled to his side, faced her, and held her snug. That hard muscled body drew her like a magnet. The pulsation in her loins met with an equaled throbbing hardness pressed to her belly. Her reasonable deductions alerted her to his erection looking for an entrance in her clothes like some errant rogue.

Brogan moaned and he mumbled some words that almost sounded like a female's name, but not hers. She wanted to hit him, but had no rights when it came to his dreams or his life. She had her own destiny, and regrettably, it did not include him. It made her think of the betrothed she'd never met. What he was like and why he would not even come to Avalbane and look upon her once to see whether he should marry her or not. Of course, it was not uncommon to have a marriage arrangement for years before the event took place. And then, from what Brogan had mentioned of the man, Lord Torrick's son was in the same position as herself. He had no choice in the matter, only a duty to obey a father's edict.

155

† † †

Brogan looked at Brie, sitting with a serious expression on her face.

"Ah, my pretty Lass, do not look so grievous of our situation. I may be in bad shape but it is only a pain that ye could take away with another kiss," he joked, trying to dispel the throb in his cock.

"You shouldn't have any pain," she said with a puzzled expression.

"Aye, maybe I do feel better in some ways, but that of one."

"What one?"

He reached out and jerked her down to him.

"The one that wants to be smothered by the recesses of your body."

She leaned on his chest with a quizzical sparkle in her eyes. She still had the virginal naiveté to understand his meaning.

"Kiss me, Lass, and make the ache depart."

"I do this and then I demand you get well," she murmured against his parched lips.

He had not expected her to kiss him. When she did, he took her in his arms and pulled her down closer. He gathered her face in the frame of his hands. She laughed a little as he pulled her over and put her on her back.

"You should rest more." She held a hand to his shoulder as if to stop him.

"I feel remarkably well and very stimulated by a dream of your lips kissing all over me." He loomed over her, waiting for her to deny him. Seeing the shimmer of her needs so exposed, he knew she wouldn't.

"Imaginative, aren't you?" She blushed and he knew why.

It was not wholly a dream. He woke and found her kissing an arc of rainbows over his loins. Her soft moist lips cooled the heated skin and at the same time caused a fire in his belly. What man could not wake to the vigorous rush of blood giving him an erection by the dainty fingers that touched with curiosity?

"Instructive." He pushed up to his knees.

He grinned at the widening of her violet eyes. She didn't take them off his hard cock jutting from his body. Her presence aroused him too much. All his dreams were not fantasy and all his wishes were granted. He knew that the moment her slender warm fingers wrapped around his shaft. Her mouth fit over the head and he found a sense of home in the cavern. She sucked on him harder than the last time. Her aggressive fondling brought him to orgasm quickly. He wanted to linger there in her hum. The juices dripped on the verge and she pulled free.

His chest heaved, the sensation died back. He waited for her to say something and then he pushed her to the ground. His eyes stayed locked to hers. He yanked at her gown to get it up her legs, over her thighs and beyond her entrance. He could bury himself deep and free himself or take the longer route and drink of her first.

Brogan chose the sweet taste of her delicious cunt. He slid down and licked a hurried swath that parted her labia and her legs. She threw her knees out and he shoved his hands under her ass to lift her to his mouth.

He teased and caressed her clit. It swelled and hung distended for him to nip and tug. She squirmed and wiggled her bottom. Her whimpering dragged him deeper. He thrust his tongue to fuck her cunt and alternated it with dips of his fingers into the gushing tunnel.

"Oh God, Brogan, let me up, please let me up," she whined, not making her pleas very demanding.

He rose up instead and drove himself into her hot core. Her breath stuttered with surprise, yet he gave no mercy. He rammed deeper and harder. Up on his hands over her, he used every ounce of his strength to impale her. Her pants escalated and her fingers dug into his arms deeper. She squeaked and squealed. Then when all her vocal cords broke into a shrill ecstasy, he came readily with her. He had waited for her to climax. He had waited until the intensity of their combined orgasms took them beyond anything they shared. Even after her lovely sound of exhaustion died down, he pumped the very last of his plentiful fluids into her.

He leaned down and kissed her deeply. Long and hard, he held her mouth trapped. She gasped for air and he gave little as he devoured her breath. It seemed a long time before he lifted up and looked at her. The watery violet stare, full of distress and something that bespoke of regret, worried him. It hit him harder than he could imagine. In his rush to make love to her, to fuck her sweet body until he couldn't anymore, he put her in a hazardous position toying with her emotions.

Brogan cupped her cheek and stroked a hand down her neck.

"We need to get up now, Lass." He eased off her.

He helped pull her gown down. Not for her modesty as she seemed freely comfortable in letting him look. He wanted her dress concealing all the finer reasons for him to harden and have at her again. Her parted legs left a pink slit with a rose bud of a clit exposed. He covered her and took her hand to pull her up.

"You should still rest. You have a fever and you'll only make it worse," she told him.

"We have to get to Kylemore. Thane will send his armies tenfold with the news ye carry. I have to be there when he comes. There are greater reasons now for me to kill the man than before."

His hand glided down the back of her head. With Thane dead, he could free Queen Rhoswen from the marriage contract. Without that hanging over his head, he might pursue a woman more to his liking.

"You are in no condition to ride," she argued, trying to twist away from him.

"I have no choice. Maybe I will have time to lounge about so carelessly once we are in Kylemore and ye could join me there in me bed." His arm circled her waist, squeezing her back against him.

"You presume too much from me. You are a means to my ending in Kylemore, nothing more."

The marble face, smooth of emotion, went even colder. In the complexity of her mission to fulfill her duty as messenger, he could see her employing every devious plan necessary. She need not be a master in all endeavors because she was a quick study. It very well could be she used her natural feminine charms to advance her cause.

The thought seemed too ridiculous and too hurtful. It didn't make it go away.

"Let us go," he ordered. "We have got a ways to go yet."

† † †

Brogan paid a villager a rightly good sum for their hospitality and they left. The silence between them held as they rode. Brienna had considered her tone may have sounded harsh, but she had to stop the perilous madness developing between them. Once he found out who she was, he would understand and nothing more would pass between them. His loyalty to the Torricks would outweigh his needs since it had already been clear to her he took some pride in honor.

When they had come back along the sea late in the afternoon, Brienna felt that gnaw to her stomach again. She didn't want to say anything, afraid he would bring up being with her sexually again. She couldn't bear to hear his elegant voice speak of their matched wishes. Only, he had to eat too. She watched him sweat with the exertion of riding, and to allow Brogan a chance at rest even though he was being quite stubborn, feigned a feminine weakness she did not possess.

"I'm hungry. Can't we stop yet?" she whined, producing an act from Medora's wide and well-rehearsed collection of grievances. Medora loved to whine over everything and Brienna had listened to it often enough. She also fell victim to giving into it.

Brogan stopped and looked back at her. His simple nod was all she needed to know she had triumphed. She would get to eat and Brogan would get to regain some of his strength.

"We will find some shelter for the night and then I will see what I can hunt up for us."

He moved slowly at dismounting the horse. She considered if she couldn't have done more healing for him. A relapse would slow them down. Neither of them wanted to put further delay in getting to Kylemore. Their needs were basic. Protect all from Thane.

They walked along the precipice of rock and Brienna couldn't help but stop to look at the sea. So far from where she lived, she felt in a different world. She'd visited other places with her father over the years. Seen many lands, different cultures and she found this view the most spectacular.

"It's beautiful here. I should love to live on this sea cliff, dance upon the white sands, and eat fish everyday," she breathed wistfully and twirled around. "I felt a great peace from the hum in that cave last night."

"The echoes of the surf can seem magical," he replied.

She pirouetted again, laughing with the secret she had of the divine magic she wished she could share with him. Spinning freely, her arms swung around. Yet, the lack of food did nothing for her balance. She felt the dizziness sway and stagger her until she stopped. Brogan's arms surrounded her. His secure hands were always there when she needed steadying. His whole body embraced her warmly. Then as if he could surprise her, he kissed her. He kissed her hungrily and she forgot all about needing food. She could only think how wonderful she truly felt in his embrace, how special he made the minutes they shared.

They dropped down to the soft patch of emerald moss at their feet. No thoughts. That's want she wanted, a mind void of reason. His hands, hot on her face, reminded her of his fever. His lips burned on hers. She did nothing but accept his dry chase to the swallowing of her throat.

From the depths of all mystery, Brienna cried against his mouth, a soundless hiccup stopping him. Bound to another man, she had to stop pretending she had the freedom to let love into her heart. Instead of Brogan asking her why she cried, he held her with a tender hug, an embrace surpassing things neither of them had to question. His large hand held her head to his shoulder and she nuzzled her face to the bristles of his neck.

"'Tis been another long day, Lass." He stroked her face. "I will go get us something to eat and then we will pick a place to sleep for the night."

Brienna nodded and shortly thereafter they parted. He busied himself with sharpening a knife on a stone for a few minutes and she watched the sea. Wiping the tears off her cheeks, she gathered her thoughts and let the quiet time hush the palpitations of her rampaging heart.

"Wait here and tie up the horses for the night, Lass. I will go fetch us something to fill out bellies."

After she had secured the horses, she looked for a place they could spend the night. A quiet, concealed niche in the rocks would be cozy and warm with a fire in front of them, she decided. She climbed down the crags and back up again. Checking each path going down, she looked for something big enough to accommodate them both. Though in her mind, it didn't have to be too spacious.

When she found the shadowy crevice in the rock that fit her, inside lay a nice sized cavern. It had a perfect feel and instinct was everything to her.

"Brie!" Brogan's voice boomed.

"Down here!" she yelled in return.

Climbing out of the crevice, the low growl of an animal stopped her. She waited, moving nary a muscle nor heaving a breath. When all remained silent except for Brogan, she began to make her way along the ledge. The tricky sounds of the waves crashing the rocks made her smile.

"I told ye to wait in one place and I find ye in another," he reproached her from atop the cliff.

"I found a place to sleep for the night," she yelled. "It's big and it's safe. No one would ever know it's down here unless they climbed along this..." Brienna stopped at the growl again.

"What's wrong?" Brogan began down. "Brie?"

"Maybe it's not so safe," she whispered and moved slowly up the narrow path.

Out of the darkness, through a slit in the rock surface, a wolf came stalking. Brienna had no idea what starving could encompass until she saw the thin, gaunt animal drooling with a predatory hunger no one could know the depths of except for him.

Brogan jumped down to the path. His actions spurred the wolf and she jumped to ledge higher up than she could fully reach. The wolf lunged at her flailing legs and missed. She crawled up onto a ledge above her, but the wolf had her gown snagged in his teeth. He tugged and shook his head dragging her back with an almost human intellect.

"Throw the knife at him!" Brienna ordered.

Her fingers sought purchase for a stronger hold as she kicked at getting away from the vicious animal. The wolf did not give up. The gown began to tear under his ritualistic shaking attack. The heavy brocade came apart at the seams. Brienna took it one step further. She unfastened the laces and shucked off the garment. When the wolf flung his head to the side, her dress came free of her legs. She looked over to see it billowing out on a stream of air and floating to the sea. Then she turned to look up at Brogan. He made noises to distract the wolf from further attempts to get to her. He challenged the beast and went stealthily toward it.

The wolf leapt at him and knocked him off balance. Both tumbled over the edge of the outcropping. They disappeared over the side of the cliff and her heart stopped.

"Brogan!" she screamed, scrambling down from her perch.

Chapter 16

Brogan's hand hit her shoe as he reached over the edge. "Well, give me a hand, Lass."

She crouched to grab his arm and pulled. His straining grunt came with the throw of his leg up.

"Come on, you stubborn, thickheaded...if you had just thrown the knife at him, you wouldn't be in this position." She labored at helping him up. "That wolf could have chewed my leg off!"

"'Tis the only knife we have and unless ye like your rabbit with hair on, then I will need it to skin your supper," he grumbled.

Hoisting him up, they fell back. He lay sprawled over her. Time had the sort of stopped feel to it as he looked at her. He tried not to stare into the mesmerizing violet of her eyes or the mirrored black pupils reflecting his expression of awe. He dropped his gaze to her slightly puckered lips and the way they almost said, *come hither*.

"Get off me." She pushed angrily. "The hair would burn off during cooking."

"Huh? I didn't think of that. Good thing I have ye along, m'lady."

She flashed him another disturbed look and he could see she'd been frightened by the wolf and of losing him. Her sudden anger reflected her frustration with those feelings and he thought it best to leave her alone until she calmed.

"The wolf is gone, so shall we inspect your little niche or maybe I should refer to it as your den since the previous occupant has been evicted?"

"It's nothing special. We could look for another." She climbed up, rather than down. "Maybe we should just sleep up here."

"Out in the open?" Brogan followed her. "It will be cold and I think I still have a fever and ye, my fair maiden, have fewer clothes on. It will be cold once the sun sets."

He looked over the length of her thin wispy under-dress. He didn't recall her having it before and assumed she got it in the village. He could not complain of the vision. Every detail of her shadowy curves formed a perfect outline right down to the triangle juncture of her legs.

"Build a fire, tend it well, and I'll be fine."

Her voice tipped the scales and went beyond suggestion to command. The spontaneous retort gave way another clue she hid a secret. All along, since even before he saw the servant Medora combing Brie's hair, he felt her not a common maid. He did not press the issue. It didn't matter her station or her standing in the clan of Rhoswen. It had never mattered to him of any woman's background.

He studied her graceful movements—the inherent qualities a Lady had before full grown. She had to be more than common and he considered how close her relationship might be with the queen.

"I will get some firewood and then I will be able to get ye something to eat." He pulled his tunic off. "Put this on. It will help keep ye warm."

"But you..." Her eyes dropped to the ground. "You'll get another chill."

"I am warm, Lass." He put the tunic in her hand. "Too warm with a fever, remember?" He smiled and went off to gather the wood.

She put up no further argument and enfolded his tunic close to her breast. He watched her as he picked up old tree limbs and stacked them in his arms. Her faraway look seemed troubled but he had no reason to pry. While he had been thankful she didn't ask much of him, it didn't ease his mind when she looked so sad.

"Brie?" He studied her for the time it took to pull her from some reverie as she hugged her body. "Brie, are ye all right, Lass?"

He stooped down and dropped the wood into a pile.

"I am fine." She shivered and wrapped her arms around her shoulders to warm her arms then, as if she had forgotten the tunic, picked it up to draw over her head. "How far before we are to Kylemore?"

"We have been on Kylemore land for half a day. The castle is still two days from here. Tomorrow night we will stay in a village and have a bed." Brogan sat down opposite her on the far side of the fire and positioned the skewered rabbit.

He looked up at the bright full moon while stretching his sore leg. The cut had gone deep to the bone. It bled profusely and he had not considered it to be a great concern. He healed fast and had the scars to prove he survived everything. Brie's frown, her doleful stare at the flames, pushed him up to sit down next to her. He put an arm around her shoulders.

"I should check your bandage," she said. "We should have stopped where there was fresh water so I could wash your leg."

"My leg will wait or do ye wish me out of my britches again?" he teased.

His jest could not even provoke a response.

They ate the rabbit and when she scooted away to lie down, he didn't make the suggestion they sleep together. Even for warmth, he'd not resist touching her in the ways that pleased them both.

† † †

Brienna fell asleep rather quickly. Another weary day had passed. Brogan's groan in the middle of the night woke her. Thinking his fever returned, she crawled over to touch his forehead. She smiled, finding him cool, the fever gone, and his disturbance just a nightmare. She thought he must have many with all the battles he'd fought. The scars on him were not altogether too numerous, yet they were there nonetheless proving he had demons in his sleep.

He shifted and groaned again. Her fingers went to his ribs.

"Brogan?" she whispered and brushed a hand over his forehead and watched the black locks fold away from his brow.

He opened his eyes and looked at her.

"I'm going to get more wood for the fire." She didn't want to alarm him with her absence and he needed to stay warm.

"Are ye cold?" He glanced at the roaring blaze before him and took her hand in his.

"No, but you..."

"I am warm enough; ye do not need to worry. I will get ye to Lord Torrick. Now will ye lie down and go back to sleep?"

Brienna nodded.

"You have to let go," she told him.

"Or ye could lay here with me." He smiled sinfully. "For warmth, of course."

Brienna lay down, letting him snuggle to her back. She didn't know how warm he would be but as for herself, she didn't need a fire to know heat. The intensity never waned as his hand pressed her belly and forced her bottom to the bulge in his britches. His fingers moved higher, cupping her breast. Kisses pressed her shoulder and she pulled her hair up and away from where he traveled to the back of her neck.

"Ye always smell good, Lass." He nipped at her skin. "Good enough to eat as evidence by the wolf."

"I feel sorry for him, so hungry."

"Aye Lass, but his death ended his misery."

His hot mouth resumed the playful kisses along her neck and behind her ear. He didn't want to talk of bad things and neither did she. She shifted to his amorous nudging. Inching his fingers down, he gripped the night dress and walked it up her legs, over her knees, along the length of her thighs and to her hip. Calloused fingers, wide palm, and a brisk caress, she rubbed her bottom to him as if she could fit any tighter.

"Relax, Lass. I will sate your lovely retreat."

His fingers rubbed her mound and her hips wriggled to his rhythmic engagement. With his hips grinding his groin to her backside, she found nothing comfortable in her position. Then his middle finger glided into the folds of wet flesh. He pushed and pulled his touch over every bump, each thin layer parted as he worked it deeper and deeper. Then like an arrow, it pierced the pinching bull's eye. Not once, not twice, not three times, he withdrew and jammed it in to the hilt of his hand.

"Brogan, don't stop," she moaned.

"I will keep ye bothered for as long as ye want." He kissed her ear.

Her body undulated to the relentless fucking he gave her with his thick finger. When she thought she could not handle more, he dipped two fingers into her sodden cavern. She jerked with spasms running a white-hot lightning even down to her toes.

"Brie, if only..." Brogan's sentence came incomplete.

She rattled in his arms, accepting the sentiments he wanted to express but couldn't. She put up a hand to keep his face near. She twisted her lips to plant kisses on his jaw. When rapture took her away from her strengths in holding him, he held her. Her orgasm increased all awareness of how her body responded to him. She could not foresee herself succumbing to the euphoria with any other man the way she did with him.

With his fingers snuggled into her liquid delights, she lay in a state of exhilaration. Her gasps quieted to muted pants and tranquilly gathered her into a sweetly ecstatic slumber. All until Brogan woke her, minutes or hours later. He didn't need to say anything. She opened her eyes, sensing his heavy breath, his hands molding and shaping her breasts beneath the night shift. His mouth wetly devoured her nipple in pleasurable tugs until she lie waiting for their union.

He parted her legs with his strong hands, his cock already released, aimed like a dart for its target. Taking a firm grip of the cheeks of her bottom, he lifted her up and in one thrust, buried himself into her cunt. On his knees, he had more power in his shove against her. The soreness had become a minimal twinge, which eventually disappeared the longer he fucked her. Orgasms discharged a hot lubricant to make his way slick and easy. She marveled how nature provided the salve right from her body to sooth all his numbing rasps to her insides.

Brienna, wanting to touch him in some way, chose to cover his hands hanging onto her bottom. The second a wave of swelling jubilation thrashed her body from side to side. A whipping snake, her body constricted on him. A wild vine, she wove her arms to his. An uncontrollable seizure of immeasurable tweaks drew her breath in and out with a plea.

"No more, oh please, Brogan, no more," she cried.

His heed did not come until he expended himself into her with a roar. Even then, sheathed in the shuddering stew of their juices, he leaned to her and kissed fervently over her face. Too weak to protest the abundance of affection, she hung in his arms as he gathered her to him. Like a babe in a cradle, Brienna relished the flourish of adorations.

Once they settled into a comfortable embrace, they both went back to sleep. Becoming habit, Brienna didn't give it a second thought to lightly kissing him anytime she woke. Familiarity still so fresh and new had its conflicts. Her greatest would be to stand in a room with her betrothed and him not see the relationship that grew between her and Brogan. During the remainder of the night, she ensconced herself intimately over, under, and along side him. While sometimes she did so on purpose, other times, she woke in delightful poses.

Near morning, she stirred to find her leg crushed between his. Her arm under his head while her other was bound to his chest with the weight of his arm over it. Her fingers moved in the thick black swirls of hair on his hard pectoral muscles. His breathing was shallow, slumbering, and calm at first. Its increase alerted her to him coming awake and it was too late when he did.

"Curiosity cannot only be one sided, Lass." Brogan rolled her onto her back and leaned over her. "And your touch sets my heart to racing with the want of ye."

"Again?" She laughed with the endearing delights of his morning revelation.

"Aye, of course again, do ye not feel how my heart sings for your lovely limbs to twine around me? Much as the ivy clings to a keep's walls, I wish to have ye surround me with your softness and your scent."

The word, *forever*, had not been spoken. It didn't mean it hadn't crept into her thoughts. She could not deny the feelings she had for him. However, she could deny succumbing to them. Brienna's hand went to his shoulder to push him away. She really did mean to fight his advances. Alas, too human too shed her wants, she folded her arms behind his neck and pulled him down to meet her kiss.

† † †

Brogan lifted slightly to look at her eyes, but she had them closed. Her hesitancy made him think again. It brought to surface where they were headed and how he had let things get out of hand. Her mouth with its irresistible puckered position took away those thoughts and he took advantage of her willingness. He savored her eagerness and pressed his mouth to hers.

"Brogan, we shouldn't." She turned her face.

"I know. We have important business in Kylemore, but...just once more, Brie. Let me into ye just once more." He rubbed a hand along her face.

She nodded and anything else he might have said stuck in his throat. Her fingers glided down his back and his cool skin quivered wherever her palm massaged, warming and loving him.

Brogan's hands worked quickly at finding their way to the bottom of her under-dress as he bunched it up to her thighs and ran his hand along the side of her leg. The velvet of her skin, warm and damp from all their previously couplings, tempted him to bathe her with his tongue. He contemplated all the things he would put finally into their embrace. Her softness pressed to him. He stroked her cheek. The ache in his ribs was only minor to that in his groin. His cock, swollen rock hard, seemed not to have recalled prior times. As if each time were the first, he felt hot and needy of her body. His fingers slid further under until he had one cheek of her ass in his palm. The hum from her enchanted with a resounding echo inside his mouth while kissing her.

The curve of her hip fit in his grip. She laughed when his fingers touched a sensitive spot on her belly. The tickling caused her to squeal and kick up her leg. He caught her knee and held the up raised leg against his side.

"Pardon me." A man coughed from behind them.

Brogan jumped to his feet immediately with knife in hand. Peripheral sight assured him Brie had tugged her under-dress and the tunic down to cover all the exposed beauty of her legs. Then she too quickly leapt to her feet.

"Jinn!" she squealed with absolute delight.

Brogan felt the pang of jealousy stab him sharply in the heart.

"Oh, Jinn, I thought you were dead!" Brie continued to squeeze the man's neck and plant several kisses on his cheek.

She reminded him of a child right then—a lovely, energetic little girl. Guilt settled in deep. He had taken the virginity of a Lass and the man she lavished affection on would know. He'd have to fight the man because he defiled the woman. In many ways, he deserved punishment.

"The brute was hurting you?" Jinn asked her.

Brogan grunted at the accusation. The man could very well see how much she'd been enjoying the fact he was prepared to fuck her sweet cunt. Though, he reckoned any excuse to try and kill him could not be held against the man since he stood holding the Lass so tenderly.

Brogan waited to hear how the man might be her father, a brother, or God forbid, a betrothed.

"Jinn, this is Brogan and he is escorting me to Kylemore...ah...to deliver Queen Rhoswen's message to Lord Torrick."

From the dark look in Jinn's eyes, Brogan considered maybe the man had been around for a few hours. He could

Sword of Rhoswen

have easily sat in the dark and watched him and the Lass coupling.

"Sir." Jinn gave a bow of his head. "I thank you for looking after the child."

"So ye serve the house of Rhoswen?" Brogan asked and tried not to look at Brie. She had not been any form of a child under his hand.

"Yes, of course he does." Brie pushed at Brogan's arm. "And put that knife away. He's a friend of mine, a very good friend."

Brogan leaned forward and put the knife in his boot. His gaze followed Jinn going to the edge of the cliff.

"Right now, I am not too happy to see him." Brogan hitched his hands to his hips.

"It was right he made his presence known." Her tone grew serious. "We weren't meant to be."

Disappointed he'd not have a final moment of bliss with the Lass, he nodded in agreement. Surprisingly, she cupped the side of his face and brushed her thumb through the course hair on his face. Before he could react, before he could hoist her up against him and kiss her, she walked away.

She went to Jinn and twined her arm around his. She gave an animated tale, pointing out where the wolf attacked her. Brogan stood in awe and watched her hair blowing in the breeze. The silken strands flapped like a golden banner. Her smile had never been livelier. It was a different side of her, a lighthearted graciousness she had hidden from him or kept shied away because of not trusting him.

"Lass, we need to go now." Brogan brought the horses over to where she stood.

"Jinn has lost his mount and will ride with me." Brie took the reins from him.

"I do not know. Your horse is small, maybe he should ride it alone and ye can ride with me." His fingers rolled over hers on the reins.

"No. I think the horse will have no problem. I'll ride with Jinn." She took her horse over to Jinn and let him help her up.

Brogan scowled with great irritation. Brie scoffed at letting anyone help her on a horse before and now each gesture, each placement of her foot was looked after by her so-called friend, and she lapped up the attention. He rode ahead far enough that he didn't have to hear her laughter. The little twitters of gaiety that burst out while Jinn, the comedian he was, told her jokes and anecdotes of where he'd been lost in the forest without a horse.

Brogan didn't trust the man. No one just got lost. Not a man that Brogan suspected Jinn was. His posture and movements bespoke warrior and not fop as he somewhat tried to imitate. They rode all day without stopping. Brogan might have suggested getting something to eat for Brie, only Jinn provided for her from his haversack.

"Brogan, would you care for a piece?" She held out a dried piece of meat to him as Jinn rode up alongside.

He shook his head and spurred his horse on to put distance between them. The cozy twosome bothered him and he didn't want to witness the overfriendly way they laughed and talked.

† † †

It took all day for them to reach the village. Brogan hardly said a word to her or the man she rode with. He had become so accustomed to having her to himself. Brienna recognized his jealousy. The endearment meant a lot to her.

The gentle stream they stopped at to water the horses made her desire a bath. She looked to Jinn, knowing he could read her like a book.

He shook his head, his eyes dashing a warning look at Brogan.

"I wish to bathe," she announced.

"Ye what?" Brogan turned to face her.

"I would like to get clean and you two might consider doing the same." She paraded over to a boulder behind which to hide her disrobement.

"Brie, ye cannot just..."

"Please turn away until I'm in the water." She stood holding her arms cross over her breasts. She knew Jinn would not hesitate. He often had to put up with her whims of swimming naked. She could only trust Brogan to show the same manners.

When he didn't look away, she walked out from behind her stone shield and headed for the water. His face pinched with her defiance and then softened to the sight she knew he loved to ogle. The corner of his mouth twisted up with the hint of a devilish smile and then he rotated on one heel.

"Do ye care to inform us on how long ye shall bathe?"

"Until I feel clean."

She swished the water between her legs and while keeping a steady watch on Brogan, she ignited the powers to heal her hymen. Brogan had come into her enough to keep the tear from healing on its own. In an instant, all soreness of the raw area vanished.

She bowed her head, feeling a loss already of the intimate moments they shared. They could never be again and she needed this opportunity to make herself ready for the stranger she would meet. She couldn't take the chance of angering the man she married. Besides, with Jinn along, there would be little chance for Brogan to have his way with her.

She splashed the cool water a few more times to rinse the stickiness of passion from her skin. Returning to her clothes, she dressed and they resumed their ride.

They tied their horses to a rail and went into the tavern. Brienna smiled with the recollections of the other place and looked for the big galoot that might grab her. She had a dozen that seemed eager, only Jinn stood to one side of her and Brogan the other. They were the deterrent to the rancorous men alive on ale. No one would dare challenge her staunch sentries.

The girl coming toward them had that same smile of willful pleasure at seeing Brogan. He, on the other hand, at first didn't look interested. Not until he looked down at her and she saw him forming his revenge for making him experience envy.

"Maggie, my bonnie Lass." He picked her up by the tiny waist and spun her around. "I do not suppose ye have some rooms to let, do ye?"

"Two." She grinned. "And of course, ye won't be needing one of them because ye are always welcome in mine."

"I will still take the two for my companions." He jerked his head toward them and put an arm around Maggie's shoulder. "First let us see to some food, some ale, and some fun." He drew her to him tight. "Of course I do not need them all in that order."

Brienna took Jinn's arm and led him to a table so she didn't have to watch Brogan's masculine display of a portentous ass. It was disgusting and made her chest tighten with a strum of pain because she wanted him to be her pompous idiot.

"Find me a shirt," Brogan told Maggie.

He took a mug of ale and leaned on the bar.

"Where are the musicians and the merrymaking of the Kylemore people?" Brogan shouted.

In moments, music trilled and song broke out.

Maggie returned with a shirt and after Brogan put it on, he spun Maggie into the dancers. One time around the floor and then he handed her to another. Her face crumpled with the rejection. Brienna sighed with the empathetic sadness. Brogan turned the head of every woman he met and she didn't like to think how she fit into place as just another sappy victim.

"Brie?" He held his hand out past the nose of Jinn. "Would ye do me the honor?"

Victim or not, she leapt up from her stool and into Brogan's arms.

They danced a jig around and around until thirst had them gulping ale. First Brienna would down half the tankard and then Brogan finished it off, demanding another. Hour upon hour, Brienna laughed and flirted with men she danced with. Only Brogan was the one she wanted to be with.

Staggering up to him, she flung her arms over his shoulders. She watched his face bow down close. The tremor started at the ground and flowed to her fingers nervously tapping the back of his neck. He had a way of looking at her so she always felt awkward and naked.

"I can't dance anymore," she sang.

"Then maybe ye should sit."

She looked at the stools no more than ten feet away.

"I can barely walk as well." She giggled.

"Then I will carry ye."

Brogan swept her up and she nestled against his chest, glad he took the hint. She didn't have to make any encouraging remarks as to taking her somewhere so they could be alone. Each long step he took went in the direction of the stairs.

"Where are we going?" she inquired coyly.

"I am taking ye to your room. I think ye have had enough to drink."

"You had just as much as I did." She hiccupped.

"Aye, but I am larger and can handle more than ye."

At the base of the stairs, Brienna stared into Brogan's eyes. He stopped moving and looked over her shoulder. She turned her head to see the sour expression Jinn wore on his face.

"Jinn, tell him I can handle myself quite well." She dropped an arm out to him.

"Maybe I should see you to your room," Jinn replied.

His small brown eyes narrowed on Brogan.

"No," Brienna whined. "Brogan is very capable in seeing me to bed." She smoothed a hand over the strain of muscle under his tight shirt. "He's very competent in seeing to all my needs tonight."

"Brie?" Jinn practically gasped.

"I'm not a child any longer, Jinn. You can't tell me what to do." She held her hand out again and this time he kissed her knuckles.

"Good night," he said, stepping aside.

Brienna curled her arm tighter around Brogan's thick neck. She rode in his arms as if she weighed no more than a butterfly. She appreciated a man with his strength. But then, his brawn was not the only thing attracting her like a honeybee to a flower.

"He's in love with me," she said to Brogan for an excuse. "Poor, poor Jinn has always been in love with me."

"I can see how that is possible."

She watched him flip the latch and push open the door. He stood her on the floor and she staggered to grab a table. Her laughter filled the room with an unreal loudness and she clamped her mouth shut with a smidgen of embarrassment.

She swayed as she glided to him and stood toe to toe, not touching and now unwavering.

"Why do you wait to kiss me?"

"Ye are too drunk."

"I – am – not – drunk!" she declared. "I'm feeling good and have all my senses." She twirled around the room.

"Except common sense."

"Are you always so arrogant?" She pulled the tunic over her head and dropped it to the floor.

She bent down to lift the bottom of the under-dress and found her head swimming with dizziness.

Brogan grabbed her before she fell. She crowded to him and looked up through her watery eyes.

"Love me?" she whispered.

He stood her back from him.

"I cannot."

She put a hand to her lips to stifle the cry of her humiliation. His simple words sobered her mind and crushed her heart in one blow. She had not meant for him to actually love her. She meant to say make love to her. The misspoken idea came with devastating results she didn't know how to accept or recover from.

Brogan took off the shirt and the one that bound his ribs. He stripped off his boots and britches. The hot tears stopped flowing down her cheeks the moment she stared at his beautiful body.

She swallowed hard. Already disillusioned by men, she saw while he might not love her, he still desired her. She held her lower lip between her teeth. The rise and fall of her chest increased. She trembled when his hand first touched her arms. He slid them down until her fingers were in his open palms.

Chapter 17

Brogan could resist no longer in possessing her. He kissed first the moist trembling lips and then went down the length of her. Raising her gown to her knees, he kissed her thighs, but did not hold to moving slowly. The dress went higher and he chased it, her heady scent beckoning him up to the hidden chamber. And then he paused.

"Lass ye are shaking."

"It's chilly in here," she replied with the illogical excuse.

The night was very warm and he felt her sudden withdrawal from him. He didn't want to back down from her invitation. He rose up and took her dress over her head.

"Then I will warm ye."

Her breasts were sharpened and spiked by rigid nipples. He rubbed a course thumb pad over one until the whimpers were long from her. Her smooth skin had the look of exquisite, unblemished alabaster marble. Her cool slick skin allowed his fingertips to skate over the polished jewel crowning her heaving bosom. Unbinding her hair, the locks of gold fell free and he raked his fingers through the silk tresses. His exploration glissaded over her in a timeless hunt to find what pleased her.

Her head dropped back and her arms reached up while Brogan kneaded her flesh. Each grasp of her nipples and the gentle tugging made her squirm. She whined in little pants as his fingers traveled between her legs and then a finger parted her. Not only opening her to his inquisitive perusal, but to fondle the pleats of the most intimate part of her. Brie's breath stuttered in agitation. She had a vibrant hunger for attention and he tried to keep from thinking one day his Lass would be in such a defenseless position before another man.

He gripped the back of her neck and head. "I'll make ye never want another."

She nodded with her loving acceptance of his edict. He covered her mouth and poured his soul into loving her for a little while. He'd get her on the bed and sandwich the purest form of beauty between him and the mattress.

"Ye are a precious treasure, Lass." He assisted her in lying down with a hand to the back of her head and one to the small of her back.

Her breasts brushed the hair on his chest, tickling and teasing him with such overwhelming delights he held her closer.

Their mouths locked and Brogan sucked at her lips until he had drained her of all glorious hums of pleasure. Her fingers brought endless rivulets of lightening wherever she put them. They were on his face, his shoulders, and then his back. They danced on their own as the rest of her writhed and gathered to seal to the length of him.

Calming her frenzy, Brogan's fingers finally journeyed down her waist, over her hip, and circled into the tuft of ringlets between her legs. Her kisses were more aggressive on his face except over his eye still slightly puffy and cut. There she took the gentlest time to not leave it unfelt with her exuberance.

He slowly stroked the part he had made damp and ready. Only he wanted her more, he wanted her so completely needy of him, she could only think of him. Lightly fondling the first fold, she squirmed like a virgin but settled when his invasion began to part the petals of her succulent cunt. The dewy flaps twitched and juddered violently. Immediately she clenched and rocked up to his caresses fingering her clit.

His tongue made cursory laps on her collarbone and then to her breastbone. Licking between the alabaster mounds, he lapped up the sides and surrounded the peak with a wet hot circle. Brie's whines begged without words for more and he offered a single kiss to the crinkled raspberry tips. The areola looked pale in contrast to the inflamed bead of her plump nipple. Brogan bit it and grated it with his thumb until it went brighter red. Treating the other as equally rough and gentle, he didn't give up the pearl until the nips quaked.

"Brogan," she murmured his name.

Her fingers combed his hair with a fretting motion.

He laved up the hard nipples with his tongue—bathing and soothing the buds while continuing to knead her breasts. He moved to the flatness of her velveteen belly. Circling her stomach and licking into her belly button created more quivering to her skin. A long strangled series of mewls pulled him to the quiver housing her ache.

He found her erect clit waiting to be sucked into his mouth.

"Oh...no...Brogan," she cried. "Oh God no."

Her pleas started the second he tugged on the engorged knot. He dipped a finger into her cunt and wiggled it up against a sweet spot, throwing her into a frenzy. He continued to torture her sensitivities, delighting in the way her fingers pulled at his hair and then rubbed his scalp.

He stopped and allowed her a short breath. It stuck going in and he felt she'd faint with the gasping pants she took too rapidly. He pressed his face between her legs at her insistence. Her insides constricted on his tongue. Her body convulsed. Unexpectedly and quite loudly, she howled with some primitive squeal. A measure of embarrassment flooded her face when he looked up. Her skin flushing with a crimson heat glowed warm and sensuous.

Brogan came up the length of her. He stared at her red-rimmed eyes. He had made her cry and had no right to hold back the feelings he wanted to express. Except the severity of telling her things that would eventually lead to hurting her more had to remain unspoken.

"Oh Lass, ye bring the devil out in me."

He smoothed a hand over her silky head. She blinked and a lone tear careened from the outside corner of her eye, across her temple, and into her hairline. He pushed and probed her dewy portal until he slipped in the narrow channel. He retracted and thrust finding her tense and unwilling to accept him with ease.

"Relax, Lass," he coaxed. "Let me come into ye, me Lass, let me in, my lovely Brie."

He whispered her name over and over again, wishing she could always belong to him. He felt the unyielding tunnel finally give into the needs of fulfillment and he plunged into her with a sharp awareness of her pain.

"Brie?" He rubbed her hip. "Does it hurt ye?"

She shook her head and the watery eyes had been just as glassy before he sank into her body.

"Brie, tell me what is wrong."

"Just a little sting."

She rose up and hugged him. Her lips pecked kisses over his face. Her body undulated and drew him to her virginal tightness. He didn't understand it, but he wouldn't complain at how unbelievably good she felt to be inside.

"Brie?" He spoke her name apologetically. "I am sorry."

"I know," she hummed. "I know."

He had more than just her present pain to show remorse for. He had fallen far from his honorable nature. He had pursued her with vigilance. He won her over to the point they would live with broken hearts forever.

"I am sorry," he repeated.

† † †

Brienna cradled his face in her palms and kissed him lightly.

"Not for now, please."

"Never for now." He rocked on top her and the barrage of kisses began to heat her mouth. Pleasurable pains riffled and licked a blaze from her cunt to her nipples. She drew her knees up and pressed them to his sides.

This time her voice came out in gasps of elated trills of ecstasy. Her throat sung with an aria of rapture met with Brogan's groans, long and deep. He bucked and jammed into her so she squeaked each time. He went faster and faster until she held on to stay attached to him. Her legs coiled around his hips and her feet locked ankle to ankle. Her fingers clawed his back and dug into his hair so she could ride his twisting torso. Muscles once so flexible under her fingertips were taut. She hung onto him with a sinful desire to be a slave to his lust.

When the crests of the tides between them had dwindled, she felt the heated fluids filling her with every lovely dream she ever had of loving a man. She could no longer push away the emotions, the feelings of belonging to someone. She buried her face under his whiskery jaw and pressed a kiss to his sweaty throat.

He rolled off her, putting an arm over his eyes.

Brienna didn't know what to say. Everything felt so right when they were two bodies entwined. Separated, they had complicated lives in which to deal with and her greatest fear neared. He could tell her body had been healed. He didn't understand it, or question it, but she felt he knew.

Sword of Rhoswen

The longer Brogan silently lay next to her, the more her fears evolved into anger. More at herself for letting her emotions lead her down a foolish path.

"If we're done, I think I'll go for a walk." She sat up and the cool air of the room ran goose bumps over her from head to toe. The dampness to her naked skin made her shiver.

She felt like an unwilling servant had serviced her. He admitted no love and the passion and sentiments she imagined wafted out the window on the first breeze. It left her bereft of contentment.

"Are ye all right?" he asked. "I will go with ye."

"I'm fine and I don't need an escort," she snapped.

The tears lay in wait for when she could cry alone. She drew the under-dress on and then the tunic. Her hand smoothed over the fabric and she felt the ache in all the places Brogan had spent a great deal of time kissing.

She went outside the tavern. The night air refreshed her spirit. The bright moon hung low in the sky and she walked with it behind her. When she heard the crunch of gravel beneath footsteps, she turned to face the glowing circular backdrop with the silhouette of Brogan coming for her.

"Brie, come back in and get some sleep." He stopped in front of her.

"I am sorry for tonight, Lass. Ye asked something of me and I could not give ye the answer ye wanted."

"You were mistaken in the interpretation. I should have made myself clear, but as you see, the drink does cloud the mind and I didn't speak my wishes so well. I wished to lay with you and have you join me, and nothing more." She tightened her jaw and hoped he believe her partial lie.

She hopped up to sit on the edge of a cart.

"No? Then why did ye leave?"

"You weren't happy with me." She turned her face and the tears trickled down. Her chest burned with despondency.

"Not happy?" He laughed. "How could ye ever think that?"

Brienna looked at him with puzzlement. He couldn't love her, and he apologized for using her, so what else could she think?

He gathered her hair up that hid her face. "Ye pleased me immensely and if ye will come back in I'd like to get some sleep which I could do best with ye next to me." He leaned over and kissed her.

She tried to resist, only he used all the right words. Folding her arms around his neck, she let him pick her up.

"Now tell me truthfully, are ye all right? I did not hurt ye too much? I have been a boar with my rutting at ye every chance I got. I never thought to ask if ye had healed from the first time."

She put her head down on his shoulder. She didn't want to say yes, it hurt. Yes, she was sore. But she didn't want to lie, because he would know.

"I'm still a little sore."

"Don't worry, Lass. I know just the thing."

"Where are we going?" She looked back at the tavern door standing open.

The outline of Maggie stood in the frame and Brienna put her head back down. Brogan might not be hers forever, but he was hers for that one more night. She didn't care where they were going. The cool air made her shiver and his arms squeezed her.

"We are almost there," he said.

"Where are you taking me?" She heard the babbling waters and looked to the stream. "You're not going to drown me like some unwanted cat!"

"Now, hush up. I am going to make ye feel better." He stood her on the ground. "Pull up your dress." He took off his shirt.

Brienna looked around extremely reticent about a public exhibition. "You want to...out here...in the open...Brogan I..."

He wet the shirt, knelt before her.

"You can't possibly think I would let you wash me there." She gathered the under-dress and tunic tight to her legs.

"I have already seen, touched, and tasted of ye. Now let me do this." He kissed her white knuckles as they clutched at the garments. "Lift it up."

"Oh, Brogan!" She closed her eyes and pulled the clothing up.

Slow, nervous and timidly, she stopped at the top of her thighs. She just couldn't lift higher with him kneeling in front of her with his eyes trained on the sacred area. Before passion had shrouded her thoughts and it came natural.

"A little higher, Lass." He pushed her hand up and then pressed the cool wet cloth between her legs. "Spread your legs a little more."

She did so only because it did feel good. The cold water soothed the sore burn traveling deep inside her. When he removed the cloth, he kissed her legs. He traveled her hip and followed the concave across the center of her belly. He abruptly stood, gathered her up in his arms, and carried her back to the tavern, back to their room.

He put her on the bed, joined her, and after establishing a loving embrace, she went to sleep. In her dreams, they could be together forever.

† † †

In the morning, Brienna stretched on the bed and lifted her head to see Brogan had left without waking her. A habit she didn't like. She ached in all the right places. Her hands rubbed over her clothing and she gave a brief thought of healing her own soreness. She pressed her hands to her cheeks to deny the temptation. She'd not be so quick to discard the lingering effects of Brogan lust again.

She swung her legs over the side of the bed and pressed ten tired toes to the floor. It didn't stop her from dancing over to a wood basin and pouring water from a clay pitcher. From the window, she saw the drab gray appearance of the sky. A crisp dewy scent permeated her nostrils from a rain infused morning. It put a smile to her lips simply because she felt happy inside.

She went through a hastened and condensed morning ritual of cleaning her face and hands. She combed her hair back with her fingers since the comb she had fought to keep was somewhere in the sea with her gown. She shook out the tunic and donned it like a new dress and slipped on the dingy shoes she'd worn through every sort of muck like they were jewels for her feet. Brogan had made her feel so beautiful inside she couldn't help overlooking everything wrong in her filthy appearance.

The tavern was quite a bit emptier than the last place they had stayed. When she went down the stairs from her room, her eyes sought Brogan's. She had not let a thread of anxiety into her thoughts until she saw him and Jinn standing together. The expressions on their faces did not look good as she made her way toward them.

"Good morning," she sang cheerfully and put herself between the two.

She faced Jinn since he would obey her more readily than Brogan.

"I hope you had a restful night, Your High…"

"I'm starving!" She put a hand up to push Jinn. "Please fetch someone to see about my breakfast."

Jinn bowed his gray head slightly at her.

"Have you been up long?" She whirled about and put a hand on Brogan's arm.

He looked down at her. "Not long." He smiled with his mouth and the wonderful twinkle in his green eyes.

"It's raining out. Will it delay our departure?" she asked, unable to get rid of the silly smile still plastered on her face like a court jester's.

"No. I was just on my way out to see about our horses when your... your friend desired to chat," he answered.

"What did he say?" She turned away afraid Jinn had said too much to Brogan.

"Seems he thinks I might be an unsavory influence on ye. The ale was his main concern." He cupped her cheek. "He reminded me ye don't partake of such indulgences and I can see why."

"I was aware of everything I did last night." Her lashes lowered to her cheeks.

"So was I." Brogan released her face when Jinn sat a plate of food down on the table behind her. "Eat and then we will set out for Kylemore."

Brienna turned around and folded her arms as she reprimanded Jinn with only a look at first.

"I don't trust him, Your Highness," he muttered and took her arm to seat her.

"Brogan and I have come through a lot, Jinn. He has offered me protection and, in the process, has been injured by Thane's men. I fully trust him and it is my command that you trust him as well. He has saved my life and..."

"Saved your life!"

"I was kidnapped and he came for me. I fell in a river and if he didn't breathe life back in me I would have been dead." She patted his arm. "I'm in love with him. Let me have this time to enjoy."

"You shouldn't have spent the night with him," he advised. "If your betrothed hears of your indiscretion, it could cause problems."

"I'll deny what I have to and Brogan will not speak against me." She pushed the plate away no longer hungry. "I have something to tell you."

She held his hands in hers.

"You're not going to go against your father's wishes, are you?" Jinn squeezed her fingers and rubbed over her knuckles.

Chapter 18

If changing her destiny were possible, she would have done so long before this day came.

"No, nothing like that," Brienna lowered her voice. "Two days ago, we were in a cave along the sea. Brogan called it Dragon's Dare. He said he didn't believe dragons existed anymore, but I spoke to one."

"Spoke?" Jinn's silver eyebrows jumped up to brighten his bark brown eyes.

"Don't look so surprised. You were with my mother a long time and certainly she mentioned to you about the bond of healers and dragons?" She looked to the door, watchful of Brogan's swift return.

"Your mother never saw a dragon. None of us have. We assumed none existed anymore." He rubbed his grizzled jaw and shook his head. "This isn't some dream or delusion from the mead you seemed to have taken a liking to drink?"

"I didn't see the dragon. Rather I heard him breathing and felt the warmth of his exhale on my face. Then, when I requested answers or maybe I was giving them, I was imbued with knowledge. I haven't sorted it all out, but I know it holds the key to something greater than what my mother or I could do with healing." She pulled the plate toward her and began eating when she saw Brogan come through the door. "He doesn't know." She imparted while putting a piece of buttered bread in her mouth.

"So, are we set to go?" Brogan dropped down in the chair next to her and picked up a piece of cheese from her plate.

"Yes." Brienna had considered how the day should go for her and Brogan.

She had to begin seriously distancing herself from him in as many ways as possible. By the end of day, they would ride into the Torrick's castle and she would quite possibly never see Brogan again. She held her chin high and took the arm Jinn offered. This was the end of her journey with Brogan. It had a blended mixture of sadness and happiness, as she would never forget him.

Brogan said nothing when she went to the horse with Jinn. They headed out on separate horses with a burst of energy and a need to out ride the encroaching storm. Eventually they left the gloomy sky behind and while the sky held no sun, it was a tranquil blue, dotted with fluffy white clouds.

He took them across the flat meadows. Brienna inhaled the fresh scent of tansies. Thunder launched into a low muttering that reminded Brienna of the dragon's hum. She swept back hair that wrapped her face in the violent rush of wind. The darkest clouds erased the mackerel sky when the ominous gray spread. The world appeared to be closing in on them with the forecast of an advancing disaster. In moments, they were surrounded by the shadowy tempest. When the rain came at last, it was as if a cloud was rending asunder, dollops of water splat on their heads. Brienna had never been to Kylemore. Impressed by the castle's size spread over the land, it had been built clearly as a fortress instead of a home. The ravages of a battle did not deplete the imposing magnitude of her in-laws power until Brogan rode harder for the gates.

Without word, the tall, heavy iron barricade swung open and two men ran up to him. Brogan jumped down. They spoke and then he ran.

Sword of Rhoswen

"What's happened?" Brienna asked the man holding her horse when she caught up to where Brogan had dismounted.

"Lord William Torrick and his youngest son are dead, m'lady, and his other son is gravely injured. It's not expected for him to live through the night," he answered. "Thane Rhoswen's army laid siege to the castle yesterday in attempts to overtake us, but we held him back until they could no longer fight. I'm afraid they will be back with a greater army soon."

He offered the information excitedly, anticipating the encounter to exact revenge.

Brienna left Jinn to his own accord and rushed inside the great hall. She found Brogan kneeling alongside a table. A man lie stretched for viewing. Tall wrought iron stanchions with a dozen candles each were marking the four corners of the table and flowers surrounded the war-wrecked body.

It was a fitting scene for a ruler and yet it was a terrible loss. Awed by Brogan's sensitivity and emotional pain, Brienna's hand went to his shoulder to offer compassion for his open grief. His anguish went beyond loyalty and she further understood what drew her to him. He kept his head bowed in silence for a long while. She stayed silent and mourned with him.

She never knew a castle could be so quiet. The desolation of war seemed to wipe away all that existed, including the bray of an animal or the hum of the wind. Time slipped by and after fifteen long suffering minutes had elapsed, a high pitched voice rang in both their ears.

"Brogan!" The girl's voice shattered the state of bereavement. She had a storm of dark hair she left wildly free to drape her slender body as she rushed toward them.

Brogan stood up to catch the girl younger that she, but mature enough to be his wife. He kissed the tears from the girls face as he held her off the ground.

"Are ye all right, my flower?"

"Yes." She clung to his neck and held him tight. "I was so worried ye would come too soon and go the way your father and brothers have.

"Kelwyn and Irvan are dead?" He pulled her away.

"Only Irvan." She shrugged. "Kelwyn hasn't long."

Brienna felt like an intruder and she backed toward the door to give them the solitude an obvious separation as well as a tragedy needed for mending.

Outside the door, Brienna leaned upon the smooth gray granite wall. She looked at the people working to clean things up. Right all the dismantled fixtures of the castles courtyard and repair what would be most important. The silence had gone and she wondered if they hadn't all stopped what they were doing to give Brogan a moment of peace with his ruler.

She considered why she came. Kylemore didn't look like the place she could find help for Avalbane. Her only option would be to beg for William Torrick's son, the new Lord and Master of Kylemore to rescind the contract so she could seek help elsewhere. This kingdom did not have the means to help her and themselves. Then remembering the guard said the Lord's son was gravely wounded in the battle, she concluded she might be free of the marriage contract by default.

"Hello," the girl's voice spoke from behind her. "I'm Nareene. Brogan asked that I show ye to a room."

"You can call me Brie. I'm sorry for the time in which it took for Brogan to get back here. It's my fault that he was delayed." She didn't know what else to say to the girl. Who was she to Brogan and to the Torrick's?

"Brogan does what is right and ye would not have had a bearing on his decisions. He likes the adventure of being away from home. I wish it were in my power to keep him here everyday, but I don't believe anyone will ever have that sort of hold on him."

"Surely, he loves you. I saw that much." Brie pried.

"Oh, I have no doubts where it comes to him loving me. That is something he would never let me forget. However, it is not the type of love I desire from him." She gestured to a narrow and dim side stairwell for them to ascend. "We'll go this way so we don't get in the way of the servants cleaning up this dreadful mess."

Nareene opened a door to a massive room, palatial to say the least and more ornate than her own home. Where her father had sought the simple comforts, the Torricks had indulged in treasures to please the eye.

"Brogan was close to Lord Torrick?" Brienna asked.

"He was the ideal son. Brogan couldn't love his father anymore and I hate that he is suffering this pain alone, but he asked me to leave him alone." She pushed open heavy draperies to let slivers of light in the narrow windows. "His brother is not so well and will soon follow. I'd say Brogan will go to be with him shortly."

"Brogan is Lord Torrick's son?" She slumped down into a chair, feeling faint.

"Yes. Did ye not know that?" She flipped a strand of her dark brown hair back over her shoulder. It was a stark contrast to that of the pale skin of her face.

"No, he did not divulge that piece of information." Brienna's heart beat fast with the happy prospects the news brought. All her concerns of how she would deal with a man supposed to become her husband changed to challenging, yet welcomed worries of how to explain to Brogan who she was.

"He's the eldest son?"

"Yes and if my uncle had not insisted on making him agree to a marriage contract with some evil witch to strengthen our stand against Thane Rhoswen, I might have been Brogan's wife and then I'd be Lady Torrick right now." Nareene was frightfully bitter with her statement.

Brogan had kept his full identity a secret from her as well. Did he have reasons for not wanting the marriage alliance because of Nareene? It seemed conceivable he had not come for her because he loved another woman.

"Is that all it would take? I mean if Brogan were free of his contract, would he marry you?" Brienna asked.

"I'm sure of it. He told me he'd always take care of me. If possible, I'm going to get him to marry me now that his father is not here to demand he keep a bargain with a Rhoswen."

Brienna listened to the girl's words. How many more people of Kylemore despised all the Rhoswens because of Thane? Would she be safe in telling anyone who she was? For the time being, Brienna decided to keep the information to herself. Even Brogan gave her doubts to trust him after seeing his fondness for Nareene.

The girl left her to freshen up and while there was fruit in the room, she went looking for something more substantial to quell the hunger she felt. As if her mind was read, she opened the door to a servant knocking.

"Lord Torrick wishes ye to present yourself at his table for dinner in the quarter hour." She pushed past her with garments in tow. "He has offered a change of clothing so ye are more presentable."

Brienna couldn't help feeling the woman disliked her. Not only were people going to resent Queen Rhoswen for her name and her relation to Thane, they would take offense to anyone from the Kingdom of Avalbane, especially from the house of Rhoswen.

It did not take long to change her clothes. It had been the most sought after comfort in days. She quickly washed from the basin of water and donned the gown happily disregarding the item no doubt would belong to Nareene. The clean clothes made her feel much better. The servant brushed her hair and tied back the long spirals of gold with ribbons.

On the walk to the dinning room, Brienna observed the malicious stares of servants. She didn't feel safe. The people detested her and her reasons for being there. It brought to light more reasons why Brogan had never come to finalize their contract. It disheartened her to think he really was just as disgusted with Rhoswens as were his people.

Brogan stood with a far off look in his eyes when she was seated at the opposite end of a long table. He had shaved the week's growth of beard, he had bathed, and it made her more comfortable when he looked fondly at her.

Nareene sat to his right at his end of the long table. Brienna felt displaced of his affections, set so far from him.

"I'm sorry for your loss, m'lord." She watched his eyes mist and then he blinked the cloudiness away to really look at her. "And your brother?"

The sorrow she understood, only he looked troubled by so many other things that the lines in his face seemed to age him. Maybe he always looked older, but the fact he had shaved off his whiskers should have made him appear younger.

"Thank ye, Lass. Young Kelwyn will not wake before his last breath comes tonight I am afraid."

"Brogan, ye should have seen the battle." Nareene's statement lacked empathy.

Not only had Brogan said his brother lay dying, but he had lost a father and another brother.

"I was so scared they would get into the castle. I do wish ye would not go away again. It's your duty to protect me now that your father is gone." Nareene had seized his sleeve and whined over the selfish trivialities, displaying more of her lack of maturity.

"I will not be leaving anytime soon, my flower. Now eat your dinner." He patted her hand at his sleeve and then took a bite of his food.

Brienna chewed the bit of meat she took in her mouth and thought about Brogan's brother. She had the skill to heal him if his wounds were beneath her fingers. She shouldn't wait, but how could she tend a man amongst a place filled with hate? The servants only knew she came bearing a message for the Torricks and they observed her as if she were a thief that came to steal the Torricks' coffers. Her biggest question was how devout were they to the church? Did they believe in the mystics, the seers, and the healers? Or was magic an evil to them, as it was too much of the lands, including her own?

If she waited, maybe she could find a way to sneak into the room and...oh that was ridiculous. He wouldn't be left alone.

"Brie, tell us about the Queen. Brogan said she was now ruler since her father's passing. Is she like her cousin, Thane? I hear she's as ugly as a toad." Nareene giggled.

"I suppose it would depend on who did the judging. I'd guess you would not find her attractive." Brienna hid her amusement behind her hand.

Nareene was an insipid spoiled brat and she would most definitely hate the fact that it was possible that Brogan might fall in love with his betrothed.

"Nareene!" Brogan chastised. "Ye will do well not to embarrass my house with your rudeness. Brie is a guest and she will not be telling ye anything that would speak ill of her sovereign."

"Well, ye have heard it for yourself. The Rhoswen woman is a hag and ye would do well to rid yourself of any obligation to her," Nareene implored exuberantly. "Ye cannot wed such a person when I am here for ye, my love."

"Nareene, please, this is not the time for this conversation. Besides, I have it from good authority Queen Rhoswen is beautiful."

He sat still with his arms leaning on the table, hands folded over his plate as if he might be finished with his meal yet he had hardly taken a bite. Grief had claimed his appetite and Brienna sat her fork down, feeling his pain.

"Tell me if it were not for her, you would choose me." She pressed.

"If it were not for her, I would choose where my heart lay." He blinked and looked down at his plate. "Eat, Nareene, or leave the table."

The sharpness with which he spoke to Nareene kept Brienna quiet. Brogan's hands shook with the high charge of emotions. Her request could wait one more day until the passing of his father found a better place in him.

Nareene did not stop her chatter, but instead of love, marriage, and the harangue of Queen Rhoswen, she ventured to lighter subjects. Brogan made only small comments, but nothing beyond a word or two to placate the girl.

Brienna finished eating.

"If you'll excuse me, I'm very tired from the trip."

Brogan nodded and stood with a disappointed expression for her departure, but she could not sit and listen to Nareene's infatuation with him any longer. She had no idea what his decision would be regarding the contract and then there was the matter of telling him who she was.

† † †

Late that night, dressed in a nightshift and robe, Brienna stole a walk through the darkness of the castle. The cold stone beneath her feet took her through endless hallways and corridors. The walls held nothing greatly ornate beyond a few well-crafted swords. With a desire to help the man lying near death, Brienna made her way to Kelwyn's chambers. She'd make some excuse and hope she could find a few minutes to be alone with Brogan's brother.

She wasn't surprised that Brogan was there. He would, of course, think it would be the last opportunity he had to be with his brother. She hung back in the shadows of the room and grieved for Lord Torrick, the deceased as well as Lord Torrick, the man kneeling.

For a while, sparks flew between them, so did that dance on their blades. She thought in that first moment if he had said who he was and she who she was, the contract may have been forfeited for their lack of involvement. Now they had a history, a short torrid chain of events that had bound them.

She tried to imagine the muscles on his back against the palms of her hands. The hardness of his chest pressing her into the bed so that she thought she might not breathe again. He was a man to be loved and respected. A marriage between them would be perfect for all reasons.

The sob that broke the silence rendered her heart with pain. Brienna rushed across the room. Her bare feet slapped the stone floor in a hurry to comfort the man who would be her husband. He turned to her footsteps and grabbed her waist to bury his face in the folds of her clothing at her stomach.

"Hush now, everything will get better," she whispered, hugging his head, kissing the wild mane. "I promise, it does get better," she murmured into the black waves of soft and freshly washed hair.

"'Tis my brother Kelwyn, Lass. Ye would have liked him, but there is nothing that can make him better, not ye, not I."

Brienna hated to let go, but she gathered his face and kissed him lightly. "I can." She turned to the servants, waiting to do whatever they could. "Please leave us."

Brogan nodded his approval when they looked to him. They could obey no one else as long as he was present.

She put a hand to Kelwyn's handsome face so similar to Brogan's.

She gathered the bloodstained cover on his chest.

"Do not look, Brie, t'would not be a pretty sight for ye to behold." His brow furrowed as he watched her fingers.

"I'd like to ask you not to watch as well, but this is something you need know about me," she whispered.

A glow, faint and magical, rippled on the dark hair over Kelwyn. Her hand lowered and the slender tapers wavered, the light touched the wound. As if it was unbelievable to see the amber light, it was more so, to see the raw butchered skin on Kelwyn stitch together with the mystical rays.

"Sorcery?" Brogan's eyes widened. "I have met men that claimed to know of women that had the powers of an ancient sect."

Chapter 19

The healers were thought to be long gone from their world. The Silver Dragon sect had died out with that of the dragons and yet before his eyes he watched her perform a miracle. Her hands emitted light and heat. They wove the ragged flesh together, and in moments, Kelwyn was only stained by the memory of a wound.

Kelwyn's eyes opened. The color of Brienna's meadows from home flashed up and she smiled. "You should sleep, Sir Kelwyn," she said quietly and smiled at the same brilliant green irises that Brogan had. She could have loved this Torrick as easily and as much if she hadn't known Brogan.

"Are ye an angel?" Kelwyn asked. His hand lifted and took hold of a lock of her hair.

"Aye." Brogan answered. "She is my angel, Kelwyn. This is Brie." He put an arm around her waist and held her close.

"What of Father?" Kelwyn's voice came rough and ragged with emotional pain.

"He is gone, Kelwyn, and so is Irvan." He placed a hand on his brother's shoulder. "But we have each other and that I will always be grateful for. Now do as Brie instructs."

"Sir Kelwyn, please close your eyes and sleep. Sleep deeply and we shall talk come morning." Brienna stroked his forehead.

"Your care is appreciated if not by anyone else, then by me." Brogan guided Brie from the room.

"How do you feel about what I could do?" she asked, wanting to know quickly.

Sword of Rhoswen

"Why did ye not tell me this before?" He looked up as if a thousand thoughts were running through his head and then looked down at her. "My father?"

"I'm sorry, no. I have the gift of healing. I cannot raise the dead." She bowed her head; sorry it was not possible.

"Thank ye for what ye could do." He put a finger under her chin and stroked the line of her jaw.

"Brogan, I'm..." His mouth smothered the confession she readied to give. To tell him who she was and that everything could be perfect between them.

When his hands untied her robes, slithered inside to hold her waist, and then ventured to cup over her breast, she could not stop him. He kissed over her collarbone and moved quickly to the firm full breasts. His tongue ravaged the beaded tip before he captured the nipple in his teeth through the gossamer of cloth. She let out a moan of resounding pleasure and it brought more kisses through the cloth everywhere. Her legs weakened with the amount of aggression he put in conquering what was already his.

He gathered her up in his arms. She wound her embrace around his neck and let him carry her down the passage. His mouth pressed kisses under her jaw and only stopped after they were inside his bedchamber. The thud of his door echoed in the room and she looked around at the furnishings.

The large elaborate woodcarvings on the headboard matched those on the chest of drawers and also on the huge cabinet. Different fur hides covered most of the floor and a thick blanket of sheep's wool spread over the mattress.

"Brogan, I need to know. Will you marry Queen Rhoswen?" she asked as he put her on his bed and knelt to bend over her.

"That is my obligation, but a decision I have not yet made." He pulled her robe open and drew it down her arms. "It will not affect your position with me either way."

"Yes, it affects me greatly." She tugged the robe shut in the front. "So do your feelings toward Nareene. Has she shared your bed too?"

"Nareene?" He stood up and rubbed the tearstains from his face. "No of course not, she's just a child!"

"She's a young woman that loves you very deeply and wants to be your wife." Brienna slipped off the far side of the bed to use as a barrier between their passions.

"Nareene's infatuation will never be returned by me. I think of her as a little sister. I always have. I cannot think of her in any other way. I know that distresses her, but one day I will find her a husband that will worship the ground she dances upon and she will have somewhere to direct that love." He walked around the bed and fingered the wisps of hair on her face. "Ye are who I want to share my bed, Lass."

"Then what of Queen Rhoswen?" Pushing the issue instead of lying with him was a strange defense; only it was instinct that made her force the subject because she knew she would not like what she would hear. "You would be her husband and still keep other women for your pleasures?"

"I want no others, just ye."

"You would marry one and lay with another? You would wish me to be your mistress, while you make Queen Rhoswen a fool."

"Brie, I do not want to discuss her. I am sorry but inside I have a dislike for all Rhoswens and while she may be a very nice woman, I cannot dispel she is cousin to the butcher that has killed my Father." He put a hand to the bedpost and gazed at her with longing. "Now, will ye give me comfort and let me seek solace in your arms?"

The tears were building inside her like a quick spring rain that threatens to flood. "I can't." She breathed but instead of hurrying from his room, she flung herself into his arms. "I can't." She hit him, knowing if she married him, she could not trust he would not take affections with another woman. She had to have this time with him as much as he needed it from her and she quieted in his embrace.

Brogan took her to the bed. Life would be perfect if they could stay coiled and locked together forever. Brogan's fervor matched hers and they both shed tears of happiness as well as sadness.

† † †

Dawn disrupted the night with a haze of light peeping through the embrasure. Brienna lay on her side and looked at the man next to her. He slept spread out on his stomach. The room had the night coolness that should have made then draw up the covers. Alas, they had been too exhausted to bother when they fell asleep entwined.

While she debated his feelings toward her as a person and her as an obligatory nuisance, she concluded he would never be able to see past his hate of the Rhoswen name even though it was not her fault for Thane's actions. She deliberated on her next move. It left her only Thane to deal with and what she could do to save Brogan anymore anguish. She'd leave Kylemore and go to her cousin. In an offering to be his wife, she'd have him agree to never threaten Kylemore again. Avalbane would be his and any other kingdom he chose to attack. But Kylemore and Lord Torrick were never to be in his thoughts or he would have to kill her. For if he broke the one promise she'd extract from him, she would learn to kill with a swiftness only pure hatred could bring.

The sun came up and Brienna dressed. She looked at Brogan on the bed, his light snore reminiscent of other nights they'd slept together. From his contented sleep, she knew he had trusted her from the start. He had slept only prepared to wake for real danger and she'd never been that to him. Her hand hovered over him and her fingers wiggled to touch him. She snapped them back, afraid he would wake and keep her from what she must do. At the door, she turned once more and blew a kiss.

"I love you."

Her lips moved but not a sound came out.

The passage free from servants, she made her way back to her room unseen. Once there, she took ink to pen and wrote a message for Brogan. Sincere, heartfelt and straight to the point, she explained all so Brogan would not think she'd been kidnapped or worse, part of a plot against him with Thane. Then laying it on her bed, she went in search of Jinn.

† † †

Brogan looked around the room when he found his bed empty of all but himself. He dressed and went to Brie's room, guessing she attempted to be discreet. When he didn't find her there, he checked the great hall. Panic rose alarmingly fast. He checked everywhere and questioned servants.

"What do ye mean she is not anywhere to be found?" Brogan demanded harshly. "How do ye let one girl leave my castle without knowledge of it?"

The serf kept his eyes down.

Brogan continued to interrogate men and woman alike until he looked to the gatekeeper and ran down to the iron gates. "The girl I brought yesterday, have ye seen her?" he demanded.

"Yes, m'lord, she went with the other man that came with her."

"When? Why?"

"They left just at dawn. She had inquired about Duane and I directed her to his quarters. Then she returned a half hour later on a horse, with a bow over her shoulder, a sword at her hip and knives in her waistband. The other man came with her."

"And your reason for letting them outside the gate?" Brogan's fists clenched at his sides.

"She said ye had given her leave to hunt. She looked outfitted for it and she had been to see Duane. I assumed t'would be all right. Was I wrong to let her leave, m'lord? I had been given no orders that they were to be detained, especially after they had ridden in behind ye yesterday."

Brogan kicked at a wooden bucket and watched it rattle across the court. When he went back inside the great hall he stared at his father. He leaned and kissed him on the forehead.

"Safe passage to your new kingdom in heaven, Father, may your rule there be untroubled." He turned to the two servants awaiting his order. "Take him away now." He sat in his father's chair, his seat of power, and meditated on his next maneuver.

Thane would be back to try and finish them off. Brie headed perilously back to Avalbane, he assumed. She put him in the middle of protecting his providence or protecting her.

"Why so gloomy, Brogan?" Nareene danced into the room.

He dismissed her gaiety on her youth. Why should she feel sad on this day? This wretched day when his father was to be buried and his love had ran from him.

"That woman has gone," she continued. "And ye don't have to make a decision about the marriage contract now. Queen Rhoswen will marry Thane Rhoswen and he will destroy her." Nareene sat at his feet and put her head against his knee.

"Queen Rhoswen will never marry Thane. T'would mean the end to her lands and everyone else's if she gave him that much power." Brogan closed his eyes. "I will be leaving tomorrow for Avalbane and hope she is still agreeable to the marriage with me. Then I will try to get back with her warriors before Thane has time to regroup."

"Ye are wrong about her. She only looked for a way out of marrying ye." Nareene's hand stroked up the inside of his thigh and he grabbed her fingers.

"No, I think the Queen of Avalbane needs my alliance as much as I need hers." He put her hand on the arm of the chair.

"I think she was here to see that your forces were weaker than Thane's so she could pick the stronger of the two to ally with." Nareene hugged his leg as he stood.

"What are ye talking about?" Brogan pried her fingers loose. "Brie was not here as a spy for Queen Rhoswen. She was here for a message for me to act on my commitment. Now she's gone home." He missed her already and he had barely gotten to know her.

"Ye have been made a fool, Brogan. She's still making ye a laughingstock." Nareene declared, jumping to her feet. "She cleverly deceived ye into believing she was just a servant, a messenger. She is as evil as her cousin. She seduced ye and now she has gone and ye should be thankful!" She handed him a slip of paper. "I found that in her room this morning when I saw her and her man leaving the castle. That woman ye brought here was and is Queen Rhoswen.

"What is this?" He unfolded the sheaf and looked at the fine penmanship scrawled across the page.

Lord Torrick,

With your confession of ill feelings towards any Rhoswen, I will assume you wish to dissolve the marriage treaty. I will keep our alliance, however, by marrying Thane, with an arrangement that he never invades Kylemore lands again.

I do this for you, Brogan, forsaking all my principles for my heart that lays in eternal mourning for a destiny not mine. Be well, be safe, and find happiness with Nareene, as she loves you dearly.

Queen Brienna Rhoswen of Avalbane

"I have to say this for her. She does offer ye good advice. Now we can be married and live in peace. Of course, we can't trust she isn't marrying Thane to rule us all." Nareene went to hug him.

"Ye spoiled child!" Brogan pushed her away so she fell back on the floor. "Have ye no idea what is about to happen? Brie is sacrificing herself and her lands for me. It will be in vain because as much as she hopes Thane will honor her request, his hatred for me will not allow him to keep such a bargain. He'll keep that promise only until they are married and everything becomes his, then he will have the power to overtake us."

"Brogan, just forget about everyone and go away with me. We could go to England, France, somewhere that we could have children and a quiet life," she pleaded.

"Nareene, that will never happen. I will die before I leave Kylemore or Brie. I said something foolish to her I wish I could take back. If I had known who she was, she would be here right now and I am about to do everything I can to bring her back."

"Ye will never get to her before she marries Thane," Nareene screamed at him leaving the room. "Ye will never see her again because ye and I both know he'll kill her."

"Queen Rhoswen is going to be my wife and killing Thane Rhoswen will be a long awaited pleasure." He stormed out of the great hall, never looking once to the servants preparing to remove his father.

He should have been there for the rites, but his father would forgive him and wish him well on his way immediately. He gathered a small group to accompany him. Sedge, Duane,

Lorne, and Reece, whom he learned had just returned to report that Medora recovered well and had been in the position of kitchen help.

"Ye did not see the Lass, did ye?" Brogan asked. "No, never mind, she would be careful not to be seen until she was sure she was near Thane's men." He went on to explain to them whom Brie was and what she was about to do.

"She's not a stupid woman, Brogan. Maybe her plan will work and we can finally live in peace," Lorne offered his opinion.

"No, Queen Rhoswen is a courageous lady that is attempting the only thing she can think of, even if it is wrong, because of me. Whether it could work or not, I cannot let her give up her life for the sake of mine. Can any of ye say the hell with her efforts and good riddance to loyalty to Kylemore, when she should be looking out for her own people?" Brogan countered.

Pride filled his heart to see them shake their heads.

† † †

Brienna did not find it hard to run into Thane's men. They seemed to flood the forests near Kylemore. The man took her to Mackey. She had a pang of fear he would kill her.

"So, m'lady, at last we meet, face to face." He touched the back of his head.

She held her chin up.

Mackey ran a finger down her throat and dipped it into her cleavage.

"You are a sweet Lass and I see Brogan's want of you. I cannot deny you do heat a man's blood by the very sight of your smooth young skin."

"I want you to take me to my Cousin. He wishes to marry me and I am going to accept his proposal," she said, holding her head high. "So I do foresee him not wanting me any other way than as you find me now."

"Tie her wrists together," he ordered. "The Queen does have a valid point."

Brienna's eyes widened. She was not aware they knew she was now Queen. Her father's passing wasn't a secret, but then she had not let anyone shout the news from rooftops. It was a way in which to detain Thane's threat toward her kingdom.

"Ah, you didn't think we knew you have succeeded your father. Believe me when I say, not much goes unnoticed in the lands surrounding Thorndale." He circled her. "Thane wants more land and to marry you is a means to his end, nothing more. What we do to you will not affect him in the least." His vile grin warned she could not protest until she knew his intentions. Her wrists were bound tight in front of her. She held her tongue in lieu of screaming obscenities at him. A pleasure he expected and she refused to satisfy.

"Now put her in my tent," he added once they had the hemp knotted.

Brienna kicked at the man taking her to the tent. The glint in Mackey's eye told her all she needed to know. Tossed inside on the ground, she yelled out at the pain in her shoulder when she hit it on the hilt of a sword lying beneath her.

She hadn't time to think how she would escape her predicament before Mackey hovered over her and stripping off his tunic. He carelessly tossed it aside and pulled his shirt off. His muscled body had many ugly gristly scars. He unfastened his breeches and knelt down, shoving her gown up.

"You can't do this. Thane will kill you for not letting him have me untouched," she shrieked.

Mackey caught her kicking legs and spread them open. His hands moved up her legs slowly, restraining them and caressing them with calloused cracked flesh of his palms.

"Thane will believe me when I tell him Brogan had already defiled your precious body. He'll believe nothing else for the length of time you were with him. He'll have expected it and therefore I am doing him a favor by bringing you to him as he thinks you'll be." He laughed and seized the bodice of her gown. With impatience, he ripped the laces free and her breasts bounced loosely beneath the thin undergarment. He drooled during his survey and spittle dripped from his mouth to her skin.

She screamed loud. She thrashed under his heaviness to no avail. He had one hand retaining her arms above her head by a fierce hold on the coarse rope binding her wrists. His other hand roughly squeezed her breast and then swiftly went to yanking up her gown. She struggled, but each twist of her body only helped him raise the brocade further up her legs.

"Get off me, you pig!"

He silenced her with his foul heaving into her mouth. His disgusting wet kisses made her gag on his saliva trickling down her throat. When he managed to have her gown above her knees it helped her to kick violently.

"You are a hellcat to be sure. I'm going to find great pleasure in defiling your body and can only hope you are as virginal as you profess."

Brienna's chest heaved with her panting breath. She took the moments of his speech to gain some strength. It wasn't enough. Mackey ripped the muslin shell of her undergarment so the barrier of even the thinnest cloth between his gaze and her breasts vanished. He stared as if he had found some great treasure. Her eyes widened with the imminent horror and then Mackey's eyes grew painfully large. He came down on her hard.

She wiggled free of his dead weight and drew her elbows together over her chest to conceal her nakedness. Thane stood above with a sword in his hand. Her eyes flitted between his and Mackey's on the ground next to her. His fixed glassy gaze looked as shocked as she felt.

"I understand my virgin bride was on her way to join me, Mackey." He held the sword under Brienna's chin and with a quick slash, cut the binds on her wrists. "While I listened outside your tent, I understand you wanted to make me out to be a buffoon. Why is that? Have I not treated you well?"

Brienna crawled away from Mackey. She watched the life draining from his eyes. She fidgeted with the laces on her gown to tie it back together and never once thought to heal the horrid man.

"Lucky I came along, is it not, my sweet Cousin? I'm sure you would not want this boar drooling on you for very long." He held a hand out to help her up.

"That is all you have in your services, is it not? The swine of all our lands?" she spit out and got up from the ground on her own accord.

"Yes, well most are stupid enough not to try and think for themselves while others, like Mackey, do contain some intelligence. Oddly, it has proven to be a dangerous amount as you can see." He took off his cape and placed it over her shoulders. "Shall I take you to your new home now? I'm sure you have demands I need to agree to before our wedding."

"I can tell them to you now," she said. "In exchange for my willingness to be your wife, I want you to promise never to lay siege on Kylemore."

"Kylemore!" he bellowed.

She cringed.

"You would ask mercy for Torrick's kingdom instead of your own people." He laughed. "How selfish of you, Cousin, and here I thought you were a compassionate woman that was selfless."

"You'll not do anything to Kylemore or Brogan Torrick!"

"How do you know I'd keep such a promise?"

"I don't, but then I suppose you will also have to trust I don't slit your throat one night while you sleep," she retorted.

"I have a demand of my own." He paced before her. "In exchange for this pledge, I will need a child from you. You give me that and Brogan Torrick can rot in that little kingdom of his."

"A child?" She knew he would avail himself of a man's rights, however she hadn't entertained the idea she would bear his children. A much grievous oversight on her part, yet a passing she could no more prevent than her having to accept him to her bed.

"Well? Do we have a deal?" he asked impatiently.

"I need time to adjust to the idea." She spoke slow, not liking anything she had to agree to. "We wed now, but I will not lay with you for one passing of the moon. At which time I will accept your advances and bear your child."

Thane gave her a pleased twist of his thick lips.

"You are every bit as I hoped for in a wife, my Cousin. It must be the Rhoswen bloodline that leaves us cleverly intelligent. I accept your terms. Kylemore is nothing but a small piece of the world I can live without anyways."

"Then I am ready to go." She swept past him and waited outside the tent with him for horses to be brought for their ride to the castle of Thorndale.

"I have one last request of my own Brienna. I have longed to taste those luscious lips of yours. Let me have one kiss to slake my hunger for this month of celibacy you would have me endure." He put his hands on her shoulders and only after she nodded did he slant his mouth over hers.

Chapter 20

Brienna envisioned Brogan. The strength of his features softened when he looked at her. She found desire for the man that could hold pain at bay in the clench of his jaw. He had shed tears in front of her so easily it forever endeared him in her heart.

"You were thinking of him, weren't you?" Thane asked when he came away.

He smoothed a hand over his charcoal beard then raked back his greasy mud-colored hair.

"That's all right, Brienna. You can think about whatever you want. I'll not harness all your fiery independence because it's what I've always admired of you."

She climbed on the horse and looked away to hide the tears she could not stop.

Thane talked all day and when they camped for the night, he had a tent erected with many comforts for her. She didn't sleep very well. Nightmares kept her tossing in the darkness so she woke often with a tear soaked face. While regrets should have had her running to Brogan, it only left her more resolved to go through with her plans.

A day later, they arrived at the castle in Thorndale. She hadn't seen the massive structure, built on the hard work of thousands long dead, in a long time. And looking at the decaying surroundings, it appeared the spirits had stayed behind to bring all of Thorndale to a netherworld with them.

They rode across a dilapidated old drawbridge scarcely looking capable of holding itself up, let alone them as their horses clopped over the planks. The large wood gates opened and Brie looked back only once. Her fate would be sealed after she entered the foreboding maze of towers surrounded by a moat of sludge. It no longer had just the darkened waters she remembered as a child. No, it had become the cesspool of fecal waste and she pinched her nostrils shut to avoid choking on the stench.

"Ah, I see the watering hole we swam in would not suit you anymore." Thane chuckled, reacquainting her with memories of them swimming in the moat.

So much had changed since those yearly years. So many good, decent people were gone while evil spread out from Thane's lands. His dominance and diabolical ways spilled to every thing. Nothing seemed untouched by the blood flowing like wine.

"No, I should say no one has been in that quagmire for a very long time." She exhaled as they distanced themselves from the putrid stink.

"On the contrary, it so happens I had two men tossed to the murky depths before I rode out several days back." He grinned and twisted at his beard. "Needless to say, they found it neither enjoyable nor dissatisfying – they were already dead."

"So it is a grave that encompasses us." She dismounted. "Will it also be mine?"

"Nonsense, my dearest, you shall have a procession of the grandest nature. It would not do to have you tossed out like the rubbish when I am King." He climbed down and limped toward her. "Have no fear, my sweet. As long as you are agreeable, your death is many years away."

"Why go through this masquerade, Thane? You feel nothing for me but contempt. You are jealous I have the power you seek so why would I believe you would keep me around once you are King of Avalbane?"

"At twelve, you were maturing into a beauty I desired."

He guided her up the stairs and stopped at a large door into a bedchamber. His fingers gathered her hair and sniffed.

"You smell wonderful, Cousin, just as I remember, always that heady scent of your blossoming body and your active lifestyle. It can drive a man to madness. Why would I deprive myself of amusements when I can reap the pleasures of your flesh?" He slid a finger down her cheek. "Simply beautiful."

"I stink and need a bath. Would you show me to my chamber?"

"This is your chamber, Brienna. Actually, it is our chamber, but for the month you have requested, it is solely yours. I wouldn't want you to have to change your residence later. I can take another until such time you are ready to fulfill your duties."

"Fine. Now will you have a tub filled and I'll need a woman that sews to make me a wardrobe as I have nothing but this rag." She walked around and inspected the pillages he had kept for himself. Golden vases, jeweled goblets and bone handled toiletries.

"I have just the servant, a special gift to make you feel more at home." He opened the door to her dressing room. "Come in and see to your Queen."

"Your Highness!" Medora rushed to kneel at Brienna's feet.

Brienna looked down at her with relief. Yet, she had no desire to have Thane know of her affections for the woman. It would be so easy for Thane to punish her by executing her handmaid if he thought they were friends.

"I wish for Medora to be sent immediately to Avalbane. I prefer a servant of your household to attend me."

"Very well, it will be done immediately. Anything else I can do for you, dearest?" Thane waved for the girl to leave them.

"No, nothing I can think of. Wait. Do you think we can have the wedding as soon as possible?"

"Ah, that would get our month's wait started all the sooner. Is tonight to your liking?" He collected her hands and brushed a kiss over her knuckles.

"Tonight will suit me very well."

She sat and waited while servants filled a tub with warm water. She had Medora brought to her so she could bid her farewell and a safe journey. Thane went off to arrange for their marriage. It left her alone with her thoughts.

Brogan filled them. She wondered and worried how he would take the news. Would he hate her, distrust her words and brush his hands glad to be rid of her? Or would he be foolish and not look to what she did, but what he wanted?

She ordered Jinn to go home to Avalbane after they left the Torricks' castle in Kylemore. He had been reluctant at first, but when she explained he could better serve her there than he could dead, he agreed. They both knew Thane would not let her keep an old warrior as her servant. He had been afraid for her safety, but no more so than she was for herself. There was not even a thread of doubt in her mind Thane would betray her. When, how, and where were the only answers she didn't have but hoped to control. Until he brought to light his true plans for their future, she would have to stay alert.

The bath soothed her muscles. She didn't think she'd ever again have a tub filled with clean water, scented with herbal fragrances. She motioned for the servant to wash her hair. The lavender infused soap actually lifted her spirits. She pulled a piece of her hair under her nose and sniffed.

"I'm sorry." She giggled. "Reliving a memory."

Once clean, Brienna put on the gown Thane had sent to her room. She assumed it came from the spoils of war.

She stood in front of the looking glass and studied her face. It was evident she'd had the stress of the past days wearing her nerves thin. Her eyes were puffy from a lack of sleep and crying. Her skin sallow from her lack of nutrition since she couldn't eat with the sickness she was feeling since she'd left the safety of Brogan's castle.

Once she was ready, she joined Thane in the great hall. She appreciated the minimum of people attending the event of her marriage. When they were through with the ceremony, Thane kissed her hand.

"You're free to go to bed," he told her.

She didn't argue and fled the room with the greatest of relief. Besides, it wouldn't be a wedding he and his men celebrated. They would drink to victory.

† † †

The stench of ale wafting over her face made her sick. She opened her eyes in surprise. Next to her, Thane lay sleeping. His heavy rasp of steady breathing came with a low grating snore. His leaden arm folded on her stomach so the meaty fingers of his left hand could latch onto her right breast.

The dreams of Brogan caressing horrifyingly were Thane mauling her while she slept.

Brienna slid out from under the burdensome arm. She stared at Thane sprawled naked on the bedding. She gave only a second's notice to his scarred back and his hairy buttocks and legs. Then she turned away to dress and get out of the room. Her stomach turned queasily into a brew of churning bile and she dropped the gown over her head.

She followed the passages down to the dinning hall and sat at the table where the night before a feast had been spread. A variety of delicacies sat alongside meats, cheeses, and fruits.

"Is there anything I can get for you, Your Highness?" A servant stood ready for her orders and Brienna thought, *yes, you can get me a new life.*

"I'd like some food. Anything will be fine."

"Yes, Your Highness."

The woman scampered off and when she returned, she had a tray of various edibles. Brienna broke a piece of bread off a loaf. She picked pieces off and stuffed them in her mouth chewing each bite leisurely. She wondered what she would do next. She contemplated what Thane would do as well.

When Brienna finished eating, she took a walk through the halls and let more favorable memories of Thane come to mind. Somehow, she had to learn to live with him on some sort of terms.

"Your Highness, can I help you find anything?" Another servant approached her and stood ready to do her bidding.

"No, thank you. I'm just looking around on my own. It's been many years since I was here last." She had found much changed from her recollections. Thane took pride in displaying the wealth he stole from his people.

"If you like that, I'll have it put in our room," Thane voiced with a graveled harsh tone.

She whirled around to confront him about just that very subject. "For a month, that was to be my room, not ours."

"You are angry I was in bed with you. Sheer habit, I think. I drank too much ale and my servants assisted me to my room. A room they knew contained my bride." His mouth cocked with a hideous grin that reminded her of a person with mental afflictions.

"You said I could have the month."

"Without me taking pleasures, not sleeping, we'll keep the arrangement as is. I see no reason for talk that my wife has cuckolded me. What would my other women say? They might get it in their minds to refuse me." He looked around the room. "You girl, come here."

A young girl hurried to Thane with a smile on her face. She looked too happy to get the attention and she appeared too young for Thane to be trifling with the child. He twisted the girl around and held her small body tight.

Brienna wasn't prepared to see him rip the dress off the tiny shoulder and kiss the girl's tender skin. When his massive hands squeezed the girl's small breasts hard, she cried out and then giggled.

"This is how submissive you will be after the one cycling of the moon."

He gathered the wispy girl up and sat her on an oak table. He pushed her so hard she fell back on the flat surface. His large hands, gnarled from having been broken many times, shoved the girl's woolen skirt up to her thin milky thighs.

"Let me give you a presentation of what you are missing." He chuckled with a sinister harshness to his voice and then started undoing his breeches.

"You're sadistic!" Brienna shouted. "A horrid pig of a man! Leave her be."

She jerked at his arm to pull him away, but his stance remained locked. His fingers suddenly were around her throat and he pulled her mouth to his. The more she struggled, the tighter his fingers drew together. She had to struggle to get even the slightest bit of air. Her mouth hurt and her throat still felt closed off when he thrust her away.

"Wait your turn and see what else I can do to make you gasp, dear Cousin." He laughed so evilly that she could only think if she didn't get out, she would be next. She could not help the girl.

As Brienna ran across the great hall, she tried to block out the sounds of Thane's grunts of copulation.

"That's it little one. Wiggle for Papa," he groaned. "Oh yes, that's the way Papa likes it."

The sweet tinkling of her laugher and the melodic mewls were all wrong. Thane's verbalizations made her sick. She knew then that she couldn't let Thane touch her, let alone her give him a child.

Brienna ran to a door to escape. She rattled it, but the lock wouldn't give.

"Yes, oh yes," he moaned. "Oh God, you're small. Just like my little cousin. I bet you would feel good, Brienna," he said over his shoulder.

She hurried for another door. Thane's howls of culmination began pounding in her head.

"Oh, yes!" he groaned.

The girl giggled again and it seemed so out of place. So horribly unreal he could be related to her in any way. The girl's moans and giggles became incessant.

"Shut up!" he roared.

Brienna heard the slap he gave the girl. The table thumped the wall. Each crack of the wood against the stone came with whimpers.

"Stop!" Brienna shouted.

He continued to grunt louder. The girl cried. He smacked her again and Brienna looked for a weapon. Before she could move, she dropped to the floor and retched. Thane's thick strangled roar filled the room. The girl's shrill cry had the sounds of rapture not pain.

"Get out," Thane bellowed at the girl.

Brienna crawled to the next exit. She found it unbolted. Thane's hand grabbed her arm. She tried to free the vise-like grip of his claws digging into her flesh, but she might as well have tried to unlock an eagle's talons from his prey.

He hauled her up and she spit at him. The back of his hand met her face. She fell back against a similar table. When he grabbed her and hoisted her onto it, she felt panic welling inside her. He couldn't get her gown up as easily as the girl's because she fought back. He managed it to her knees before she kicked him in the groin.

He doubled over and than charged her before she could get off the table. She sat up and threw a copper bowl at him. He ducked and hit her so hard she saw stars. She heard the dress rip at the shoulder and swung her hand. It caught him on the jaw. The slap did not even make him hesitate and he grabbed both her wrists and pinned them above her head. Holding them with one hand, he mauled her breast through the thick fabric.

Brienna lay still, her chest heaving.

"Yes, that's the way Papa likes his little ones. See, you like this, all women like to feel extra special."

She closed her eyes and felt his hands let go of her wrists. He held her face and kissed her mouth hard and then gentle. She let things lull in his mind while the tornado spun in hers.

"That's it. Now we're getting somewhere." He leaned down and slid her dress up.

His hands stroked her legs. He got the dress to her knees and freed her legs. She bit down hard on his lip and kicked him away with all her might. She jumped off the table and met another blow from the back of his hand. It sent her sprawling to the unyielding cold hard stone floor.

"Don't try my patience, Brienna. I'm giving into your demands only because I want you to willingly strip for me. I want to see those delicate pink-tipped fingers stroke me with the wanton desires I draw from your fresh supple body. I want to hear pleading moans come from your throat begging me to not stop dipping my cock into the sweet honey of your cunt."

Brienna only understood one thing listening to him. She'd be dead, or he would, before he would get any of that from her.

"However," he continued and reached down, pulling her up from the floor with one hand and pinned her to him so her arms were behind her back. "Know that at any time I choose I can rip that gown from your lovely body and take what I please, as you very well know." He tossed her away with his warning and then stalked off.

Brienna slid down the wall and drew her legs up to put her head on her knees. Every ounce of her fought crying. She was so angry that it wasn't hard to hold back the tears this time. She had made a grave mistake in coming to Thane. He was more vile than she could have ever have dreamed. He had no morals and therefore he could not be trusted to keep any promises.

She sat on the floor for a long time, not caring who saw her or how it might embarrass Thane. She had seen Medora off the day before and prayed for her speedy journey. She knew she had been right in sending her to Avalbane. With the way Thane was, she didn't dare consider Medora may have already fallen prey to his rapacious lust.

"Mama. Mama."

Brienna looked up at the wee child grabbing her hair.

"Oh, I'm sorry, Your Highness. My babe just snuck out of the kitchen without me knowing." The girl Thane had just used on the table stood before her.

Brienna put her legs down and sat the wee one on her lap. "What's his name?" she asked, bouncing the child up and down on her knee.

"Soren," she answered quietly.

"What is your name?" Brienna looked up at the timid girl.

"Nora, Your Highness."

The girl that seemed limitless with life in front of Thane was as meek as a mouse now.

"How old are you?" She cooed at the child and continued to bounce him up and down to hear his burbles of pleasure.

"Eighteen."

Brienna quickly calculated the girl had been fifteen or even younger when he first bedded her, by the fact she had a two year old child.

"You're son is beautiful," she told the girl and handed him up to her.

"Yes, don't you think he has Lord Rhoswen's green eyes? He says my other wee babe more resembles him. He thinks this one belongs to Mackey." She kissed Soren's temple and held him lovingly.

"You have another babe?" Brienna got off the floor and brushed mindlessly at the wrinkles in the gown. The girl was not only used by Thane, but his men as well? The outrage she had welling in her was murderous.

"Aye, Your Highness, his name is Ronan and I'm hoping to have me a girl in five months." She rubbed a hand over her seemingly flat belly, indicating she carried another child.

Brienna went in search of a private chamber. Her husband had two children and another on the way. He bred the girl like a wild animal and she'd grow old quickly under the steady strain of childbirth if she lived through all of them.

Once she found a quiet, solitary place out of sight, she knelt down and convulsed with dry heaves. Thane's perverse life soured her stomach. For the rest of the day she hid herself away in her room. Periodically, servants would come to see if she wanted anything, but she knew Thane had sent them to check up on her.

Boredom pushed her from the room and she lingered outside the great hall to hear Thane in conversation with several men.

"Our lookouts have spotted him on the fringes of the forest," one skinny man said.

"So, Brogan has come seeking my wife, no doubt. She's a prize that even he cannot give up. Very well, lay in wait until the opportunity is right and seize him. I don't care about his men, but I want Brogan Torrick brought to me alive," he laughed. "After all, I did promise my wife I wouldn't bother Kylemore or Torrick. I have another twenty nine days before I can kill the cur."

"Yes, Lord Rhoswen, we'll see to it immediately," the man replied.

"And, Duff, remember I need him alive. However I don't care how much damage is inflicted on him before he reaches my feet." He stomped his boot to make his point.

Brienna gasped and backed away.

"You might as well come in," Thane shouted. "I know you've been listening, Cousin!"

She raised her chin and marched into the room.

"You promised."

"He's being brought here alive," Thane wheezed.

"You plan to kill him."

"Well I can't very well have him here trying to kill me, can I?"

He motioned for her to sit in the chair next to him, a seat that was not there before that day.

"You explain to him if he keeps to his lands, then we shall never see each other again. And if he does not comply, than he'll give me no choice but to kill him."

"If I do this, you'll send him home?"

"I have no wish to upset my plans with you. I intend on making you swell with my offspring," he chuckled. "And I want you to enjoy it."

"Do you not have enough children already with Nora carrying your third? How many other servants are walking around with your bastard children?" Her words were meant to be a cutting chastisement, but the effect was wasted on Thane.

"I don't know that any of the wench's children are mine. The girl has been had by dozens of my men and ridden more in one day than any of my horses."

She hated him. The graphic correlation was far more than she wanted to know. The whole affair sickened her. The mere thought of it again made her stomach flip-flop in protest of the memory of Thane's grunts.

"I don't want the child touched by anyone again. She's nothing more than a babe herself and the fact she is carrying a wee one inside her is all the more reason for her to be left alone."

"I'll give orders for no one to touch her until she's empty of the brat if that pleases you."

"It does, thank you."

She stood to go and could not believe the sight that came through the big cross buck plank doors. The well-worn steel hinges did not make the slightest noise. The man thrown to the floor cried out with a draconian pain that dropped her back in the seat.

Brogan, her heart cried.

Chapter 21

"Ah, just the man you've been waiting to have a talk with, my wife." Thane took Brie's hand in his and held it up to his lips to kiss.

Brogan picked his head up and his eyes squinted to focus on Brie. He could see her lovely face filled with sorrow before it slumped into an insipid countenance of apathy.

"Well, Torrick. Do you not want to wish my bride good fortune? I'm sorry we could not invite all nobles to our wedding, but she insisted we wed last night," he gloated. "Maybe you will have invitation to attend my coronation as her King."

Thane ran a hand down the side of Brie's face and she sat still and accepting of the man's touch.

"Why have you come?" she asked him.

While her features were unmoved by his presence and her words filled his head with things he did not want to hear from her luscious lips, her violet eyes gave away the pleading of her heart for him not to challenge her decision.

"It is your wish to stay here, Your Highness?" He bowed his head, unable to look her in the eye for fear he'd do something rash.

"I've married Thane by my own choice."

She walked to him. He could smell the lavender of her perfumed body. He could hear the catches in her breath.

"Of course I wish to stay here. I think I made it clear in my message to you that my place was here. All Rhoswen lands will

Sword of Rhoswen

be joined as they were before my father and Thane's father split the providences."

"Well spoken, my love."

Thane came to stand along side her. He drew her up against him and brushed a kiss over her lips. A moan escaped her and he hated that it sounded like pleasure. Thane sucked at her mouth and sandwiched her between his chest and the hands he had rampaging over her back and bottom.

"She's mine, Torrick, body and soul, to do with as pleases me."

He snatched a handful of her golden hair and jerked her head back roughly. He slobbered kisses along the side of her slender neck. Brogan could not turn away his eyes. He cringed each time Thane touched his Lass. He knew for certain he would kill Thane Rhoswen the first chance he got.

When Thane grabbed her breast, Brogan attempted to get up. The foot that kicked him in the ribs put him flat on the stone floor.

"Do you think I could wait for you in our bedchamber now?" Brie's voice whispered.

"Yes, a very good idea indeed. You go ready for me."

Brogan glanced up and watched her leave.

"Take him to the dungeon. Chain him to the wall and we'll decide later what to do with him." Thane ordered. "No one sees him and that includes my wife."

† † †

Satisfied Brogan was to remain alive for the moment, she ran to her room. In the trunks and cabinets, she looked for a knife, a weapon of any sort to kill Thane. She couldn't live another minute with the thought of him touching her again. Every salivating lick of his tongue to her skin left her sticky and sick.

When not even a small dagger could be had in the room filled with trinkets of his plundering villages and other lands, she hurled objects at the stone wall.

"Your Highness!" Nora wailed, rushing in the room. "Whatever is wrong?"

Brienna seized the girl's wrists. "Don't you let another man touch you, do you understand me? It's wrong and they'll be sent to hell for abusing you in such a way."

"But they give me presents. Look." She held up a pendant. A large pewter cross with a ring about the intersection of the crossbar and upright shaft. The Celtic cross had shamefully come to be a token for her promiscuity.

"Nora, it is wrong to let them treat you like this. I will give you what you and your children need. All I ask, is you have nothing more to do with any man. It could hurt your babe." She put a hand to the girl's abdomen.

"It can? But my others were fine."

"One day a man may get too rough. Please, Nora, do this for me. Thane has agreed." She saw the smile play at the girl's mouth.

"He doesn't want any men to touch me anymore?"

Brienna felt pain for the way the girl loved the wrong kind of man. She lived to please him.

"No, he doesn't and he won't touch you either until the babe is born. He doesn't want his child harmed."

"I won't do it anymore. I want Thane to be proud of me. Maybe if I have a little girl, he will love her."

"Yes, maybe he will."

Unfortunately, recognizing Thane for a beast, Brienna feared just how he would notice once the babe grew by a dozen years.

"You're so lucky, Your Highness. To be married to him and share his bed every night," she sighed.

"Lucky? It should be you that is his wife and sharing his bed. You are the one producing his children. I should never have come here and I wish I could leave." Brienna walked around and picked up the objects she had thrown at the wall. She placed them back in their original places, turning the dents away from sight.

"You want to leave?" Nora asked.

"Yes, but Thane would never let me go. I'm more like a prisoner here instead of the mistress of this castle." She sat on the edge of the bed and picked at some of the gold threads in the gown.

"I can help you leave if you really want to go." Nora smiled at her and touched her hand.

Brienna looked up at the girl. "Can you also tell me how to get Brogan Torrick out of the dungeon, because I can't leave without him?"

The girl nodded her head.

"You can?"

"I know a way."

"Then we go now." Brienna looked in the dim passageway to make sure no one lurked outside her chamber door to hear the plans she made. "We'll need a horse, is that possible?"

"Yes, Your Highness. I can come and go as I like from the castle."

"Then tell me how to get away from here."

"This way, Your Highness." Nora led her down stairwell after stairwell.

"I've never been this far below the main levels."

She had, of course, played in the castle and went many places she wasn't supposed to go, but she never went in the dungeons. To a child, the place couldn't be more scary.

† † †

"I'm sorry, Your Highness. My orders are no one, not even you, are to be allowed in the cell with Lord Torrick," the guard said.

Brogan picked up his head.

"What is your name and that of the man that did not give you new orders?"

The Lass spoke and his heart lifted.

"Thane said I could have five minutes. I have no wish to go back and tell him how I was mistreated by my request. Of course, the punishment may only be for the man that forgot to tell you. However, we both know my husband is a cruel man. He will exact punishment down the line for mere fun. It would be a shame to see you tossed in that dreadfully filthy moat."

"Well, Your Highness, I suppose it really can't do no harm, seeing how he's chained up. You be careful of him though and keep a right good distance or it'll be me head if you should come to harm in there." He unlocked the door.

Brogan stared at her as if he'd gone to heaven and they sent the prettiest angel. She floated inside the door and then he heard her speak.

"Shut the door," she ordered the guard. "I do not wish anyone to hear the vile things I plan on calling him."

Brogan watched the wide toothy smile on the guard.

"You tell him right good, Your Highness." He shut the door, leaving them alone.

Brie rushed to him.

"What are ye doing here?" he grumbled painfully when his one arm dropped.

He clutched his side.

"I should ask you the same. Thane has given me his word and you'll spoil everything by trying to take me away."

"Ye can't trust him. Thane will betray ye."

"Eventually, yes, but not before you have time to build your force stronger and prepare for him. You have a minimum of four or five months."

"How can ye be sure?" He leaned on her as she guided him to the wall next to the door.

"Now hold still." Her fingers ignited with the amber glow.

Brogan closed his eyes and could feel the healing heat radiating through him. "Lass, I could have used your mystical powers a lot through my life and for those of the men I have lost."

"You have five minutes to gain what strength you can and then the guard will return to make me leave. I can get you outside the castle to a horse I have waiting, then I want you to go home and forget me, Brogan."

"If I could do that I would not be here. Ye go with me. For 'tis the only way I will leave, Lass. Ye do not get to dictate my future." He put all his energy in pulling her to him and capturing her mouth in his fervid kiss. "I will die before I leave ye here, Brienna Rhoswen. I love ye."

"I'm married," she cried under his lips.

He devoured the tremble to her words with promises. "I will be annulling your marriage personally. Ye belong to me by contract and by love. I will release ye from neither." He held her face. "I did not misunderstand ye words in that note, did I?"

She shook her head. Her sweet kisses over every inch of his face with tender adoration gave him the strength he needed. Her surrendering tears gave him the mindful will to triumph. The proffering of her devotion was the last fortification he needed.

"Oh, I love you so much," she murmured, clinging to him. "I'm sorry I didn't trust you could want me."

"Do not be sorry for anything, Lass. I should never have said what I did about the Rhoswens. Thane is the only one to taint the name and I will make sure he is gone and soon forgotten." He kissed her wet cheeks. "I promise no one will ever punish your heritage because of one bad seed."

The rattle of keys in the door separated them. Brie stepped aside so he could grab the guard. He hauled the dimwitted fellow into the cell and promptly knocked him out with a well-placed blow of his knuckles to his face.

He took her hand and let her lead them through the dungeon passages. When another guard came along jingling keys and whistling merrily without care, Brie shook his hand loose. He stayed hidden while she moved into plain sight.

"Excuse me, but Thane told me I could find a door this way. Would you mind pointing the direction to me?" She coyly smiled and batted her eyes at the young man.

"I can show you, but the door is locked, Your Highness."

"Oh that shouldn't be a problem. He gave me a key. Of course, he wasn't sure this is the right one. Could you tell me if it will work?" She held the large ring up with the key she used to unchain Brogan.

"No, Your Highness, that one will never work. This here is the key. I'll show you the door and let you through."

"Oh, would you? I wanted to take the short way around to my husband and I'm already late."

Brogan peered around the corner. He watched Brie charm the guard, and then she gestured for him to follow. He kept to the alcoves and side passages until they reached the door. He waited until the man unlocked and opened the door. Once Brie was outside, Brogan rushed the man. He hit him as hard as the last guard in his way.

The horses stood a short distance from the door. The one thing they hadn't counted on were the sentries and their keen eyes from atop the turrets.

"The prisoner is escaping!" A voice rang the alert.

"Your Highness." Brogan boosted Brie up onto her horse and then mounted the other himself. "I suggest we do not dawdle too long in this spot."

The horses jumped the hedges one after the other. Brogan's hit with an unbalanced thud and he barreled over the horse's head to the ground. He hit hard and moments later, another horse leapt the wall of greenery and he saw the hooves coming dangerously close toward him.

He rolled into the stream and painfully learned he broke his arm. The horse cleared him and the man jumped down to attack. Brogan staggered to his feet to defend himself the best he could. His eyes went past the man.

"Keep going!" he ordered Brie when he saw her spin the horse back toward him.

She came like a thunderbolt and in seconds knocked the man from his feet with her swift kick to his back. The man fell, face forward into the stream. Brie swung her horse around and skidded to a stop. She hopped down and ran to Brogan.

"'Tis busted pretty bad," he said, looking at her examination of his arm.

"Ah, m'lord, have you know faith in what your eyes have shown you before?" She smiled.

She laid her hands to his arm and traveled from finger to shoulder with the amber glow caressing him. The warmth tingled and soothed so it felt better than new.

"Come here, my enchantress." He lifted his arm over her head and drew her against him. "I do not want ye to ever put yourself in harm's way again for me."

"You really think there is time to argue this now, Lord Torrick?" She kissed him and pushed back out of his embrace. "We should go."

"Lass, I hope ye do not go lighting the fire in every man's heart or I shall truly have a hard time keeping ye mine."

He swung up behind her on the horse and they set off on a gallop for the woods before any of Thane's other men could find them. They rode until the steed lathered. Brogan feared they could push him no further without his collapse. He slid off the horse. Brie slid down into his arms. She had the vim and vigor of any able-bodied man. He found it hard to deny her the respect of equality, but he liked when she let him treat her like a woman.

"Why are you smiling?"

"I never considered I could love a woman."

She hugged him and he groaned.

"Oh, Brogan, your ribs."

He watched her fingers light-up. Her hands floated over his chest. He gripped her fingers and pulled them to his lips. "'Tis enough, Lass."

She nodded.

"They will look for us to head straight to Kylemore. 'Tis time we work toward the same goals. We will take shelter for the night and come morning, go back to Thorndale."

"Return to Thane's castle?"

"If ye do not wish to go, I will not make ye, Lass, but I have to go back and finish off your husband. He will not take from me all that is mine. My father is gone and I cannot bring him back, but I will not give him my home or..." He elevated her chin and kissed lightly her soft lips. "My heart."

"I go where you go and nothing could ever change my mind." She folded her arms over his shoulders and brought him down to kiss her again.

"Must be wee fairies spinning those magical spells about," a man said from a cart they had not heard roll up to them.

"Nay sir, 'tis only the charms of one wee Lass that has me heart captive." Brogan looked over the cart of hay pulled by an ox. "Might ye be interested in trading your conveyance for this fine horse?"

"What is wrong with the horse that you would offer a more valuable animal for these rickety trappings?" He looked at the horse with a skeptical scrutiny.

"M'lady is tired of riding on the creature and your hay would give her a softer ride. Besides, we need a place to sleep so it will serve us well."

"I don't know. That looks too good of an offer. Did you steal the horse from Thane Rhoswen's estate? That man plagues us with his taxes and if he finds out we have a horse of his, then hell will be to pay for sure."

"I will not lie to ye, sir. We did take the horse but he will be more interested in the fact that I stole his wife." Brogan waited for the man's reaction.

"In that case, you keep the horse and I'll offer you my home to sleep in. Anyone to do something as foolish as that needs all the help he can get." He pointed to the back of the cart. "Tie your horse on and climb aboard. We'll be to my village in the quarter hour."

"Thank ye. I am Brogan Torrick and this lovely lady is Brienna Rhoswen of Avalbane."

"Avalbane, huh? I cannot believe that you have joined leagues with the devil, m'lady. King Padric Rhoswen has always been against Thane Rhoswen of Thorndale."

"My father, the king, is dead and I made an unwise decision. Lord Torrick is going to correct that." She put her head against Brogan's arm while lacing her fingers with his.

"Lord Torrick? Of Kylemore?" he said with amazement.

"Brogan's father was killed by Thane's men. So there are many reasons for Thane to part this world." She hugged his arm tighter.

"Yes, many reasons." He nodded.

The man asked no more questions and they rode along to a village of about two dozen ramshackle huts.

"The night gets cool, Your Highness, and the comfort of our home is the least we can offer the Queen of Avalbane," the man told her.

"What is your name?"

"Elgin, Your Highness."

"Elgin, we require a modest amount of food and the privacy of a night under the stars in your wagon. That is all. For this, we will be grateful." She took his hands. "And I need not ask you keep our presence to a minimal amount of people. It is for your safety as well as our own."

"You need not worry, Your Highness, no one here would give Lord Rhoswen a drink of water let alone information." He brought them a loaf of bread, goat cheese, and a chuck of salted ham. A considerable bit more than modest, but she accepted his kindness.

"Why not sleep inside their hut?" Brogan asked after he had his fill of the food.

"Because I'll not have them sleep outside for the sake of my comfort and while they could remain inside with us and then we could not be alone." Her fingers skated down his chest over the blood spattered, filthy shirt. "Tell me this is not the time, the place, or that you don't want to touch me as I want you to."

Brogan unfastened her gown enough to draw it off her shoulders. The pearly skin begged his lips to touch light to the softness. He expected the thin under-dress he'd seen before. He found her barren of any other garments. He kissed the gold brocade down lower, until her arms lifted out of the sleeves. The fabric hung on her breasts.

Brienna pulled the laces loose and lowered the gown herself. It caught to her hips and she pushed it free. He looked over the curves. He felt them while she pushed his shirt up and kissed his ribs.

He dropped his britches and he picked her up to lie in the hay. His hand cradled her head and he followed the contours of her face to find a flaw, there was only one, a tiny scar on her neck that he had put there.

"Why did ye not heal this?" He kissed the blemish.

"I was deserving of this infliction for the one I gave to you. I could not heal yours so I would not heal mine." She twisted her head to have him kiss over the scar again.

"Lass, I do not fault ye for what ye think ye had to do." He rubbed his finger over her bottom lip.

"I waited my entire life for you," she purred. "I've given myself to no other but you."

Chapter 22

Brogan left her mouth with serene splashes of his tongue over the pale pink tips of her breasts. She shivered and the areolas shriveled in protest to the cool breeze. It made the tantalizing pearls larger and more prominently peaked for his lavish attention. He bathed the spires, lapping up the vibrating beads until they softened into radiant scarlet mountains.

The moans of extreme rapture moved Brogan from her breasts down to her satiny flat belly.

"Ye are exquisite, Brie," he hummed over her flesh making it quiver with excitement.

Her fingers raked fistfuls of his hair in agitation. He moved lower and licked the sensitive inside of her supple thigh. The skin quivered and he rubbed over it with his palm to quell her nervous shutter.

He put his arms under her thighs and gripping her buttocks, he gathered her up to lap at the soft fleece nestled between her legs.

Her hips rose with spontaneous eruptions. Brogan drank in the angelic flux of heaven before lowering her back to the hay.

He mounted her. The instant her body involuntarily bucked and jerked, he filled her with his hard throbbing cock.

"I love ye, Brienna Rhoswen. I will love ye forever," he whispered in her ear.

He kissed her mouth tightly until her jaw stopped trembling.

He made his thrusts slow and gentle until she fell into a rhythm with him, engaging the fervor in them. Brienna's fingers were like a flurry of fairies tapping up and down his spine. Her body quaked with turbulent spasms that made her hips grind to his harder. He delved deeper with his intrusion and loved the way she wanted him. His accommodating lurch of stabs inside the tight sheath brought out choked whines of ecstasy. Her fingers ensnared his hair and she gave him no liberty to move from her greedy mouth.

She sucked at his tongue. Licking over it greedily. He perused her mouth in the same manner so she kissed him with her wild abandon. The exhilaration shackled his mind. The lust in which he hungered to sate, the thirst for her love, he devoured. Her body convulsed with a wicked enthrallment. Brogan pounded in hesitant jolts and his grunted voice, thick with emotion, ground out sentiments she deserved to know.

"Trust that I will love ye forever, Brie," he groaned.

Her chest heaved in gasped breaths. Her hard nipples tickled his chest hairs and sent sizzling streams of fire shuddering to his cock.

The delicious woman bathing him in her hot juices drove him closer to the edge of ejaculation. Her sultry whimpers, her ecstatic whines, and the speckled kisses she pummeled his face with were an added bonus to the way her body responded to him. He'd never had a woman so freely relinquish herself to the passion of lust with such reckless ardor. Brie's intensity in conquering passion's yearning matched her fierce skill with a sword. Their joint climax exploded the silent night with their carnal cries. Brogan muted most with his kiss so the animalistic sounds of copulation did not bring villagers to their bed of salacious indecency.

"Lass, ask me to take ye away from all this madness of our lands and I will whisk ye away to a distant shore where only we exist." He rolled to his back, keeping her a part of him.

"I would if I thought we could be eternally happy without another thought of our clans, but I know guilt would destroy us. But for these times we can share, know my thoughts will never venture outside of this paradise we steal from heaven." She kissed his chin and snuggled into his body.

He reached above them to take a blanket Elgin had lent them and fluffed it in the air so it floated down over them. The wool offered warmth and concealment of their nakedness until later, after Brogan took his lover to the brink of madness in ecstasy again.

Heaven could not offer him anything better than the fetching hush of love the Lass breathed upon his chest in her slumber. She laughed when he tickled her ear with his tongue.

"Ye know we need to go soon, Lass."

She smoothed over the lines in his face with her fingers. "I know."

"Ye could stay here and wait for me. Ye know I would feel better for it." He sifted the fine threads of her hair through his fingers.

"I go where you go, remember?"

"I can only but ask ye, Brie, I will not order ye." He kissed her nose and then got them both up from the bed of hay.

"It is a good thing you do not try. To think you would even be so bold to suggest to the Queen of Avalbane you might tender a command is pure arrogance, m'lord."

He tossed her back in the hay.

"Good morning." Elgin made his way to them. "Your sleep was well?"

"Very well." Brie jumped off the wagon and brushed the bits of hay from her dress.

Brogan pulled pieces from her hair.

"Excellent. I've had my son equip a horse for your travels. I hope it will be far from Thorndale." He waved to a lad no more than ten.

"Thank ye Elgin." Brogan clasped the man's extended arm. "When Thorndale falls, if ye wish to make a new life somewhere else than in the shadows of that decaying castle..." He pointed up a hill where a lone spire protruded. "Come to Kylemore."

"Or Avalbane," Brie added, nudging him.

"Aye, or Avalbane." He draped an arm over her shoulders and hugged her.

Elgin left them to go.

They took the familiar route and Brogan let the countryside flash by with cautious observance. From the emerald green pastures rolling out like a jeweled carpet to the thick forests with a blur of trees forming gray stripes, his peripheral vision watched only for movement.

"Nora told me a different route that we could take and I think the one over the back meadow would hide our arrival best," Brie voiced.

"Aye, of all the ways in, I think that may be the safest." He reached out to invite her hand to his. "No gallantry beyond what will keep ye from harm, okay?"

"Brogan, I can't promise you that."

"Lass, please!"

Brie shook her head. "I won't promise it. You can't make me turn from helping you if I can."

"Your Highness." He heaved a big sigh. "Ye vex a man to no end."

"But you still love me, don't you?" she coyly teased.

"Aye, Lass, nothing ye could say or do would change that." He smiled. "Maybe I will grow to like my feathers ruffled by ye.

Now do ye think ye could give my vain ego some slack and let me go first?"

"After you, m'lord." She waved her arm in a flourish and gave a nod of her head.

† † †

They found the castle a shell of stone. Thane had taken every able-bodied man to Kylemore. Brogan looked at her with a dreadful consternation. He feared the worse for his lands.

"Your Highness, come to your chamber quickly. Nora has been calling for you." A woman rushed to her.

"Why? What is wrong?"

Brienna only gave Brogan a fleeting glance before she ran to what had been her room for only one day. Nora lay in a tangle of bloodied sheets moaning with pain.

"Oh my God!"

"Lord Rhoswen beat her until she lost the babe then had his way with her. The blood doesn't stop."

A woman sat on the far side of the bed stuffing wads of cloth between the girl's legs.

"She's been crying for you all night."

"Nora, I'm here, Nora."

"Your Highness, he said he made you a promise. He said you told him not to touch me until I wasn't carrying a babe inside," she sobbed. "He said he could make that brat come out immediately. Why would he hurt me? I've always loved him."

Brienna's jaw trembled with the horror of what could only be her fault. She held the girl tight and kissed her head.

"Oh God, Nora, he's not a man. He's a demon that plagues us all with cruelty. I'm so sorry." She held Nora tighter and rocked her gently.

"Who'll take care of my babes?" she cried weakly.

"I will, Nora. I told you I'd always take care of you and your children. I promise you they will grow up with every luxury I can afford them," she cried harder, feeling the girl's life slipping away. "Nora, oh please, Nora, don't leave us."

Brienna laid Nora back on the pillow and without another thought to the servants in the room she laid her hands over the injured part of the girl's body. She concentrated with the urgency but the soft healing light would not glow from her hands.

"Brogan?"

He took her hands. "What is wrong? Why are ye not healing her?"

"I don't know. I just don't know. I've always had command of the power."

"Lord Torrick?" Nora looked to Brogan.

"Aye?"

"Queen Rhoswen. You'll take care of her?"

"Aye, Nora, always."

"Good because Lord Rhoswen said he was going to kill her. I don't want him to hurt her like he done to me."

Brienna watched her eyes drift shut.

Brogan pulled her up from the edge of the bed and held her.

"It's my fault. If I hadn't interfered with her life, if I'd just stayed here, she'd be alive." She cried with racking sobs she couldn't control. "I've done something terribly wrong and I don't know how to change it." She looked at her hands. "Yesterday, you... I healed you, why not Nora?"

"Come on, Brie. We have to go to Kylemore. I know ye are hurting, but we have to go."

"Brogan, if you don't kill him I will. He took that girl's life and that of her babe out of pure hatred for me. He can't be allowed to destroy anymore lives."

She rubbed the tears from her face and looked at the two women with their heads bowed in silent mourning. "I'll be back for Nora's children. Please take care of them until my return."

"They'll be well looked after, Your Highness, you need not think of them."

"They are Rhoswens and by right and my pledge to their dead mother, I fully intend on caring for them personally."

"The Queen and I will be back for the wee ones after we settle some business in Kylemore."

"Yes, m'lord."

He kissed Brienna's hand. "We will raise them as our own, with our own," he whispered.

How could she love him more than she already did? He knew her heart and mind so well at times. It would seem destiny made their marriage arrangement, not their fathers.

Brogan stopped and held her back when a man came bounding up the stairs toward them. They had been wrong thinking no one had been left behind. The man charged Brogan with his sword, but missed as he twisted away.

Brienna lifted a vase. She saw Brogan's eyes turn on her with a want to stop her. But he grinned, knowing he could not tame her so long as the winds swept the land.

"Now, my Lass." He pushed the man further past him so he fell to the floor and Brienna crowned the man in the head.

"Some use comes from Thane's plunders," she said, looking at the brass urn. "Oh look, he has ruined it." She showed Brogan the dent. "And my sword!"

The man groaned and she hit him again with the urn. Brogan picked up her blade. He hefted the weight of it in his hand and then offered her the hilt over his arm.

"Your sword, Your Highness." He bowed his head.

She felt safe in the presence of her sword. It had been her shield, her guardian, and it symbolized her mother's strength. It was the one tangible item that linked her to Argola Rhoswen aside from herself. It held sacred the inherent mystical healing powers her mother had transferred to her. She hoped, having it back in her hand, she'd learn why she couldn't heal Nora.

"Do be practical, my love. You bested me," she said with a desire for Brogan to be as safe as she felt. "Therefore, it should be you that carries it. But remember, it is mine, and I will want it returned."

She took his hand instead of the sword.

"I do not know that Kylemore can handle another attack from Thane if he has taken everything he has got there."

Brogan helped her up on a horse and gave her the sword. She saw worry in his eyes and she knew what he wanted without his words.

"I have to ask ye for help," he said, rubbing her leg.

"Anything, Brogan." She looked down at him with some elation he could humble himself to ask.

"Your army. Can ye get to your..." Brogan held her hand tight. "I do not want to send ye, but..."

"I go where you go, Brogan. As to the forces of Avalbane, I have already sent Jinn and Medora. They will bring the help Kylemore needs. I never believed Thane would keep a promise to me."

She bent and kissed the scar she had put on his hand. He held her face and kissed her lips.

"Beautiful and smart." He smiled.

"Yes, and it would have done you well to have come for me a long time ago, Lord Torrick."

"Forgive a fool, Your Highness." He bowed his head. "I did ye, as well my father, a disservice in not fulfilling the contract immediately."

"I'll not hold it against you as long as you remedy it and soon. I've grown fond of the Torrick name."

† † †

They traveled by day, by dark and took to sleeping only a short night. There was no time for anything in their quickly formed nest other than the few hours sleep. By the third day, they heard the roar of war and raced for the castle.

Brogan charged his horse through the gates of his castle. Brienna stayed beside him as she promised. Swords clashed and bodies fought so there was no telling who was who in the throes of the fray.

"Find Nareene and see to her safety," he shouted above the din of warriors and tossed her sword to her.

"Be careful."

She followed in the wake he created—with his horse, his foot, and the spear he pulled from a dead man's back. She hoped it was no one she knew. When he leapt off the horse, she had to trust he'd be all right. He had gone against bad, he'd fought against evil, and he had survived before.

"Go now, Lass."

One of his men tossed him a sword. He wielded it in defense of the onslaught of men and she hurried up the stairs into the great hall.

She went carefully through the door. The quiet chilled her and she ran up the stairs to the second level. The familiarity of the place warmed her heart. She traveled along the corridor and glanced into rooms.

"Nareene?" she called out, looking into each room.

The silence disturbed her.

"Nareene?" she whispered louder.

The castle was surprisingly quiet yet somewhere she could hear talking. Normal voices that seemed calm, undisturbed by the flurry of aggressions outside. She stopped to look out the embrasure and saw the fighting in full force. Her eyes scanned the courtyard for Brogan and she could not discern him from any other warrior.

She continued to move along with the idea that Nareene had expressed a fear of the last battle and thus she considered the girl was in hiding. Then she heard the voices again and she stopped to listen outside the door of one bedchamber.

"Ye said ye would marry me and we'd rule all three kingdoms together," Nareene whined.

"Ah, little buttercup, you are the impatient one," Thane chuckled.

"'Tis been a year. Do ye know how sick it made me having to pretend I wanted to marry Brogan? He thinks this little kingdom of his is enough! He did not even want to marry the Princess Rhoswen before she was Queen because he believed he could keep ye at bay. What a fool."

"Calm down, my petite. I hardly see a child in you anymore, Nareene."

Brienna backed from the door slowly.

"Ye will kill her, won't ye?" Nareene cooed. "I hate the woman."

"Yes, but why hate buttercup? Does Brogan's affections for her spark your jealously?" he asked with an amused tone, suggesting he did not care for Nareene anymore than she probably cared for him. They were nothing more than two vultures with self-centered quests.

"I should be asking that same question of ye," she whined. "Besides, I want to be Queen."

"You have no worries; you are all I need, my sweet. Now come over here." His voice croaked with gentle coaxing.

"And ye will kill Brogan?" she sang.

"They'll both hang from my drawbridge gates, just for your pleasure."

Brienna bumped into the wall and her head hit a shield. It rattled against the stone and she turned to run for an escape down the stairs. The men coming up grinned. Especially McCollum.

She spun and found Thane planted in the passage. Nareene held his arm.

"Look, she's even made it convenient." Nareene looked to the men behind. "Kill her."

"Now hold on there." Thane put a hand up to his men. "I don't know that I want to dispose of my wife quite so quickly."

Nareene whined alongside him and stomped her foot.

"Now, my sweet, I haven't taken over Avalbane yet and I may need her to lay the groundwork for us. We mustn't be hasty in our greed." He stepped toward Brie and she lifted the sword.

"You'll never get Avalbane or Kylemore." She swung the sword hard and caught the man next to McCollum first. He fell back and his shriek blended with the thump of his body on the hard stone. His cry made her cringe, but she didn't have time for her misplaced empathy.

"Get her, you fool!" Thane ordered the other man standing back shocked by her ability to wield the sword.

"She's..." the man started to complain.

"A silly woman. Are you going to let one scrawny little lady make you cower? You kill her now. I've other things to attend to," he ordered the man and then looked at Nareene. "Are you coming?"

"I wish to stay and watch her die." Nareene smirked.

"Whatever you wish, my dear."

Thane moved stealthily around Brienna. She was a danger to him and he knew not to take chances. It didn't prevent her from feigning a lunge at him. The problem was the other man blocking any attempt she might make.

"Goodbye, Cousin." Thane disappeared down the stairs.

"Kill her." Nareene taunted the man with threats. "Kill her now or Thane will hear about your refusal."

Brienna smiled at him. "I'm very good with this." She reminded him, brandishing the sword as if it were a feather under her spell. "Are you going to let this child dictate what you do? Believe me, you run and I'll make sure she doesn't tell Thane you choose to save your hide instead of dying for him or this little brat."

McCollum stepped closer. "Problem with my leaving is I got a crow to pluck. You ran me leg through with a blade and I ain't rightly goin' to forget it."

Nareene practically danced with delight.

"So you reckon on seeing how skillful I am when my hands aren't tied. You are either brave or an imbecile. I'm going to say the latter since you fight on the losing side."

"No way for you to know Thane will loose." He grinned.

"What, your hearing isn't working?" She nodded to the window. "Sounds like a whole lot of cheering for a battle, don't you think?"

He cocked his head.

Nareene ran to see for herself. "No!" she wailed.

"What is it?" McCollum asked.

"The banners of Avalbane!" Nareene spun around. "Kill her this instant. Her armies have surrounded and infiltrated my home!"

Chapter 23

The man gave the idea one last consideration and then turned to flee. Brienna grabbed Nareene by the wrist, but she put up a fight. She had two options and only one prevailed. She dropped the sword and swung a fist at Nareene. It connected to the girl's jaw and while it hurt, she gritted her teeth to bare the pain.

"That's for your disloyalty to Kylemore, especially to Brogan." Brienna reached down and grabbed the stunned Nareene by her arm and hauled her to her feet. "Give me any trouble and I may have to kill you before you get a chance to plead for your life to Lord Torrick."

"Ye both are dirt on my shoes," she screeched, stumbling alongside Brienna's forceful urging to go with her.

"You are a stupid child." Brienna picked up her sword and made her walk in front of her. "Thane is a pig and you're blind if you can't see he's using you."

"Thane loves me. We met six months ago and have been meeting secretly ever since."

"Loves you? Thane doesn't know what love is. I saw him rape a girl your age."

"He's kind and gentle and ye don't know what ye are talking about. Ye are bitter because he doesn't want ye."

"If that is the case, then I can only feel relieved. Thane Rhoswen is a black mark on my family's name. I'd rather be dead than ever have the abhorrent miscreant touch me." She shoved Nareene down the last few stairs.

When Nareene fell to the floor, an arm wrapped Brienna's waist from behind and another wrenched the sword from her hand.

"Lovely of you not to take too long to join us," Thane whispered in her ear as she struggled.

McCollum helped Nareene up off the floor.

"I'll kill her myself!" Nareene took a knife from McCollum's belt and thrust it toward Brienna.

She squeezed her eyes shut against the oncoming pain and then opened them to the small squeak. Thane held her sword out. Nareene looked wide-eyed at him and then at her stomach. The point of the blade was in her firmly so when Thane jerked it free, she collapsed in a heap at their feet.

"Sorry, little one. Plans you knew nothing about just can't be altered." Thane shook his head. "She was a fiery sweet thing. I'll miss her."

"She loved you." Brienna stared at the girl on the floor.

"Yes, that always does make it easier to have complete control." He looked over the sword and dropped it down on Nareene. "Brogan finds her and your weapon he'll only be able to conclude the worse."

"He'd never believe I killed Nareene." She squirmed in his arms.

"He won't want to, but what else could he believe when she is dead by your sword and you're gone?" He dragged her through the great hall and out a back entrance.

"I'll never stay with you." Brienna attempted to kick and twist to get away.

"I only need you for a little while, sweet Cousin. Just as soon as you get me a drop of the Silver Dragon's blood and then you'll be free to go." He thrust her at McCollum and mounted the horse.

Brienna was stunned. McCollum hoisted her up to Thane and she couldn't comprehend what he was asking of her.

"The Silver Dragon is a myth" She forced a chuckle. "Dragons don't exist anymore."

"Well then your life will be short lived once we get to Dragon's Dare. If the Silver Dragon truly is extinct, you will follow that same path." He kicked his heels into the horse.

"Why would you want a drop of blood from a dragon anyway?"

"Your mother was a healer and don't pretend to think I don't know you are one as well. I've done a great deal of studying over the years, listening to all the tales, and piecing together all the legends. One drop of blood from that dragon by a healer's sword will give me the powers tenfold of any mystic healer that has lived before. I'll live forever with the gift of life. For all eternity, I can heal myself and my armies. Nothing will stop me from ruling this land and the world.

"What makes you think I'll help you get anything like that?" She clenched her jaw tight to keep from turning on him in her fit of rage.

"Because on our little journey I'll tell you a story about your mother and how she died."

"My mother died from a fever when I was twelve years old."

"And just after that event, did you not find it odd your father and mine no longer communicated?"

"My mother died from a fever," Brienna repeated, unable to keep the quaver from her voice.

"My father learned she was a mystic healer and tried to get her to divulge the secrets she held about the Silver Dragon."

"Like father, like son," she breathed. "Evil seems to be hereditary in your branch of the clan."

"Name it as you'd like, but what you know and can do is rare and should be used to their fullest extent. I've reports of you healing your wounded that have battled my forces. Do you know how I retrieved that bit of information—by you Brienna, by your goodness. In a rush to heal, you laid your hands on one of my men and he remembered everything. He was a greedy man that I rewarded very well."

"No doubt a reward he didn't expect."

"I was protecting your secret, Cousin. I couldn't very well let the man run around the countryside, spouting off your practiced sorcery. How would it look on our family name?" He laughed.

"You were going to tell me about how my mother died."

She didn't want to believe him, yet she never really believed her father's story of how her mother died either.

"Later, when we set up camp for the night," he replied.

She looked behind them and saw McCollum and two others followed forty yards behind. It would make escape hard, so she decided to wait for a more opportune time. Besides, he had piqued her curiosity greatly by mention of her mother. Her father would never tell her anything specific about her mother's life as a healer. He claimed not to know, but she knew it was a lie. What she remembered of her mother was a loving woman that adored her father. If Argola loved Padric only half as much as she loved Brogan, then she would have told him everything.

The day passed quicker than she thought it would. Thane was for the most part pleasant, thoughtful and generous with his stories about when she was little. She didn't let the false front he put up distract her from knowing he was still the same cruel man that hurt a young girl so badly she died. She pitied Nora's babes for having him as a possible father and she was going to make sure he never had an ounce of influence over them. Brogan would make sure that Soren and Ronan came to live with them. Brogan would make sure everything was all right. It was what she had to believe for her peace of mind.

† † †

Brogan looked at the man under the point of his sword. He'd seen men shake and then he'd seen men tremble. The young fellow he held by a boot on his chest and sharp steel at his throat quaked.

"Tell me again what it is ye overheard your master tell McCollum," Brogan insisted.

He couldn't believe the tale being told and before running off on a wild goose chase, he needed to hear it again.

"Lord Rhoswen said that he wasn't to kill the Queen, but to play along with whatever Nareene said. Then, if defeat looked imminent he was to get the Queen to him so they could go to Dragon's Dare."

"Why?" Brogan pushed the blade firmer into the man's flesh.

"I don't know."

"Kelwyn, get a handful of men together," Brogan ordered.

"Ye are not going to believe him, are ye?" Kelwyn questioned in disbelief.

"Aye."

"Ye cannot. It could be a trap set up by Rhoswen. Ye cannot even be one hundred percent positive his wife was not part of a ploy to get ye and your best men away from Kylemore." Kelwyn rubbed his face. "I will grant she did a good thing for me, but then when did a woman not use trickery to her own advantage?"

Brogan grabbed Kelwyn's arm and pulled him away from the man on the floor. He didn't give it a second thought the lad quickly scampered off. He had the information he needed.

"Listen to me, Kelwyn," Brogan growled in his brother's face. "The Lass is our best ally. Ye would not question a thing she does if ye knew her the way I do. It is her very army here that saved us from defeat."

"Ye are talking about her doin' that magic thing."

"That woman means the world to me with or without magic. Now go get the men. I want to leave within ten minutes." Brogan ran his fingers through his hair. "Oh and ye have dirt on your nose."

"Dirt?" Kelwyn's face twisted up, confused.

"Nothing." Brogan pushed him to go.

Brie was caught in every thought. He might have laughed at his mention of dirt on his brother's nose, if he wasn't caught in a very serious problem... how to help Brie.

He joined Kelwyn outside the castle.

"Less than five, Brogan, we are ready in less than five minutes." Kelwyn smiled at him.

Brogan nodded his appreciation.

They rode hard, hoping to catch up to Brie. When darkness fell and the sky was void of a single star, they were forced to bed down for the night. Sedge told him his tent was ready, but he couldn't find a way to lie down and sleep. There had hardly been a night that passed that he hadn't slept alongside Brie, now he gave pause to what he'd do if he lost her for good.

"Cannot sleep?" Kelwyn put a hand on his shoulder.

"If there was ever a time I could have died, it was when I saw her kiss Thane to prevent me from fighting them all to get to her." He watched the black sky, praying it didn't rain and at the same time hoping Brie would have safe shelter.

"Ye are worried what Thane will do with her," Kelwyn said. "Ye know if he was taking her to Dragon's Dare, he needs her for something special. He will not want to ruin whatever he has in mind."

"That is the only thing keeping me from riding through this Godforsaken black night to find her. However, I have a fear of what Brie will do. She may be Queen of Avalbane, but the Lass is a warrior in her heart and soul." He held his hand out to Kelwyn to see the healing wound he would not let her heal. "First time I met her, she bested me with a blade."

"Ah, beautiful and deadly! I can see your attraction to the pretty part, but the lady wields a weapon by both sword and hand. What was Father thinking, making ye sign a contract of marriage with her?"

"I have never known him not to have the same appreciation of the wenches I do, maybe he saw in her what he saw in our mother. It would be nice to think he met her and immediately thought she perfect for me. Yet, ye know as well as I do this was to be a marriage of convenience, an alliance between Avalbane and Kylemore, benefiting us both where Thane was concerned."

"Well, I know it sure is a good thing her army came when they did." He patted Brogan on the shoulder. "I am sorry what I said about not trusting her. It came out before I even thought about all she has done. We could not have lasted long today without the help. And that night I was wounded...I did not dream her presence, I know, but tell me it was real."

"She is a mystic healer. What we have heard is true and she is not evil. She believes in God and has all the same values as we do. She has not said much about what she is because she was raised to keep it a secret. At the same time, I know she does not understand it fully. I felt her heal me one day and the next she seemed to have lost her powers."

"The power she had." Jinn appeared from the trees, "She has passed on."

"To where?" Brogan turned around, not wholly surprised the man eavesdropped.

"To the child she carries, I assume."

"Child? Kelwyn, get everyone up. We will ride by torchlight." Brogan hurried to his horse.

Within twenty minutes, they were making their way through the forest by the blaze of rags twisted on clubs of wood.

"Do you think this is a good idea?" Jinn asked Brogan. "If we're traveling in the wrong direction, it'll put us further from the Queen instead of closer."

"We are aimed in the general direction. Ye need only inhale and smell the sea," Brogan assured Jinn as well as himself. There was no room for second guessing himself.

"I did not like the advantages you took with Her Highness when I came upon you." Jinn offered his feeling on their first meeting. "My first instinct was to kill you."

"I can appreciate that." Brogan smiled, hoping the darkness shielded his amusement from the man. "And now?"

"I've watched the two of you together. The Queen has been wearing her heart on her sleeve where you're concerned."

"And how do ye feel about that?" Brogan pressed the man to admit, Brie and he fit like the stars and the moon.

"I'm satisfied with her decision." He released the information with a little reserve and then added, "I've seen you give her your heart in return and it can only mean good for this country to have rulers not at each other's throat. Your honor is commendable."

"Commendable? I have never heard anyone praise emotions as if they were defined actions. I do not have a strategy or a need for any plan to be praised on."

"It is commendable because you express openly what many men do not." Jinn put his hand out and touched Brogan's arm. "It is the deepest form of commitment to offer all of yourself, instead of just the man for a marriage."

"Aye and I have no problem with speaking the words, Jinn. I love the Lass with all my heart and will do everything to keep her safe." Brogan thought of Brie and while he worried over her as he should, he had the strength to remember she remarkable adaptability of taking care of herself.

"A hard feat to keep her safe as you are learning, is it not? Her Highness has a mind of her own," Jinn said.

Brogan chuckled. "She does at that and all the better for me because I will never bore of her."

Chapter 24

The glow on the beach was the sign of their arrival. Brogan had Sedge, Lorne, Duane, and Jinn handle the men in the camp while he and Kelwyn snuck into the cave beyond them. Daylight would have been nice, except they had left it behind in favor of traveling.

He motioned for Kelwyn to lag back as he proceeded into the darkness. Beyond the gapping entrance, he found another fire with no one. Brie's voice took him deeper into the cavernous hole.

"Your father murdered my mother because she refused him and you'll have to kill me as well," Brie dared.

"Do it and I'll let you go back to that Torrick." He handed her a dagger.

"I don't believe you." She spit and swung the blade at him.

Brogan came out of hiding. He held Brie's light-weighted sword with one hand and waved it at Thane. "Ye want to make deals, Thane, then come to me." He curled a finger at him. "Come on. Why not fight someone ye have a chance against? The Lass is too good for ye in many ways. Especially in swordplay and I'd hate to see ye die too quickly." He slowly circled to cut Brie out of their path.

Brogan lunged at Thane and then he saw Kelwyn. He had joined them at an inopportune time. Thane grabbed him and held a knife to his throat.

"Do you still wish to say no to me, Brienna?" He pushed Kelwyn to walk forward. "Get the blood of the dragon now, and just to be on the safe side, give her that sword, Brogan."

Brie rushed to Brogan and took the sword.

"He did not harm ye?" Brogan whispered, holding her arm and trying to inspect her.

"No." She shook her head.

"NOW!" Thane demanded. "Or would you both like to see how sharp my knife is on this lad's throat?"

"Give me my sword, Brogan." Brie had her hand around his on the hilt. "Brogan, please."

"She cannot just walk up to the dragon and stab him," Brogan argued. "That would be suicide for anybody."

Thane narrowed his eyes. "Then go with her and the young one here will await your return."

Brogan took Brie's arm and led her toward the hum. It wasn't the surf echoing as he had thought. Brienna put her hands up and the amber glow emitted with a brilliance lighting their way.

"I thought ye could not do that anymore," he said.

"I'm not doing it, the dragon is," she replied and kept advancing slowly.

The closer they got the vision before them illuminated with a white glow. The albino dragon sat ready for them and Brogan stood ready to push Brie away from any danger.

"I need one drop of blood," she said.

"I do not think this is the best of ideas." Brogan released the sword in his hand. "What does Thane want with the blood anyways?"

"The power of life. With one drop of the Silver Dragon's blood cut into his body, Thane can bring back the dead." She gulped loud enough for him to hear as a whoosh of hot air breathed across their faces.

"Bring back?"

"Yes," she whispered. "Thus he could cure himself over and over, living forever as a pestilence on this land," she lamented. "You saw Thorndale and the ruins it has fallen into. He's a disease and by one drop of the Silver Dragon's blood, he would be an indestructible plague left to ravage the land and our people."

"Well, we cannot let him get that kind of power."

"And we can't sacrifice Kelwyn so I see no other choice. We'll just have to think of a way to stop him once Kelwyn is safe."

"Ye take the power of life for yourself and then ye can bring Kelwyn back from the dead," Brogan suggested.

"I don't know if it even really works. We can't put faith on happenstance being in our favor when it comes to your brother's life." She looked down at her hands.

Brogan tried to take hold of them but the intensity of heat burned his fingers.

"Lass, your cousin does not plan on letting any of us live after tonight." He spoke quietly as if the softness to his voice would change the meaning of his words. "But 'tis your decision. I am here to support what ye decide.

"Brogan, it's time." She raised the sword and the glow flowed from her fingers down the wide steely blade. "The sword of Rhoswen will meet its origin for the first time since its creation."

† † †

All myths of the sword became more real to Brienna. She only ever half-believed the Rhoswen sword was made from the Silver Dragon's scales and steel. Her hands quavered as the sword's vibration sought to take her to the dragon. She knew the weapon was more than a means to protect. It was the key to the life's blood of everlasting eternity. All the sensations she had felt only briefly that one other time she was with the dragon were now magnified and she had the understanding of centuries.

Brienna stepped forward and then turned back to Brogan. "I've got my power back and I'll cure the wound Kelwyn gets as long as you get Thane away from him right away."

"Do not let the dragon's magic fool ye, Brie. Ye said yourself the power is gone and 'tis not ye lighting up your hands as if they were flames."

"I don't understand. You can see for yourself the amber glow radiating from my fingers. You can see its transference to the sword." She questioned his doubt and her own because something told her he was right. "My mother said she lost the power when it transferred to me."

"Jinn said it was upon conception."

He glanced back where they knew Thane held Kelwyn prisoner. He thought the same thing as she did, his brother may already be dead. What would prevent a man racked with so much evil from disposing of one more threat?

"You talked to Jinn about my powers. He's never said anything to me. He, like my father, pretended to be dumb on the matter." The emitting amber glow reddened with its intensity. "Well if that's how I lost...." She lifted her eyes to him, coming aware of what he tried to tell her.

The distraction of the sword faded in comparison to the onslaught of news so wonderful it seemed wrong to feel happy at that moment when all looked so bleak. A babe grew in her womb, a beautiful child she and Brogan created out of passion. The bondage of their love had been consummated with permanence and she couldn't let anything destroy what they produced.

Brogan put a hand to her cheek. "I would say we gave each other a lot more than our love that night in Elgin's wagon."

The momentary thought of that night brought a soft curve to his mouth and she loved him more for his brave front. She could sense his unease for what she had to do.

"I'm carrying your child?" She touched her stomach and then swiftly spun from him before he could stop her.

"Brie!"

The flaming breath of the dragon shot out above her head. It wasn't a misdirected aim or an angry reaction to her advancement. The Silver Dragon beckoned her with his challenge...he dared her to be courageous. When all legends fade, it is usually to the waning truth of reality. The Dragon's dare wasn't for man. It was for mystic healers to present themselves to face danger and magic of the highest form.

"I do this for all our sakes," Brie announced. "I do this to save one, to protect all," she proclaimed with it set in her mind she would do as Brogan suggested and take the blood unto herself.

Brienna stuck her sword into the toe of the creature and pulled it out swiftly as if to inflict as little pain as possible on the dragon. The emanating glow from her hands and the sword extinguished in a flash of lightning that shot forward. She dropped to the ground when the breath of the dragon inhaled deeply, pulling, dragging every flicker of the amber power from her fingers and the sword.

Within seconds, Brogan ran to shield her body with his and the dragon exhaled flames. They shot straight out within inches of their heads. He took in another labored breath, leaving them seconds to rise up on their feet and run. The second blast of heat unfurled above them and they knew the Silver Dragon had spared them with purpose. Whether it was because of the babe or by accident, Brienna questioned not the divine luck following them every step they took.

"Did you get it?" Thane asked too eagerly as they emerged.

Kelwyn elbowed him and ducked the dagger as Thane took a swing at him. His surprise was only a flash in his eyes when he mistakenly let his anxious greed guide his judgment. Thane Rhoswen had let his guard down at the wrong time.

Brogan seized the opportunity and rushed at Thane who no longer had a weapon in his hand. He tackled him to the ground and fought to gain the upper hand. Brienna, still shaking from the release of power, watched in silence and in prayer.

"Are ye all right, Your Highness?" Kelwyn put a hand to Brienna's shoulder.

"Yes," she answered and looked to him when his hand covered hers on her stomach.

"Are ye ill?"

"No, not ill, Sir Kelwyn."

"With your leave, I will see to helping my brother." He bowed slightly and danced around the two men wrestling in the damp sandy floor of the cave.

"Stay back!" Brogan ordered, commanding him through gritted teeth. "This scum of the earth is mine."

Brienna put a hand to her lips to still the quiver of apprehension. She couldn't heal him if he got hurt. Thane's grunt relieved and grieved her. She turned around, not wanting to see the life force ebb from his eyes when Brogan rose to his feet. The knife had found a place in Thane's chest and it was done. The menace and scourge to their lands ceased to exist.

Brogan put his hands on Brie's shoulders and turned her to face him. He took the sword from her and sheathed it in his belt. Then, as carefully as a man might touch a fragile bird's egg, he put his hand to her stomach.

"I wish to fulfill the marriage contract as soon as we return home, Your Highness."

Brienna flung her arms around his neck and crowded to retrieve his kiss.

"So shall it be," she murmured to his hot breath mingling with hers.

They weren't given long for the torrid passion to escalate beyond the first stages of their embrace before someone coughed behind them.

Brogan turned his head.

"Aye? Can ye not see I am busy tending to the affections of my Queen?"

Jinn clamped a hand on his shoulder.

"Time enough for that later. You two will have to curb that appetite when in public or the people of Avalbane will think their rulers are in love."

"I will shout it from the castle spires if need be so no one will question my devotion to her, Jinn."

Brogan squeezed her gently. She would have to explain while she carried a child he need not treat her as one.

"Thane's men?" he inquired on a serious note.

"Scattered to the far corners of the land, I'd say."

"Good. Let them fold back into mankind and become noble warriors as they were before Thane's influence." Brogan walked Brie past Thane's lifeless body. "Bury him where he lay. He wanted to be part of the Silver Dragon then let him be entombed in the dragon's lair."

The sky had cleared and millions of bright stars twinkled against the blanket of blue-black. Brogan kept his arm snug around her. They strolled along the fringe of water sloshing to shore. Kelwyn had brought him a blanket to drape around her shoulders. He rubbed a hand up and down her arm every time he felt a tremor ripple through her.

"When we leave here, I'd like to go to Thorndale first," she said. "I want to raise Thane's children with the love and privileges they're entitled to."

"I said it before and I will say it now. We will raise and love them as if they were our own. They are the future rulers to our lands as equally as our children will be. I promise, Lass, I will love them no less." He stopped her and looked down at her stomach. "However, they are not our own and I think it will be right when they are men, they are told they are Rhoswen's. The name should live on with their children and then maybe they will have a chance at washing away the distaste people of lesser knowledge have about the Rhoswen clan."

"I like that idea. Without it, I'm afraid the Rhoswen name would die in disgrace. No one would ever know it was by one man evil tried to prevail."

"Soon, Lass, ye will be a Torrick as I promised, but know that I will see to the care that the Rhoswen name is not forgotten."

"Brogan, you'll not be disappointed our firstborn will be a girl, will you?"

"Nay, a girl would be nice if we're to have the two boys as well. It shall give me a wee one to spoil as she should be spoiled. Is this something ye already know?"

"I haven't the gift of healing anymore because the power has passed. It only goes to a girl child."

"I will not ask why that is. We have already seen what one man would like to do with such power. I think women are gentler in their ways and have a deeper compassion than what is taught to the male offspring." He kissed her temple. "A daughter will be grand."

Brienna sighed with a contentment she hadn't felt in a very long time. All was right with the world. As she prayed it would, everything fell into a proper place. What started as an advantageous union between the Torricks and the Rhoswens was given credence as fate. What threatened to be a passing affair was graced by God to be a timeless love.

Brogan stopped her at the farthest reaches of the beach, distancing them from all the men. His fingers sifted through her hair dampened by the sea spray.

"I love ye." He bowed his head down to capture her smile in his kiss.

"I love you too." She kissed him and nuzzled her face to his bristly cheek. "I do hope you've already picked out a private place for us to spend the night."

"I have." He pulled her into a small cave. The stars offered a glistening light off their reflection in the trapped pools of saltwater on the beach. "Will this do?"

"Very nicely." She slid the blanket from her shoulders and fanned it out over the sand.

Whether they were alone or a thousand people watched, Brienna didn't care. She drifted down on the blanket with Brogan. Nothing could gain her attention more than his kiss that held the promise of forever.

Epilogue

"Will you still take on mistresses?" Brienna's new sword hit his.

She fenced him back to a stone pillar in the courtyard. A pastime and a pleasure, they practiced together for fun and for a future they prayed would stay peaceful. For such a pastime, he had a delicately thin blade made. He couldn't keep her still, but he could reduce the stress of carrying anything heavy while in her condition.

Her old sword they retired to a wall much like other relics in the castle. The kind of peace they felt had no need of weapons and for a time, he knew she'd allow him to pamper her.

"No because I already have one. I may be married and in love with my wife. A woman to whom I have the honor of calling Queen Torrick, but my heart will belong to my Lass."

He rushed her and pinned her petite frame to a wall with his chest. He felt hers heave and he looked down to the very familiar pearlescent mounds of flesh straining under the pressure of his weight.

"I love you, Brogan Torrick, but I win." She smiled.

"It could never be as much as I love ye, Lass, and how do ye figure ye win when I have ye trapped?"

Quickly he read her thoughts and they became his, he had forgotten her hands. He leaned away and glanced between them at the knife she held in check. His hand wrapped to the back of her head and held firm.

"It does not look good for ye to best me every time, Lass, especially in front of the little ones."

They both looked over to Soren and his brother, Ronan.

"I think they're too young to take much notice, my love."

"I think they will end up learning to be warriors from their new mother if I do not make some sort of showing."

Kissing the sweet coral lips, he waited for just the precise moment. When she dropped the knife, he grabbed her hands and pulled her away from the wall to hold her against him.

"You better hope the only fighting you have to do is with women, my king. I don't think kissing men will produce quite the same affect as it does on me." She laughed when he swept her up in his arms.

A servant ran to collect their weapons and put them away and they continued their daily playacting battle with each other in their bedchamber.

"Brogan?"

Brienna lay nestled in his arm and her fingers circled through the swirls of hair on his chest after the sweltering heat of their passion ebbed.

"What is it, Lass?" The palm of his hand lay on the slight swell of her gravid belly. That she carried his child was the pinnacle of their love and he kissed her forehead lightly.

"Will we love each other forever?"

"Forever, Lass, it will be forever." He leaned over her and gave way to the idea they'd not be getting up any time soon.

Samhain Publishing, Ltd.

It's all about the story…

Action/Adventure
Fantasy
Historical
Horror
Mainstream
Mystery/Suspense
Non-Fiction
Paranormal
Red Hots!
Romance
Science Fiction
Western
Young Adult

http://www.samhainpublishing.com

Printed in the United Kingdom
by Lightning Source UK Ltd.
118899UK00001B/113